Praise for *Unsheltered*

'*Unsheltered* reads like a thriller, is utterly convincing in all its
invention, and kept a hard hold of me from beginning to end.'
Elizabeth Knox

'Li is an unforgettable character, whose scars are as
compelling as her extraordinary resourcefulness – she
powers an urgent, heart-stopping novel.'
Emily Perkins

'*Unsheltered* is a fist-clenching, breath-holding,
heart-accelerating reading experience. Clare Moleta writes
with clarity and force, conjuring a terrifyingly real world of
environmental desolation and bureaucratic mercilessness, but
also, vitally, one in which empathy, love and hope stubbornly
persist. In temperamentally tenacious and teeth-grittingly
tough Li, Moleta has created a heroine who is utterly believable
in both her ambivalence about becoming a parent and in her
single-minded determination to keep that child safe.'
Emily Maguire

UNSHELTERED

CLARE MOLETA

SCRIBNER

SCRIBNER

First published in Australia in 2021 by Scribner, an imprint of Simon & Schuster Australia
Suite 19A, Level 1, Building C, 450 Miller Street, Cammeray, NSW 2062

Sydney New York London Toronto New Delhi
Visit our website at www.simonandschuster.com.au

SCRIBNER and design are registered trademarks of The Gale Group, Inc.,
used under licence by Simon & Schuster Inc.

10 9 8 7 6 5 4 3 2 1

A catalogue record for this
book is available from the
National Library of Australia

9781761100758 (paperback)
9781761100765 (ebook)

Cover design by Sandy Cull, www.sandycull.com
Cover artwork by Kate Breakey: 'Desert Cottontail', from the series
Las Sombras/The Shadows, silver gelatin photogram
Typeset in 12.5/17 pt Adobe Garamond Pro by Midland Typesetters, Australia
Printed and bound in Australia by Griffin Press

The paper this book is printed on is certified against the
Forest Stewardship Council® Standards. Griffin Press holds
FSC® chain of custody certification SGS-COC-005088. FSC®
promotes environmentally responsible, socially beneficial
and economically viable management of the world's forests.

For Leon and Franka, my best place

To Margot,
thankyou!
clare

Contents

Makecamp   9

The northern highway   61

The inland sea   101

Transit   183

The range   243

This land, this red land, is us; and the flood years and the dust years and the drought years are us. We can't start again.

John Steinbeck, *The Grapes of Wrath*

Author's note

The setting of this novel is Australian but not Australia. Geography, distance and time have been altered, some things moved around and others invented entirely.

This is how Weather came.

They were out in it, the two of them, yelling and laughing till they choked on the rain. Then they were quiet, just standing in it. Dust to mud under their feet and the smell of wet pulling up memories like fish. Li fell against Frank and he licked rain off her.

I bloody told you, he said with his mouth on hers. Didn't I tell you we weren't going anywhere?

Yeah? Well it better stop soon or it's gunna wash everything away.

You're a hard woman to please.

They danced a bit, tried to. Slow mud circles with the rain running them together. She couldn't tell if it was his hair plastered against her forehead, or her own.

He turned his face up to the rain. Let's go and get her.

They'd talked about it before, tried to imagine what it would be like for Matti the first time, and Li could hear his regret that she wasn't with them now. But she wanted to go inside with him, wet like they were. Pulled him towards the door with her hands

1

at his belt. And then over his shoulder she saw Matti running down the driveway towards them, running hard through the rain as if it was something to shelter from. When she got close enough Li saw that she was crying. It irritated her that Matti was having this reaction, and not the one they'd imagined for her.

It's all right, she said. You don't have to be scared of it.

Frank crouched down in the mud. What's wrong, beansprout?

And Matti said, Robbie went past the bend and he won't come back.

Robbie was Carl and Angie's boy. A quicksilver kid with a light in his eyes that came straight from his mother. He was six and Matti was five and they lived for the same things: matches and pocketknives and secret hideouts. When they were together you couldn't break in. His fast grin was just for her.

Li had thought they were at Angie and Carl's and Angie thought they were with Li. They'd been playing in the storm-water pipe for weeks and nobody knew. And Matti and Robbie, they didn't know what it was, what it was for. Who would have thought to tell them? Neither of them had ever seen rain.

The drain grate had rusted through. It wasn't hard to lever it up and drop down into the cavity under the road, where the dry concrete pipes led off on either side. The two of them had been going down there after school, taking torches and lollies and leftover sandwiches, chalking how far they got and daring each other to go further.

When the air turned thick and electric just after four o'clock, they hadn't felt it. Didn't see the sky fatten like a bruise, bringing people outside to look up and remember. Matti was at the first bend and Robbie was up ahead in the dark. He'd just yelled back that he'd passed her chalkmark when she wet herself. She hadn't known until right then that she needed to go. She started shuffling backwards without telling him she was leaving.

Why not? Frank asked later.

And Matti, head down, Because I peed.

It was so easy for Li to imagine her down there with her undies and the front of her T-shirt soaked, elbows raw and stinging, overwhelmed by shame because Robbie would have to crawl through it too.

And when Matti came out backwards into the heavy purple light? That was harder to imagine. Did the world smell changed? How did she make sense of the water that started leaking and then flooding from the sky; the noise of it?

She told Frank, I thought I'd got to the sea. She said she called to Robbie down the tunnel but she couldn't even hear her own voice.

Angie and Carl left town a few months later. Their millet was ruined anyway. Li had known them more than ten years, Frank since primary school, but they didn't say goodbye and Li thought that was right. She couldn't look at them without a debilitating sense of relief.

People said they'd gone down the highway to Valiant on the edge of the Gulf coast. Valiant was the only city in West. It was a place you could go and try to forget things. But most people figured Angie and Carl would only stay there long enough to buy their way onto a boat and get across the Gulf to East. Why not? Why not leave this whole unsheltered state behind, if you could?

The newspapers said Weather was better over east, not so fierce yet. And the three External Border precincts were there – maybe Angie and Carl could find a way into one of them. Start again, sheltered. Maybe they could outrun Robbie.

The last story Li heard was that they were in a makecamp outside Sumud, trying to queue or buy their way inside. It made sense. Sumud was the closest XB precinct, just across the Gulf. The man who told her that story was a customer in the hardware store – he'd hardly known Angie and Carl. She didn't tell Frank. It would be tough hearing about his oldest friends third-hand.

Ange told Li something, though, the one time they talked after the flood. She said she'd decided to live. I can't leave Carl on his own with it, so I'm gunna keep going.

How? Li was standing on the verandah, holding her casserole, because Angie hadn't asked her in.

You just decide to. Every time I stop, the hole opens up and I wanna fall. All I wanna do is fall. The only way I know not to is just keep deciding over and over. Everything's a decision now. Opening my eyes, putting clothes on, eating, going outside. Nothing just happens.

All the neighbours had helped them search. The roads were under water, rain still belting down, and they could hear it roaring in the drains beneath their feet. They nearly lost Angie trying to climb down into the pipe; Frank had to drag her out and hold onto her. Someone brought a concrete cutter and tried to dig up the road to cut through the pipe. The hole they made filled up with mud and Carl dug in it with his empty hands.

*

Leaving was a decision for Angie. For most people it just happened. Because after the flood came howlers so vicious that the smell of them coming made you freeze up. Then the drought again, and then fire. Within two years everything was gone. When Li and Frank and Matti walked out of Nerredin onto the highway, all that was left was the pub and the ruin of the old school building. But Robbie was the town's first real victim; their unbearable, inadequate offering against what was coming. Robbie was the end of Nerredin.

Matti wouldn't talk to Li about it, not ever. She shouted and pushed her away, ran out of the house. But Frank said she asked him one question. Where will Robbie wait for me?

And Li was glad it was Frank because she didn't know the answer, had never known it since Matti was born. There was nothing here for a child, but they'd had one anyway. Like Angie and Carl had Robbie.

What Li knew, what she understood before Frank, was the size of Weather. People could build their firebreaks and desalination plants and early warning systems and bunkers, but they couldn't withstand it. Nobody could.

She would have gone sooner but Nerredin was Frank's home. So she waited for him to understand that home was finished. That all they could do now was try to keep their kid alive and look for somewhere safer.

The night before they left, they slept in the pub, bedding down on a single mattress on the floor. Their house, the olive grove, gone. Everything stank of ash. Others talking or sleeping around them – the ones who'd hung on, like them.

The three of them had a long walk ahead, through the hot season, to reach Valiant. It would be hard on Matti, but Matti wasn't sleeping. She had lost Goldie, her rag horse, as they ran from the fire and now she held tight to a new wooden horse Frank had carved for her, small enough to fit in her hand.

Li felt Matti watching her in the semi-dark but she kept her eyes closed until she heard her roll over to face Frank.

Dad, are we going to live with Hani and Auntie Teresa and Uncle Navid?

For a bit, yeah. Till we find somewhere else.

And is Hani excited about meeting me?

Keep it down, beansprout. People're sleeping.

But is he?

I bet he is. I bet he's jumping off the walls and his mum's saying, Calm down, mate, don't bust a gut before they even get here.

Matti wriggled, pleased, pushing backwards into Li. Her hair smelled of smoke. How long till we get there?

It's a pretty long way. We'll be walking for a few weeks.

Every day?

Yeah, but we'll stop and have a rest when it gets too hot. It's gunna be good. You're a good walker. And we can make up some new games.

Like what?

This kind of talk would keep Matti awake all night. But Li didn't want to stop them, she just wanted to pretend she was asleep so she could hear it up close, the way they were with each other. How Frank made it sound so easy.

Matti said, But are we going to stay and live in Valiant?

You plan on doing any sleeping tonight?

This is my last question.

Okay. Well, we'll see what we can find for work. Find you a school to go to.

Matti had had six months at Nerredin Primary before the first howler tore off the schoolhouse roof and sent the teacher running back to Valiant. Homeschool since then, for the kids that were left. They'd shared it out, taught what they knew.

And if we can't find anything for work and a school, then will we go across the water on a boat?

How about you stop worrying about everything, Frank said. Let's just wait and see.

Li tried to read his voice, because they hadn't talked about this. About East. Getting to Valiant was what they'd talked about – how far a kid could walk in a day. Heat. Where there might be water and how much of it might be contaminated by ash. They'd talked about the size of the flat where his sister and her husband lived with their three-year-old son, above their garage and repair shop. There might be some work for Li there, and Navid knew people down at the port. That was far enough ahead for her. But even blinded by the loss of Nerredin, Frank might still think bigger.

What's it like inside the walls? Matti asked.

I don't really know, sprout. A bit crowded, maybe? But you and me and Li don't take up much space. Except when your mum sleeps sideways.

Did he know she was awake? Did he understand why she wasn't helping with this, why it was better left to him? She couldn't look Matti in the eye and talk to her about the future.

So, will we go inside them?

Maybe. Maybe we'll find somewhere we like more, that's not inside the walls.

Like where?

I dunno. Somewhere with a bit more room, maybe.

Dadda?

Matti.

Okay, but would there be horses there? Cos there probably isn't room for horses inside the walls?

Sleep was coming, closing Li down. But she could feel the wire wound tight in her child. Four nights ago Matti had lost Goldie running from the fire. Yesterday she had seen the black ash of her home. Two years since the flood – nearly a third of her life. Did she even remember Robbie?

Where, Dadda? Where are we going?

Frank touched the back of Matti's head and she burrowed in against him, away from Li.

Go to sleep now. We're going to go to the best place we can find.

Makecamp

Li woke like she was climbing out of a hole. Cold. Something pressing on her eyes. She tried to open them but the dark knuckled in under her lids and she squeezed them shut again. Something clothy and claggy inside her head, every thought was like lifting weight. It hurt to breathe and there was pain or the memory of pain at the surface of her skin. A sharp antiseptic smell. Underneath it, sweat, dust, dank concrete. No sounds from makecamp, no voices, but she wasn't alone. She could move her hands but not her arms. Fear arrived too slowly. Matti, she thought.

A woman said, She's awake.

People breathed around her, bad air and unwashed bodies. She listened for lighter breath, a faster heartbeat, for anything childlike. There was something she needed to remember.

It's okay, you're safe. The woman turned away and spoke to someone else. Get Rich.

Her voice was familiar but Li couldn't do the work of placing it. She was sinking back down in the hole, her head filling up with glue.

*

Rolling a six is the best, Matti said.

Yeah? Li was half listening. The burn had gone out of the sun and the highway to Valiant was soft and warm. Their best walking hours ahead of them. What does a six get you?

Well, two things. You can add *or* take away six points from your total points, depending how close you are to winning. *And* a truck stops and gives you a lift.

How far?

It depends.

She clawed up and out again, got clear. She was lying on a hard surface. There was a delay between her and the pain, between her and thought. Her arms were tied, she couldn't lift them. Something was wrong with her hands and her face. Why couldn't she open her eyes? People were talking but no one talked to her. No one told her what she needed to remember.

Matti, she said, and her voice was blurry in her own ears.

There was a low whistle, a little way off. Sudden quiet movement around her, then a different, waiting quiet. She flinched as a hand came down over her mouth, but lightly, briefly.

The woman said, Shhh, up close, and Li smelled her fear.

Then a man called, We're good. It's Rich.

The sound of a metal shutter being wrenched up. The man spoke quickly to someone else and the shutter came down again.

There were no shutters in makecamp, no one would waste the metal. She was somewhere else. Somewhere closed in but big enough to make echoes. Footsteps on the concrete, getting louder. She tried to make her muscles work, to get ready.

The woman said, She's in and out but she's awake. Then, to Li, You want to sit up?

12

Her first try brought on cold sweat and a rush of nausea. The woman steadied her while it passed. Take it easy, you're pretty drugged.

She tried again and sat up slowly.

I'm Safia, from the ready shop. You remember me? The woman was untying something at Li's waist. We had to do this to stop you from scratching.

Li felt her arms come free of her body. When she started to speak she coughed and kept coughing until the woman held a bottle to her mouth and she resisted and then swallowed water and worked to get her breathing under control. Pushed the bottle away and discovered each of her hands was bound with cloth. The padding made her clumsy and her skin felt raw under the fabric. She touched her bandaged hands to her eyes; they were bandaged too, and the side of her face and neck. Pain pushing up through whatever drugs they'd given her.

Matti, she said, her tongue thick and slow. Matti?

No answer. Her arms went wide. Where is she? Tell me where she is. She lurched forward in the dark, fighting nausea, reaching to drag Matti in out of empty space.

Your daughter's not here, Safia said. We haven't seen her since they cleared makecamp.

Li stopped moving. Everything stopped. When?

Two days ago.

Two days. Black noise came rushing in but she clenched her fists and the pain brought her back. What happened?

You don't remember?

She was trying. Remembered Matti saying, Don't go tonight. She remembered smoke. Running till she couldn't breathe or see.

Safia filled in the gaps. XB Force and loud hailers and dogs. Batons, studded gloves. Tear gas. Saltwater cannons. What had happened to the people who tried to gather up what they owned, or stay, or fight. What happened to the sick ones. How fires had started and were left to burn. Too much useless information. Two days. Two nights. Where is she where is she where is she —

Don't do that.

It was a man's voice. She realised she was trying to pull the bandages off her eyes but the bandages on her hands were getting in the way. She sensed him move to touch her and reared back.

This is Rich, Safia said. He's okay.

I was a medic. In the army.

Nobody said *am* anymore. Almost nobody.

Safia said, He's the one that got you out. The relief medic gave you oxygen, she got us water to cool the burns, but Rich did the rest. Kept it all clean, measured out the doses. He's the reason she left us medical supplies instead of handing you over to XB Force.

The man, Rich, let Safia vouch for him. Li could feel him breaking up the air close to her but he didn't try to touch her again.

Where are we now?

Port Howell, Safia said. The industrial zone. They won't find us here if we're careful.

Port Howell was where the boats came in from West. Where Li and Matti had landed three months ago. Half a day's walk from makecamp.

Rich said, They set up a holding centre.

She faced him blindly. Where?

Bout twenty clicks north of the port. Anyone who didn't get away got taken there for processing.

The black noise receded a little. Li grabbed onto this place where Matti could be. Afraid, waiting for her to come, but fed and hydrated. Sleeping inside, with a blanket, with other children, while someone in a uniform guarded the door.

She kept her face turned towards Rich's slow, easy voice. I need to get there before Agency does. If she gets processed without me, she'll be an unaccompanied minor. I don't know where they'll send her.

Safia said, They might have already processed by now. And if you turn yourself in and she's not there, they won't let you out again.

Then I won't go in the front gate.

Rich said, You never seen a holding, have you? It's not makecamp.

She hadn't but she knew the difference. There was no fence around makecamp, you could come and go as long as you didn't make trouble. A holding was built to contain. She'd need to get close without being seen, need something to cut through the fence. It was so hard to think through the drugs.

We have a phone, Safia said. We could arrange for you to call someone inside, find out if she's there before you turn up at the gate.

Why was Safia helping her? The question slipped away. She nodded. That'd be good.

So you gunna let me do this now? Rich asked. Find out if you can see before you start making plans?

Okay.

Okay. He did her eyes first. His hands smelled of alcohol. He was careful, deft, but she could feel a tension in him, something coiled. This was just a precaution, he said. You burned your eyelids and maybe your corneas, too, but we couldn't have a proper look because of the bucket of shit we were in at the time.

He loosened the last bandage and lifted off the padding. One eye, then the other. Some kind of gel pasted into the hollows so the fabric wouldn't stick but it still felt like removing a skin. Nothing to stop her from opening her eyes now, except the fear

ould change when she did. And fear was a waste

opened them the action felt complicated, mechani-
cal. The light broke in and then in a little while she could see.
His eyelashes first, each one. Then his face near hers. Bearded.
Intent on the job. Behind him, layer after layer of light, back and
back, as though that skin coming off had brought everything
into relief.

You right?

She squinted, nodded slowly. She didn't remember him from
makecamp but people came and went.

The swelling'll start going down soon, he said. You've lost your
eyebrows and your eyelashes and you're gunna have some scarring.
He held her chin lightly and turned her face to the side. You got
a couple of nice blisters there too; they could still get infected.
I'll put a new dressing on. He lifted her chin to inspect her neck.
This looks okay. Lucky you were wearing so many clothes.

She wasn't wearing them now, just her singlet. The way Matti
had slept in the tent on the road to Valiant, when they could
keep clothes on her at all.

Safia said, We had to cut most of them off you. I'll go and get
your pants.

It crashed back in, the terror of Matti in the world without
her. Without Frank. Li pulled free of Rich, sucking air. For a
few seconds she couldn't even think. Just blind, useless panic.
Then she forced it back down and made herself look at where
she was. An old factory. They were in an alcove at the back; she
could see metal roller doors across a space broken up by floor-
to-ceiling pillars and old packing boxes and what was left of
conveyor belts after everything useable and portable had been
salvaged. There were three other people in the alcove, apart

from Rich and Safia, but she was pretty sure she'd heard more voices than that.

What is this?

This? Rich glanced around and back at her. This is our reward for waiting nicely.

Frank used to do that, she thought, offer a joke like a small present. Rich was unravelling her hands, now, inspecting. They felt tender in the air.

Wiggle your fingers, he told her. Make a fist?

It was sharply painful when the skin stretched across the back of her hands. Her fingers looked okay though. He rubbed anti-biotic cream lightly onto the burns.

These're healing up pretty good, he said. I got some gloves for you.

How do they feel? Safia was back with her pants and boots.

I can use a phone.

We're going to need your help first.

Li focused on this woman she knew the same way everyone in makecamp had known her, through trade. Safia had given her credit on ready meals when she and Matti first got to makecamp. She said, I need to use the phone.

Not yet.

They'd got her out alive, treated her with medicine they could have traded. Drugs that had stopped her seeing what was obvious. She kept her eyes on Safia.

Phone doesn't work, does it?

Safia didn't flinch. Adam found it on a salvage run. We think it's patchable.

Li had done a few patches for her in the first weeks in makecamp, mostly phones and radios, to clear her debt. Then three men had come to her tent. One of them took Matti outside while the others explained that patching was already staked out and she was interfering with trade.

Who would I call?

There were some older kids in makecamp who had a phone.

Safia must have seen in Li's face how unlikely this sounded.

They kept it quiet. Mostly rented storage in the shop, but they had it when XB Force came in. We saw them get put on the buses to holding. I can give you the number.

If I patch.

If you patch.

Li's head was clearing and the whole deal felt thin, stitched together. They needed her till she patched the phone. How did she know anything on the other side of that was true? What if holding was bullshit and Matti was still waiting right where she was supposed to, back at the Kids' Tent?

I want to see makecamp first.

Safia shook her head. She's not there, Li. Nobody's there.

Rich said, Camp's finished, you understand? They demolished it. Bulldozers, the whole thing.

I understand. Did you see my daughter get on a bus?

Rich sighed.

Then I'll start at the camp, Li said.

She remembered the early dark. The two of them zipped in together, Li's body cupping Matti's, the sleeping bag tangled around them. Smell of mould and her own sour breath.

She listened to makecamp waking – tent zips tugging down, quiet prayers, radios, someone pissing in the dirt close by, footsteps and low voices in multiple languages as people joined the food queue.

Matti said, I miss Dad. He always woke us up.

It felt like a slap. Matti hadn't talked about Frank since the night they left Valiant, huddled together in the crush on the deck of the fishing boat. Almost two months.

Ask me what else do I miss.

What else do you miss?

Matti breathed, thinking. His voice. And the fun stuff we used to do, like when he swang me round and round and threw me on the couch. And when we played the Best Place, like if I rolled a five or a three or something, he always gave me chances.

Harder not to remember in the dark. Matti scrambling up off the couch and launching herself onto Frank. We're gunna *wrestle* and there's *no* Stop It!

Li rolled away and tugged down the zipper, letting the cold in. Come on. Breakfast.

They waited in the queue while it got light and then they kept waiting. The kitchen van was relief-run on donations, but there was no movement from inside yet. There wasn't always food. She was worried about Matti's toes and fingers, the raw spots on her skin, about the small bones she could trace in her back. You couldn't see them under the oversized jacket but she'd felt them in the dark. The cold season had barely started and already it was hard to stand for this long. How bad would it be here in a month? Li saw how Matti leaned forward slightly, leading from her nose. Their place in the line was okay – they should get millet, maybe beans too – but there was the queue and then there was everyone around the queue. She was tense all the time watching them, especially the younger men, trying to gauge who she could face down. She held her body stiff, elbows ready, and tried to cover all the angles.

Do you know how seconds work? Matti asked, looking up at her. So, you count to sixty and when you get to sixty it's not seconds anymore, it's one minute! And then you keep counting and it's seconds again! And when you count to however many minutes are in an hour, it's hours!

Eight years and two weeks old. When you taught your kid at home, around everything else, it was easy for things to slip. Matti had learned time here in makecamp, where the days kept passing and passing and nothing happened.

Makecamp was an unsanctioned waiting room between unshelter and shelter. It came and went – set up, got cleared out, resurrected itself as close to the XB as possible, on the unused scraps of land that floated between Port Howell's jurisdiction and Sumud's. It was somewhere people could get to.

This makecamp had lasted fourteen months. It had its own newspaper in five languages. There were communal cooking areas and portable toilets, three food shacks and a bakery, the ready shop for basic supplies, places to rent tools, get a haircut or a translation or a bucket shower. There were prayer tents, koffee shops, a library van. All the usual Trade services at inflated prices but there were relief groups that came and went too, blurring the line between what you had to pay for and what you could get for free.

The camp hugged Sumud's perimeter fence, always in sight of the highway where trucks carried goods to and from the unsheltered regions, through a checkpoint about fifty k south of Port Howell. The checkpoint was the only official break in the fence and it was guarded twenty-four hours by XB Force. Come too close on foot and you risked getting detained or shot. Every truck was searched. Driver IDs and customs paperwork vetted, cargo checked, undercarriage swept for jumpers.

From the checkpoint the highway ran inland through the No Go, straight to the XB's southern gate.

Li looked past Matti to the perimeter fence. They could always see it, wherever they were in the camp. High, spike-topped welded mesh panels, stretching out of sight in both directions. Warning signs repeated in pictures and languages. She wondered if Angie and Carl had stood in a queue like this, looking at the same stretch of fence, if it had got them anywhere.

The fence was just Sumud's first line in the sand. On the other side was the No Go – the same grey scrubland but with hills in the distance. Beyond the hills, out of sight, was the XB itself, the wall around the precinct of Sumud. People said there were only thirty or forty ks between the fence and the wall, but in that open ground there were XB Force patrols and no presumption of innocence.

Li said, Don't go out there again.

But Sulaman's dad lets him go, he just says be very careful.

If Sulaman gets shot that's his dad's business. I don't want you playing in the No Go.

Matti looked down. I wish I never told you.

Yeah, well. Li took a breath and let it out, watched it fade in the air. I'm glad you told me.

The queue shuffled forward a step. Matti said, You know what? What?

Me and Shayla and Sulaman, in the No Go, we found a big tree that was dead. And there was a big stripey lizard living inside it. This big.

Huh. You see any other animals out there?

Rabbits. And pigs. I mean, I didn't *see* any pigs but there was poo everywhere. I thought there might be horses in the hills, but probably not.

Something started taking shape in Li's head. Something trade-able that no one had staked out yet.

I don't really want to go out there again anyway, Matti said, because of the Takeaway.

It brought Li back sharply. The Takeaway was an old terror, she hadn't heard Matti talk about it in years.

Matti looked at her, pupils expanding. Li remembered her on the boat, twisting and crying through sleep while they crossed the Gulf. Because of Frank, she'd thought. But the Takeaway came earlier, back in Nerredin. Was Matti already afraid of losing them, of being lost to them, then? Before everything was consumed and nothing was left standing and nobody came to help and they had to walk. Like all the others.

Frank would have said something right but Frank was gone and Li didn't know how to answer these fears. Tell her the dark was benign and no one would hurt her?

She said, Just stay outside the fence.

All the way back to makecamp Li kept having the same unfinished thoughts. Rich had volunteered to show her the safest way after dark – a long slow circuit from the factory through Port Howell's industrial zone, avoiding security patrols. The third night since the camp was cleared. She kept groping for action, decision, a way to claw back the time. Over and over her mind dragged her back to the fence with Matti on the other side.

Mum, look!

But she wouldn't think about that. There was nothing there that would help her. She needed to pull herself together, work out the next step. There had never been any records of who was in makecamp, but someone must have kept track of the eviction, checked off status numbers before people were transferred to holding. There were always parents or reliefers at the Kids' Tent to break up the fights and hand out the stuff. Someone would have made sure all the kids got out.

She kept looking across for Frank, to say these things out loud or ask what he thought, kept forgetting it was Rich. He was nothing like Frank, except for some economy in the way he moved. And the joking where there was nothing funny. He'd given back her flint and steel and her knife in its sheath, but her sharpening stone was gone. It wasn't clear to her yet why he was helping her. He didn't seem to care about the phone.

All the times Matti ran away back in Nerredin, they'd only lost her once. Not even in Nerredin. They'd gone to Warrick for a Mynas home game, three families in Kit and Ivan's van. In the crush out the front afterwards Li let go of Matti's hand to reach for her wallet.

The backs of her hands hurt through the gloves. Rich had said she should keep them on as long as she could but they were too white, too visible. They were on open ground now, between the highway and the perimeter fence, with nothing but scrub for cover. Rich kept pace beside her, alert in all directions. He'd offered her a ready bar. Told her there was a fence around makecamp now, too, right around the site, to stop people going back in. That there were patrols. After that he seemed to know enough not to keep talking.

They'd found her at home, after loudspeaker announcements and searching the grounds with dozens of volunteers. When Li got back to the house after dark, frayed and panicky, the radio and all the lights were on. Matti had fed the chooks and washed herself and she was trying to make pikelets. A taxi driver leaving for Nerredin had recognised her and dropped her home. Her face was a mess of snot and flour and she looked up at Li without forgiveness. You shouldn't have let go of me, she said.

They stood at the western edge of the camp and looked through the new fence. They weren't far from the main cluster, where she and Matti had slept. Safia and Rich had said makecamp was finished, that there was nothing to see, but she could see everything. There were the food shacks, there was the ready shop, the stinking toilet block, the rows and rows of tents with their tarp extensions and washing lines and murals and cooking fires and solar hook-ups. Over there was the patch where Sulaman's family had tried to grow food. There was a relief truck, or maybe it was a water truck, and then it all collapsed in on her and turned to ash. The truck was a metal hole, black and buckled, and the queue had moved somewhere else.

And right in front of her, on the other side of the mesh, had been the Kids' Tent, where the reliefers handed out pencils and vitamins and jumpers and old shoes; where parents took classes with donated books. Those kids Matti ran with didn't queue at the Kids' Tent, they mobbed and wheedled and grabbed. Got done by Medical for scabies and fungus and footrot. Matti came back all hours and not often empty-handed. Fruit sometimes, or bottled water, a toothbrush, a balloon, a lice comb.

You ran straight at that tent, Rich said. I had to drag you back.

A capful of bubble mix, once, that she'd saved so Li could blow it with her. That was a good day.

You seen enough?

She could hear in his voice that they needed to be gone, but she held onto the wire with her gloved hands and kept looking at the place where the Kids' Tent had been, where she'd told Matti to wait for her.

The Takeaway is a man and he's way up high and if a kid goes somewhere without a grown-up, he'll reach down and grab you up and take you.

Rich said, Kids got out. I saw them.

And she had to believe him because she didn't believe Matti was dead. Maybe those other kids, not Matti. Matti was smart.

She was little and she was fast and she knew when things were going wrong. She knew how to get out.

There were lights along the highway, a vehicle moving towards them.

We have to go now, Rich said. He put a hand on her shoulder and she felt that tension in him again. Twisted free and rammed her elbow back into his ribs. He breathed out explosively. When she spun around, he was bent over, hands on his knees, and she waited, with her hand on the knife, for that coiled thing to snap. Then he laughed quietly and raised his head.

Wild woman, hey? All right, you take your time. He looked past her at the lights on the road, started backing cleanly into the scrub. But Li, if you get caught, you can't help her.

She had borrowed wire-cutters from Amin against the promise of meat. Made the first snares out of fencing wire, wrestling the strands into slip-knot loops that left her thumbs and forefingers aching. She made Matti show her where the kids went under the fence – a hole in the sand behind some bushes at the far eastern end of the camp. She cut into the fence just above it to make it easier to get through.

The first time Li went across it was just before dawn. She had warned Matti the night before that she was going. Told her to stay in the tent as long as she could after she woke, and then look for Sulaman's parents or Shayla's in the food queue and stand with them so she wouldn't get pushed out. The Kids' Tent usually opened around ten. If she wasn't back by then, that's where Matti had to wait for her.

Matti had taken a long time to fall asleep but she didn't wake when Li left, and Li didn't look back.

The No Go was sand and scrub and stringybark, noisy now with the early racket of birds. The kind of country that tricked you into thinking it was flat. Once she went over the first low rise and lost the fence from her sightline, everything took on a different scale. The night's condensation pulled up the smells of earth and leaf and salt, smells that were in the camp, too, but masked by cooking and fires and bodies and mould and untreated sewage.

There was spoor everywhere – signs of rabbits, roos, feral dogs and cats. Pigs too. She was going to need a knife. She moved in spurts at first, tree to tree, on high alert for vehicles or human movement but there was just the occasional sound of a truck out on the highway to Sumud and once an XB Force vehicle inland, moving away into the hills. On the other side of those hills, she knew, was the XB. The actual wall. It felt as distant now as it had before they crossed the Gulf.

She laid the first snares a few kilometres from makecamp and got back to Matti in the food queue before it started moving. Matti hugged her quickly and held her hand all the way to the front. When Li went back across early the next morning, there were two rabbits in her snares.

The third time, she went late in the day and took Matti with her. The sooner she knew how to get her own food, the better. But things started going wrong before they were even across. Matti had told Shayla and Sulaman to meet them at the fence, had promised they could learn too.

Li saw them waiting, serious and expectant, for this sanctioned adventure in the No Go, and sent them packing. Telling two kids was like telling half the camp. She tried to stay calm in the face of Matti's fury, explain what she should have understood, but in the end she had to shove her under the fence.

Walking wasn't a problem for Matti after the weeks on the road to Valiant, and she was already used to watching out for XB Force. She was good at spotting spoor, too, once she forgot to be mad. Li sent her up a tree after a bird snare and was reassured by the sprung, economical way her child climbed. But the dead honeyeater was harder for Matti than Li had expected, and when they found a young rabbit still struggling in the last snare, she cried and wanted to take it back to camp, alive. You could patch her, she said.

Li showed her the mess of its leg, told her that letting it live would be cruel as well as stupid. When she broke its neck, Matti beat her with her fists and shouted at her, out there in the open, still not dark. Li had to slap her quiet. She crouched in the bushes, holding her still, and listened until she guessed they were safe. She could feel Matti's outraged breathing, her strong, skinny body struggling to contain it, and she regretted the force of the slap.

Sorry, she said.

I'm not listening, Matti growled.

So Li talked to the back of her child's head in the dusk. Told her that she had to look after them both, trade for what they needed, and teach Matti to do it for herself. That was more important than the rabbit.

You're just saying that cos you're a human. If you had a baby rabbit, how would you feel?

They had raised a kid who could think like this because until a few months ago she had never gone hungry.

I don't know, she said. I don't have a baby rabbit, I have a beansprout. And she heard the wrongness of it. The trespass.

Dad had a beansprout, Matti said. Not you.

28

Walking back to makecamp after dark, they were quiet. The moon lit their way patchily, betweens scuds of cloud. Li was thinking she'd been wrong to bring Matti, it had been too soon. Matti had already made her first snares, and it would be easier now Li could trade for more flexible wire. She would make her practise until it was second nature. She'd teach her to skin and gut the kill, how to cut the bladder out without contaminating the meat. How to check the heart and liver for signs of disease — their trade would be worthless if people got sick from it. Li had been a little older than Matti when Val started teaching her these things but Val had had time on his side. Matti was smart and she was quick. She already knew how to draw water out of leaves, how to make a basic still. Li would bring her out again, just not straight away.

Mum, Matti said.

This was a new thing. Since the boat. Before that she had only been Mum when Matti wanted something. Otherwise she was Li, and Frank had been Dadda and then Dad.

Mum. See the jumpers?

They were near the fence now, parallel to the highway. Li saw the headlights coming and pulled Matti down but Matti was looking at something closer — a brief flaring of torches, shapes moving in the roadside scrub on the other side of the fence. The truck was almost on them, gears shifting down as it began the uphill stretch. They stayed low and watched the jumpers swarm the road, leaping, clawing, climbing. They went for the sides, the tailgate, tried to pull themselves under the moving vehicle. Matti was still and attentive in Li's arms. One of the figures turned to pull someone up behind them and lost their grip and fell.

I'm going for the kids, Matti whispered, because they're faster.

The truck picked up speed and the jumpers fell back. They walked or limped into the scrub and out of sight but a few of them stayed, crouching beside bodies on the road. Li listened to them crying in the dark and held onto Matti like it was only her arms keeping her clear of the wheels.

They got back to the factory after midnight. A woman Li hadn't seen before was on watch. They had a fire going in the alcove. Half a dozen people slept around it, huddled in blankets. Rich left her and went over to the packing crate that housed his sleeping bag.

Safia was sitting up by the fire, drinking koffee with Adam, who did salvage runs. They watched Li come.

Where's the phone? Li asked.

Safia looked at Adam. He handed it over carefully. It was an older model, the passcode worn into the keypad, plenty of surface damage. The charging port needed replacing for a start. She took the back off, held it up to the firelight.

Adam said, Can you patch it?

She focused on Safia. Do you have my kit?

Safia produced the flat leather pouch from inside her jacket. Li took it from her, flipped it open across her lap and went through the screwdrivers, the needle-nosed pliers, the picks and hooks and fine-tipped tweezers, the fishing magnet. Everything in its place. Safia had kept this from her to show that she could.

So, can you? Adam said.

Maybe.

We took a risk helping you.

Li looked at him. He was barely out of his teens. She remembered him hanging around the ready shop with a dozen others like him, all vying for jobs from Safia.

Where are you going to charge it?

I've got that covered. You just need to do your job.

Can you find me another model like this? she said. Two would be better.

Broken ones. Maybe.

Broken is okay.

Safia gave Li Adam's sleeping bag to use while he was gone. She slept uneasily. Once she woke to find Rich beside her, offering painkillers. When she woke again it was getting light and Adam was back with the parts she needed. He looked like they'd cost him but Li didn't ask.

By the time she'd patched the phone, it was full daylight. She woke Adam and he took it and went out again. Now she had nothing to do the pain reasserted itself, and the sick tense of time passing. Then Rich and one of the others came back from the port with bottled water and food from the relief groups; bread and beans and four hard-boiled eggs. More koffee.

We're not the only ones, he said. They reckon we'll be all right if we stay out of the nice end of town and don't piss anyone off. Sumud just wanted the camp gone, and if Sumud's happy, Port's happy.

Safia said, What about Agency?

Agency's got enough on their hands. They're not gunna come looking.

He'd brought yesterday's newspaper too. Makecamp was still burning on the front page, under a headline quote from Sumud's Chief Security Officer. *Nazari's message to Gulf people smugglers: 'Your trading model is over.'*

Adam came back when they were finishing breakfast. He bypassed Li and gave the phone to Safia, who checked it over while they all watched. Then she entered a number into the keypad and handed the phone to Li. It was fully charged.

One call, she said. There's credit.

Li walked away to the far end of the factory before she pressed call. It only rang twice.

Who is this?

My name's Li. I need to ask you something.

Li, the boy said. Are you my contact now? I have dollars.

No. I'm unsheltered, same as you.

How'd you get this number?

Safia from makecamp gave it to me, from the ready shop. She said there were three of you and you might be able to help me.

Silence. If she pushed too hard he might hang up, so she waited. Her hands hurt. In the midmorning light the factory looked like a ruined church with its concrete pillars and remnant fires and bird shit. All the glass had been salvaged from the windows. And Matti had spent another night alone.

Are you there?

He breathed out, a hard whoosh against her ear. It's just me now. I can't waste the battery.

Don't hang up. What's your name?

A tiny pause. Arsalan.

I'm trying to find my daughter, Arsalan.

You think she's here?

Maybe. I hope so.

How old?

Seven. Eight. She turned eight. She was at the Kids' Tent when XB Force came in.

The Kids' Tent caught on fire, he said.

I heard they got out, got taken where you are. He didn't answer. Are there other kids in there without parents? Young kids?

Why don't you come and see?

The little fuck. You know why, she said. If she's not in there and they hold me, I can't look for her. Silence again, but he hadn't hung up. She could hear some kind of repetitive banging in the background.

He said, over the noise, There are no little kids here now.

You sure about that? Her name is Matti. A different, sharper silence. Li's heart rate spiked. You know her? You know Matti from makecamp?

She had a horse she carried around.

Yes. *Yes,* that's her.

She's not here anymore. Agency took all the little kids yesterday.

For a second she couldn't get air in. But she *was* there? You saw her?

I saw her get off a bus. And then I saw her at processing.

And she was okay, she wasn't hurt?

They put those ones in a different container. Like, hospital container. Or they died and they took them away. Matti looked okay.

Li felt her legs going. Got her back against the nearest pillar and lowered herself down.

Where did they take them?

People said north. I think there was a problem about keeping kids here, a legal problem. They're going to take all the under-fifteens but they started with the little kids.

Are you sure it was north?

Lady, I don't know. They wouldn't send them south, would they? I just know they had a bus and they took the little kids first. Must be a long way north cos they haven't come back for the others yet.

How many did they take?

She almost heard him shrug. How many you can fit on a bus?

Fifty kids? she thought. More if you packed them in. That meant Agency paperwork, something on Matti's record. She needed to get to the Source Centre.

The banging in the background got louder and there was yelling now, too. The boy talked over it. I tried to get on the bus because people say Agency treat little kids better, so I thought it might be a better place, but they ran my status.

When did you turn fifteen, Arsalan?

Two months ago. People say I look younger.

So he was out of time, she thought. The day he turned fifteen his status number would have gone into the ballot, and now he was waiting to find out if he was going to be shipped to the Front. Maybe this month, this year, maybe ten years from now when he was starting to feel lucky. And this was Matti's future, too.

Recruiters came yesterday, he said. I got a choice. I can join up, voluntary, or Agency sends me back. He sounded different now, engaged. She needed to finish this, but it was hard to resist the idea that she was making a trade here. Stay on the phone a bit longer, keep listening to this kid and maybe someone would do the same for Matti.

Do you have anyone to go back to?

They don't send you all the way back, they just leave you on the highway somewhere. You don't know much.

No family then. No one in holding and no one outside waiting for him. She forced herself to say it. You'll get paid if you join up.

He laughed, a disgusted sound. Army came round makecamp every week saying that. Get paid, get fed, place to stay, better than this place. Take charge of your future. Like I'm supposed to put my hand up to go to Wars? At least with the ballot I get a chance.

So, what are you going to do?

I'm going to keep trying till I get inside, he said. I still have some dollars for the trucks. I had a contact before but he's not calling me back now.

What will you do inside? She wondered if he thought it would be some kind of happy ending. Everyone knew there was no quota for queue-jumpers.

I'll find my brother. He got in two years ago. The banging got so loud that Li lost his voice for a moment. Then he said, I want to go to school again and eat challow and play footy. Mostly I hope I find my brother.

Arsalan, she said. I have to go.

Matti always wanted to play this game where you're trying to get to the place you'd live if you could live anywhere. You know? The Best Place.

Yeah, yeah. The Best Place. But I think she thought it was a real place. She used to get in fights about it. She said it was better than inside and she was going to go there. Some of the little kids believed her.

His voice was so close. Li could almost touch her.

Lady? Wait, Lady?

I'm still here.

It's good you're looking for her.

Li stayed where she was, with the phone to her ear so the others wouldn't know she'd finished the call. Yesterday. She'd missed Matti by one day.

Now what? It made sense that they'd go north. There was nothing south between here and the ocean except the checkpoint in the fence, and if Sumud was willing to take busloads of unsheltered, makecamp wouldn't have been cleared in the first place. Agency wouldn't ship unaccompanied minors back west if there was no one there to claim them. She'd asked around when they first got to makecamp and everyone said the same thing. XB Force might but Agency was government and government was still signed up to conventions. That only left north.

Further down the factory, the others were keeping their distance, pretending not to watch her. She turned her back fully. She had never thought she would call this number. Frank only ever asked her about it once, after they'd got to Valiant and he was wearing himself out in Agency queues, searching for ways in that didn't exist.

You could ask him to sponsor us, he'd said. He might have connections now. He might be happy to do something for you.

As if she would have asked Chris for anything. It had caught her off guard, that Frank still thought this way about people. She told him she'd already searched the Source directory. That either Chris was dead or he didn't have a phone. Had Frank believed her or had he just decided to let it go? She'd found the number years and years ago – long before she met Frank. Just to know he was still in the world, to place him on the map. Not ever to call. She used to recite it in her head when she was walking or falling asleep, over and over until it had a rhythm. Later, in Nerredin, she gave that up, never thought about him, not really. But when she reached for it now, the number was right there.

She got up as she dialled because she needed to be on her feet for this. While it rang her heartbeat raced ahead of her. Such a small thing she was asking, in the scale of things.

The voice that answered was completely unfamiliar.

She said, Chris?

Yeah.

It's Li. She waited for him to speak. When he didn't, she said, Do you know who I am?

Li. Another pause. Right. I guess. I guess I'm surprised that I'm hearing from you. Under the shock, his voice was rearranging itself, setting up lines of defence.

I need to ask you something.

I don't think that's a good idea.

Li pushed past his wariness. My daughter and I have been in the makecamp outside Sumud for the last three months.

You have a kid? He sounded confused, like this wasn't what he'd expected.

Yeah. XB Force just cleared the camp. We got separated. I don't know where she is now. She heard the news like it was being reported about someone else, someone more careless.

How?

How what?

How did you get separated?

I was. She cleared her throat. I was out of the camp when it happened.

Right. Silence again. A harder, assessing silence. And what is it you think I can do?

Fuck him, what did he think she thought he could do? She took a shaky breath, couldn't afford to alienate him. Agency took the unaccompanied minors north, she said. I heard there's another holding up there, somewhere along the XB. A place they keep kids.

Okay.

So, you're in Fengdu, right? You have a phone. If I give you her status number, can you make some calls, find out where that would be?

Why don't you make the calls?

It was possible that he didn't know. She said, I can't call into those places. They'll just put me in a queue till my credit runs out. She heard footsteps, turned. Adam was striding down the factory floor towards her.

Look, Li, Chris said. I'm sorry, but you've got the wrong idea about how things work inside. I don't have any special access to the Population Distribution Agency or anything else.

Bullshit, she thought. Said, You have sheltered status. They'll tell you things they won't tell me.

I don't know what you've heard, he said, but the Agency doesn't have two sets of rules.

Maybe his calls were monitored. She'd heard that happened inside. Adam was in front of her now, lit with indignation, holding out his hand for the phone. She knocked his arm aside. Chris was telling her to log a missing-minor claim.

I don't have a number they can call me on.

That doesn't matter. He sounded impatient now, done with it. The Agency doesn't call. You need to follow the Source procedure and they'll contact you that way when they have news. Okay? I have to get back to work.

Let me give you her status, she said. In case you change your mind.

I can't help you, Li. He started to say something else, something placating. She hung up.

One call. Adam's voice went high. The trade was for one call.

I needed two.

You think you're the only one trying to find someone? You didn't even put in for the credit.

He stepped towards her and then froze when she raised the phone above her head and drew her arm back, ready to throw.

You think you can put it back together? They stayed like that for a few seconds and then she thought that this was a waste of time. Dropped it into his hands.

You're welcome, she said, and walked away from him.

They'd crossed the Gulf in the dark. The man sitting next to them in the press of bodies on deck was crossing for the second time. He warned her to keep Matti's clothes dry, unfastened his life jacket and pulled his T-shirt up to show her the scars of chemical burns from fuel mixed with saltwater. The first boat had capsized just outside the port. He made it to land and walked to the makecamp, but two weeks later it got shut down and he was sent back across the Gulf.

There's a new makecamp now, he told Li, closer to Port Howell. From there you can try to buy a sponsor inside Sumud, or maybe jump a truck. He said most people off the boats ended up in the makecamp, unless they'd made an arrangement.

She knew about the new makecamp from Teresa and Navid. Teresa had told her she and Matti might have a better chance of getting their change-of-status claim processed now, without Frank. And then she went out of the room and they listened to her crying.

The man looked Li in the eye. You have to be careful in a place like that, he said. A woman and child alone.

Matti slept and slept across the Gulf. She slept like she'd been awake for years. She cried in her sleep and Li couldn't reach her, could only sit holding her, in her own sickness and fear. The moon came out and showed the black horizon all around them. She thought how fragile their continent was, with the sacrifice zones encroaching from the north and the oceans rising around the edges, taking back its low places. Matti had never seen the sea before they came to Valiant. Navid took her down to the port one day when Frank's shift was finishing.

She wanted to know why the water was just lying there, Frank told Li afterwards. Why no one was using it. So I showed her the desal plant, explained how it works.

You took her in there?

Not inside. Jesus. Anyway, she wanted to know once we use up the sea, what else will people drink? Navid told her beer. But then he starts explaining how the Gulf's just one little bit of all the water and I showed her a couple of freighters on their way to the precincts. She's nodding, like it's all making sense. And then she says, So can we walk out to those boats?

The nausea passed and there was only the rocking that went on and on. Her head so heavy on her neck. Frank, she thought, it's your turn. But she felt the weight of Matti, the bulk of her life jacket, felt her breathing, still breathing. Darkness everywhere, the deck slippery with vomit, Valiant behind them, West behind them. Frank. Waves lifted the boat and the man beside her started praying. She looked east, she thought it was east, searched for the lights of Port Howell.

The nearest Source Centre was about an hour's walk from the factory, on the western edge of the industrial zone. Closer in, most of buildings had their lights on and their windows intact. There were vehicles moving in the loading bays, shiftworkers stacking and unloading and yelling to each other, security guards smoking in doorways. Early afternoon, a cold grey rain.

At the edge of the zone she saw the port. Gulls circled the freighters coming in from the Gulf and there were tankers queuing up outside the desal plant. Something bottomless opened inside her. The desire to fall was so strong that she had to step back. Closed her eyes to steady herself, and when she started walking again she only looked at what was right in front of her.

The Source Centre was crammed into a single shopfront between the hammam and the Dollarzone. It was the closest one to makecamp, so Li and Matti had come here once a week to check on their claim. Almost a forty-k round trip. They got up in the dark and came home in the dark. The walk was too much for Matti so they got a taxi back but the camp price was double local price and it could go higher depending on the driver's mood and how desperate the passengers looked.

Back in Valiant, Frank had queued every weekend for two months to get them pre-registered under the skilled worker and food security categories. Now Li was waiting to be contacted about registration. Once you were registered, you waited for clearance, pending sponsorship. Then, if an XB precinct opened a quota, you looked for a sponsor inside that precinct and got your sponsor approved. Then you could apply for change of status under quota.

The queue was shorter than usual this time – it looked like clearing makecamp had been bad for business. There were wharfies and factory and plant workers, and a handful of other evictees like Li, trying to blend in with the legitimate unsheltered, the ones with a home and a job in a hometown that still existed. She used to bring the plastic sheet and the sleeping bag so Matti could rest while they queued. Sometimes they got onto a machine before closing and sometimes the signal didn't drop out before Li finished punching in all the numbers. There was never any progress on their registration but she couldn't know that for sure unless they queued.

She stood in this queue for two and a half hours. Every time she shuffled forward she reached down to drag Matti with her and Matti wasn't there. She rocked on her heels, chewed her lip, tested the flex of her fingers, anything to stay in motion. Hours already since she talked to Arsalan. Almost four days since they'd cleared the camp. Maybe Matti was safe for now but Li couldn't keep her safe. That depended on Agency and Agency had cracks you could drive a truck into. So easy to lose one skinny girl who couldn't tell the time yet.

Acid rose in her stomach and her burns throbbed, in spite of the painkillers Rich had topped up before she left the factory.

44

People looked away from her too fast. She kept her eyes down, read the graffiti on the pawnbroker's wall, the words she knew or could translate. *Refuse the Ballot.* You saw that in every language, in West too. *The Whole Game's Rigged.* And scrawled over but still visible, *We Decide. Terrorists Go Home.* That was an old one, like a history lesson about missing the point. Matti had struggled over *terrorists.* What if they can't go home? she'd asked.

Li's face felt raw where her eyebrows had been. She tried to remember the burning tent, the heat of it. What she remembered was Matti at the fence, her fingers curled in the wire. *Mum, look!*

She got to the front of the queue. The shopfront window had *Single Source of Truth* stencilled on the glass in the official yellow and a government-approved price list underneath. An armed security guard out the front was checking everyone's status. Inside there were six machines under strip lighting, with access to printing for an extra fee. A Cnekt slot for phone-credit top ups. There were newspapers available for reading on a table along the back wall, but only one chair, for the second security guard.

Li found a free terminal, swiped her card and logged on. Barely enough credit. She scanned the Source newsfeed first. More photos of the camp demolition, XB Force in riot gear, medics carrying a burns victim on a stretcher. Statements from health and security officials in Port Howell. It all looked familiar but not because she remembered it. She'd seen it all back in West, in newspaper coverage of other makecamps, other demolitions.

There was nothing about unaccompanied minors.

She checked Matti's status for an Agency update – maybe even a note about her being taken. But there was nothing. Just the pre-registration claim, still stranded at Stage Two Request, dependent minor.

The child who stared out at Li from the screen was a few years younger, hadn't fully grown into her eyes yet. This status-record Matti felt immensely far away, as if Li had lost the years since the photo was taken, too. And then she realised this was it, now, this was all there was. The photos had been in their tent.

Lodging a missing-minor claim took her right up to closing time. She punched numbers and watched the clock, her stomach tightening every time the page froze. There was no save function. When she was halfway through the form, the signal dropped out and she had to start again. She had to enter her status at every new section and every time she typed *unsheltered*, half the fields disappeared. She hesitated over *Employment or means of support*. The olives, the hardware store in Nerredin had been legitimate. In Valiant they'd put the garage and the salvage depot and the desal plant down on their pre-registration, plus agricultural skills. Leaving it blank wasn't an option. She didn't know how patching was regulated in East but it was all she had now.

A pop-up warned her she had three minutes. If she didn't submit the claim before the terminal shut down she'd lose it all, lose another day tomorrow starting from scratch. The last field was a contact number. Probably Chris was right, they wouldn't call, but she couldn't take that chance. It might be days before she found another Source centre further north; what if some Agency employee checked Matti's status in the meantime and saw there was a claim? Teresa and Navid had a phone for the repair shop but what could they do, all the way back across the Gulf? And unsheltered. She knew what it had cost them to get her and Matti on that boat.

One minute.

She put Chris down. Hovered over *relationship* and then typed *relative*. Whatever he said, she didn't believe he was powerless, not compared to her. And she had to believe he wouldn't be able to live with himself if he got the call and did nothing. Because he owed her, really he owed her his life.

Walking back to the factory, she thought about the last time she went into the No Go. Less than two weeks since the first reports of fever and makecamp was a sprawl of contagion behind her. She moved as fast as she could, watching for patrols, listening for movement. Smoke was rising north of the camp. That made sense. Port Howell authorities wouldn't want to burn the bodies too close to town.

Four days since she'd been through the fence. Matti would be back in the tent by now, hopefully sleeping. Li could do what she needed to and be back before she woke.

The first snare was on open ground about five hundred metres from the fence. It held a rabbit, partly eaten and starting to stink. She cut it loose, threw the carcass away into the scrub so the smell wouldn't drive away new kill, and then reset the snare. Kept moving. Two days without sleep, waiting to see if her child would live. The next two snares were empty and she was grateful to conserve the time and effort.

A few hours south, dusk and temperature falling, she saw the highway in the distance, cutting inland across the flat of the No Go until it got lost again in the hills. Nothing moving, and she'd be hard to see in this light, so she kept heading towards it, carefully, on a diagonal. There was an ache at the base of her skull that she was trying to ignore. Two more snares to check.

Just before full dark she heard engines and flattened herself in the scrub while the tankers roared past, headlights boiling. Water runners. They travelled in convoy now, belting through the

No Go in daylight if possible. This one must have got delayed. It wasn't the jumpers they were worried about, it was Trade. Trucks had been ambushed in the No Go, food and medicine lifted, water siphoned off. That was why all the drivers were armed now and most convoys carried security. She hadn't run into any Trade out here yet but she'd heard stories in makecamp about things that happened further north – trucks and tankers hijacked, disappeared up into the sacrifice zone.

Her head was thumping now and the ache was spreading slowly through her bones. Resetting the last snare in the dark, her hands were unsteady on the wire and there was a spinning lightness behind her eyes. She made it to a patch of stringybark with the idea of digging a windbreak, but she was sweating, off-balance, a tide surging in her ears. She managed to get her pack off and pull out the water bottle but not to open the lid.

Fever held her down in the hole. There was somewhere she needed to be but whenever she tried to climb out, Frank started talking again, explaining the rules. You know your problem, Li? Every time you throw, you're betting on a five. See, Matti, she figures things can go any way – sooner or later she's gunna roll a six. That's why she wins. A fluorescent light buzzed on in the swirling black and there was a clock ticking and someone breathing behind her, but not Frank.

She woke clear but weak and in terrible thirst. She was shaking and too cold to function. It was light. The sand under her was wet and her clothes were soaked with sweat or dew. In a few minutes she steadied enough to get the lid off her water bottle.

Matti had been alone all night. She would think Li had been hurt or killed, that she wasn't coming back. Would she do what Li had told her and wait at the Kids' Tent, or would she come into the No Go looking for her? Li stood shakily and lifted her pack. She would just check the two snares that were directly on her way back. Go into makecamp with fresh trade if she was lucky.

Get up. Slowly.

She was so focused on the gun that it took a few seconds to register he wasn't XB Force. No uniform. And it was just him. He'd found her by accident; he looked surprised, anyway. She stood up and stepped away from the cover of the mallee, from the snare she'd just reset and the fresh kill.

Where are you from?

Port Howell.

Liar.

A couple of metres between them. She kept her hands at her sides.

You're makecamp, he said. Why are you across?

Looking for food.

His eyes moved past her to the shrubs, but the pistol stayed steady. In the No Go? That's not how it works.

People like him brought the food. People like her paid for it. That was how it worked. She said, I don't have enough trade.

He was dressed like her, shabby, colours of sand and scrub. But the pistol looked army issue – the kind you could get if you had backup. That meant he might have bullets too.

Catch anything?

Not yet.

Harder than it sounds, huh? he said. You shouldn't be out here alone.

You're out here alone.

He grinned at her. No I'm not.

She didn't let herself look behind him, didn't take her eyes off him.

You should get back inside before you get yourself shot. He looked down her body and up again. Think of something else to trade.

He took a step towards her. She brought her hands up and he stopped. Said, You're bleeding.

No.

Let me see.

I'm not bleeding.

Two more steps and he jammed the gun into the soft place under her jaw, dragged her arm up, rigid, in front of her face. Then what's this? Huh? What's this? He slapped her with her own hand. Forced her hand into her face and rubbed it back and forward, smearing the gore. He pushed her away onto the ground. Raised the gun.

Show me what you've got.

She started to get up.

No, stay down. Crawl.

Her body shook, disobedient. She crawled and breathed, felt his eyes, the stones and brittle grasses under her hands. Towards the mallee, with him behind her. *But Mum, if you die first, where will you wait for me?* She crawled in an arc, a little to the left of the shrubs. A little more to the left.

You lying bitch. He moved past her eagerly towards the kill, but a little to the left. Where she had led him. Her disobedient body, the rock under her hand.

The snare took him clean by the ankle and flung him forward. He shouted before he hit the ground and the pistol went clear without discharging and she sprang onto his back and brought the rock down on his head, hard, twice. Left him face down and picked up the kill without turning her back on him. He didn't move. She couldn't afford to lose the snare but her hands were shaking too hard and her body would not approach him. There was no time anyway. If he hadn't lied the others would have heard him shout, they'd be coming now. She picked up the gun. It wasn't loaded but that didn't make it useless.

Walking back, she kept telling herself to run but her body wouldn't do it. She was so tired from the work of fever. Her bones were rubber, she was dried out inside and the steady thumping in her head was back. She needed to see Matti, know she was okay. Take the kill to the ready shop. Safia would keep it cool for a cut on her trade. Then drink and sleep. Not dream. She would never bring Matti back out here. The pistol was tucked into her waistband, against the small of her back, and she wondered what bullets were worth.

She heard it first, before she smelled the smoke. Started running.

Rich was on lookout, he brought Li in. Any news?

She shook her head. It had taken her too long to find the factory again – too many empty buildings with broken windows. There wasn't a lot of light left when she recognised the lettering over the entrance. ort Howell Pack ng Compan.

Come over here, he said. Someone wants to talk to you.

It was already night inside, almost colder than outside but they'd lit the fire again. Rich walked alongside her easily. He was solid, muscular, everything about him was capable.

Most of the group were sitting around the fire, eating out of bowls they hadn't had this morning. A metal pot of soup or stew sat near the fire. No sign of Adam, but she saw a bicycle, propped carefully against the wall, and there was someone new sitting on a packing crate talking to Safia while the others listened in.

This is Yara, Safia said when they reached them. She's with Friends of the Camp.

Yara stood up. She was young, early twenties at most, and Li thought she'd seen her before, maybe in the kitchen van or the

Kids' Tent. Friends of the Camp was the main relief group in Port Howell. She shifted the pad and pen she was holding into her left hand and held out the other to Li. Assalamu alaikum.

Wa alaikum assalam. Do you know something about my daughter?

Your friends told me. I'm very sorry. What I know for sure is that the Population Distribution Agency took a busload of unaccompanied minors from the holding facility up the Northern Highway yesterday morning, to a temporary facility up there. At least seventy children. We tried to take statements from them, get a list of status numbers, but we couldn't get access.

What temporary facility?

We were told they're setting up in an old army barracks north of Kutha. They're going to hold them there while they try to trace relatives.

I know where that is, Rich said. That place got decommissioned years ago.

Yara passed the pad and pen to Safia. Why don't you finish the list? She turned back to Li and Rich. There's a larger group but they could only spare one bus. I saw Agency staff loading food and bedding. Cooking gear, camping gear, high-thermals.

Why would they need camping gear?

Barracks'll be pretty basic, Rich said. They might end up camping inside.

Yara said, It'll be better for them up there. She looked straight at Li, trying hard for adult certainty but her ladybird hairclip gave her away. There's about another thirty older minors in holding, waiting for the bus to come back. We're trying to monitor their wellbeing but we have to reapply for access every day.

Li stopped listening. Something was loosening its grip a little in her chest. This was how Frank saw the world, she thought.

This was the system working. She hadn't kept her daughter safe, so now government was doing it for her. It was just hard to have faith in it. She realised Yara was asking her something.

Is there anyone in West who could claim her?

She hesitated, unwilling. My sister-in-law and her husband back in Valiant. They might.

That's good, Yara said. They'll try them first but their tracing database is a bit of a mess. I think you have time to get to the barracks first.

What happens if they can't trace? Rich asked.

Yara nodded, thinking. If it's just a few children left they might try to negotiate a limited humanitarian intake with Sumud, but that won't be quick either.

Li said, I've already lodged a missing-minor claim. How far is it?

Kutha's almost three hundred kilometres north. Yara looked at Rich. I'm not sure about the barracks.

Bout another two hundred from there to the turnoff, he said. Big walk.

Li said, I'm starting tonight.

There are taxis running up the highway, Yara told her. Do you have any dollars? Li shook her head. Watched Yara sifting and discarding options. Let me see what I can do, she said.

She turned back to talk to Safia and Rich explained. Friends of the Camp had been waiting on two containers of supplies to help winterise makecamp, mostly donations from inside Sumud. The containers had cleared customs the same day the camp was demolished.

They offered the stuff to holding, he said, but holding won't take it. They don't want to winterise, you betcha, that'd just make it harder to shut the place down. They want everyone processed and gone.

If the supplies weren't unloaded by the end of the week, they'd be sent back to Sumud, so Friends of the Camp were distributing them on the quiet. Rich had heard about it from Yara in the port that morning, told her where to find them.

Yara and Safia were talking through their list. Do you have any tents? Li asked.

Yara looked up. No, but we have plastic sheeting. We have groundmats, sleeping bags, cooking gear, ready meals. I can get you some high-thermals too – the nights are going to get colder. She lifted the top page of her pad, tore off the one underneath, and passed it to Li, with another pen. It was a list of supplies in neat, handwritten bullet points. Write your name at the top. Circle what you need. I'll bring the van back after dark.

Before Li left Port Howell, Rich gave her back the empty gun. Self-loading nine-millimetre, semiautomatic, he said. Army issue. Not easy to come by was what he meant.

She resisted the memory of the trader pressing it into her neck.

Rich said, I reckon if you can get hold of a pistol, maybe you can get hold of bullets too.

So the others didn't know. Li put it in a side pocket of the pack Yara had given her, crammed with gear. She tested the weight, checked the straps and buckles. She'd need to dirty it up a bit or she'd be a walking target.

You can't get lost, Rich told her. The highway sticks to the No Go, so you'll be hugging the fence the whole way. There's a bit of a town called Ruddock about two hundred clicks north. Just get through there. You can resupply in Kutha, should be Source there too. Not much left in the way of towns further north, it's mostly dust and salt now. Great big salt lake up there. So. After Kutha the highway starts veering north-east, around the XB. The old army-base turnoff should be signposted, unless someone's nicked the sign. Barracks is about twenty clicks down that track.

He told her about water supplies and where relief was most likely to be set up. It all sounded plausibly first-hand.

She said, Did you come down that way?

I been all over.

You ever see Agency using barracks like that?

He rolled his shoulders back, wincing at some twinge. I couldn't tell you, Li. I don't go visiting bases for the happy memories.

Safia came over. Good luck, Li, she said, I hope you find her.

Li nodded. She didn't trust herself to speak and after a minute Safia went back to the group and the gear she was sorting and distributing. Li wondered if she'd find a way to take a percentage. In makecamp Safia had always found a way to set herself in the middle of things and get people to work the angles for her.

You know she's most of the reason you're walking around now, Rich said. Condition you were in, you wouldn't have been any use to your kid.

She couldn't deny what he was saying. And maybe there was something wrong with her that she didn't see it like he did. But she wondered if he saw the other possibility: that Safia had protected Li, protected her hands, because she needed a phone. And while Safia was waiting to get her phone, Matti had been processed and put on a bus.

He hauled up the shutter. You should get out of here before Adam gets back. He'll wrestle that pistol off you and then he'll pistol-whip me for giving it away.

The punchline was in his body this time, in the ease that said he could kill Adam bare-handed without breaking a sweat. Nearly made her smile.

Walking out of the factory, she thought that it wasn't Safia she'd been lucky with, it was Rich. And that probably she should have said it. Then a wind from the north-east carried the bitter burnt smell of makecamp, and she forgot him.

In the Nerredin hotel, three nights after the fire, people had talked quietly in corners or listened to the radio, or slept. Some of them had had time to take their own bedding from their own houses. Beer was on tap but no one was drinking much. Stitch, the Janovich's dog, moved among them, pausing to be greeted.

The Janovich twins, Toby and Jay, were playing pool. No one had told them to go to bed and Matti had sat up late watching, hovering in case they let her have a turn. Now she was asleep on a mattress at their feet and they stepped around her, maintaining the irregular thock and clunk of their game.

Li and Frank sat near them at the bar. Li was drinking whiskey for the first time in years, but not enough to dull the clean lines of movement in her head – the route she was mapping, the things they needed and how to get them. Frank was carving something out of an olive branch he'd brought back from their grove that afternoon, walking among the charred trees until he found one the fire had only licked over. Already a shape was emerging under the borrowed knife.

He looked up at her, the drink in her hand, at the half-full bar. Huge Wednesday night, eh?

You keep saying how I never take you anywhere.

He grinned, went back to it. Last Saturday's paper lay unopened on the bar beside her. *Government promises 'robust discussion' with XB precincts over quotas.* She sketched the highway south over the sports section, the distance between towns, the bores she remembered. Three hundred k to Valiant, give or take. She'd never been there – it hadn't been on the circuit. Didn't know Frank's sister either. Teresa had moved down to the city before Li met him. They'd have to walk in the cooler hours, build in rest days for Matti. She figured two weeks, two and a half.

They news came on the radio. Kit went behind the bar and turned it up. The situation was still unpredictable, fireballs to the north and east. Most people with vehicles had already gone. The rest were staying put for now, waiting for the DES to give the all-clear. At least here there was nothing left to burn.

He said, She's going to be cranky as shit in the morning.

Maybe she'll just wake up and start playing pool again. What are we going to feed her?

More kelp? I think those three already ate all the crackers. He held the wood away, considering. Did you see when she tried to sink one and she whacked Toby in the nuts with the other end?

Nerredin's finished, Li said. Nobody's coming to fix it, nobody's coming back.

He looked at her like she was incomprehensible. Don't make it sound like nothing. This is our home. Hers and mine anyway.

Li looked away, focused on Matti, sleeping bag thrown off, limbs starfished. One hand gripped the balled-up tea towel Frank had put there to stop her reaching for Goldie in her sleep. When she looked back at him she could see that he was sorry but what he said was, Why is it so easy for you? He meant, to uproot, to walk away. He was asking if she'd ever really been attached. And she didn't know. Because now that there was nothing to hold onto, it didn't feel that different. Maybe she felt relieved that he had to carry this with her now, instead of her carrying it alone in preparation.

Blunt fucken knife, he said.

She looked at the gouge in the wood, watched him start, patiently, to fix it. Matti's room had been full of Frank's small, strange animals. The accumulation of all her seven years.

Kit Janovich came down the bar to check their drinks, a burn dressing on her bare arm. We're leaving the day after tomorrow, she said. We can give you a lift as far as Warrick. Ivan has a cousin there we can stay with while we look for a place to run further south. She refilled Frank's glass and looked around the pub with tired eyes. We've been talking about it since the first howler. No one'll buy this. We tried.

She went to get the twins to bed. Li nudged her glass against Frank's. What do you see? If we stay.

His hands went quiet. When he grinned at her, finally, she had to look away. We could run the pub.

Niche market. We could call it The Oasis.

I reckon. Take turns being the customer.

She listened to Toby arguing with his mother, the late Weather update, snoring. Frank's eyes moved over the dusty sherry glasses on the top shelf and the Christmas tree, hung with Jay's origami stars. Ivan was up on a ladder, taking down a wall-full of licence plates from decades of vehicles abandoned on the highway outside town. The metal was worth more than the pub now.

Frank shook his head, nodded. Drank. After a second, she drank, too. He saw it now. In the process something in him had been reduced. She hoped not too much because she would need all of him, they would need all of each other for what was coming next.

It's all gone, she thought and felt light, almost giddy, in the presence of the two people she loved who were with her still. Frank put the little horse on the counter. In the light from the bar fridge, it wobbled but it stood.

The northern highway

The bus had refuelled at Kutha three days ago. Li heard about it at the relief station on the way into town, from a local couple in their sixties who refilled her waterbag and offered her a choice between bean- or vegetable-based readies. They didn't know where the bus was going but the woman said there had been government workers in and out of town earlier that week, and talk about traffic on the old army access road to the north.

The cashier at the truckstop hadn't been rostered on three days ago. Couldn't tell her anything about a bus full of kids. We get a lot of vehicles through here, she said.

There was a young woman in the phone box outside the truckstop. She was actually on the phone. Li hadn't come across a working phone box in over a year. She glanced in as she passed but it was just habit; there were too many people around for her to try any salvage. The woman looked back at her and the side of her face and neck were pitted with black dots of shrapnel.

Li went across the road to the newsagent and offered her services for a twenty-dollar top-up for the Source booth on the

63

main street. She patched the internal antenna on the owner's radio but she worked too fast, made it look too easy, and he refused to finish the trade until she got his daughter's old baby monitor working too.

He backed up the story about the bus while she patched. It been at the truckstop for close to an hour. He'd thought it might have had engine trouble but it took off all right in the end.

Kids getting on and off the whole time, he said. No supervision. Wandering in and out of here trying to steal stuff. Peeing on the side of the road, some of them.

When she described Matti, he shrugged. There were that many kids, I'm surprised none of them got left behind. I couldn't even swear they did a headcount getting them back on the bus.

Walking out past the revolving book rack she heard Matti screaming but it was only in her head. She went down the road to the Source booth and queued to check on her missing-minor claim. No response, no update.

It was six days since she lost her, the end of the sixth day.

When she left the factory, late on the fourth night, she had walked to the eastern edge of the industrial zone and then cut around a checkpoint on the main road into Port Howell, through the No Go to where it joined the highway. She'd been walking north for forty-five minutes when a taxi slowed down behind her. The driver was going as far as Ruddock. He added up her bandaged face and the fact that she hadn't come through the checkpoint and named a price she had no hope of paying, but his tray was half empty and when she handed him all the dollars Yara had given her, he didn't stop her climbing up. Ruddock was five days' walking. It was worth all the dollars.

There were four other passengers. Three of them looked like they were going home, supplies piled up around them. They were relaxed and social with each other and they ignored her, like they ignored the old man huddled in a corner He looked familiar but it was probably just because he looked like makecamp. Li wondered how he'd got through the checkpoint. She pulled the new hunting cap down over her eyes and looked away.

The outskirts of Port Howell gave way to crops and greenhouses, hulking outlines of glass and plastic.

Ruddock was a one-street town. The driver let her off at the far end and she walked north until morning. There was no cloud cover. A vivid moon. Company trucks and water tankers and road trains filled the air with noise and dust. She didn't meet anyone walking but the roadside was strewn with rubbish and shit. When she saw the fires of a roadside camp up ahead of her, she crossed to the other side and moved past it quickly in the dark.

Her breath cut the air but the high-thermal gear and the hunting cap kept her warm as long as she kept moving. And moving kept her mind quieter, made it easier to keep the fear at bay. She had a three-by-three metre plastic sheet and a couple of two-by-twos, a lightweight groundmat and rope, and a high-thermal sleeping bag. She had five days' worth of readies, a small first-aid kit and a torch. The pistol and her knife. She had her toolkit on her belt and her own flint and steel, plus a box of waterproof matches because Yara had offered them and they weighed nothing. She had Yara's pen, too. The heaviest thing, apart from the pack itself, was the five-litre waterbag she wore under it. The mobile weight of it against her spine was a reassurance.

When the sun was high enough to give some heat, she had left the road and made camp in a stand of silver wattle. She bagged a branch with plastic, tied it off. Ate half a ready and drank a little. The fifth morning. Already she could feel the distance accelerating again and fear rising to choke her. Dark pictures in her head.

Exhaustion took her down but in sleep she waded through sand and Matti was always just ahead of her, just out of sight across the drift, pushed away by her approach.

In the late afternoon she woke and drank the water she'd harvested, finished the ready and got back on the road. In the last light she saw that the country west of the highway was cropped with millet and murnong, beans and chickpea and kangaroo grass. On the other side, a little way off to the east, was the perimiter fence, and then bush and low brown hills, and somewhere beyond them, the wall. XB Force patrol vehicles a long way way off in the No Go.

Between the highway and the fence was mostly scrub. She passed people setting up camp for the night, spoke to a few of them. They were coming from further north, heading for Port Howell. A family remembered a bus with Agency branding going the other way. There were kids, their son told her. I was waving and waving at them. They invited her to share their camp but as long as there was a clear sky she preferred to keep moving through the coldest hours. It was safer, quieter. The trucks were like clouds blowing past, nothing to do with her.

Walking came easy. Li had walked through her childhood with Val, town to town on the circuit, and after Val she'd just kept walking. The settled years in Nerredin had softened her a bit but she'd got all the blisters she was going to get on the road to Valiant. It was Matti who'd slowed her down. Frank too, if she was truthful. Her makecamp boots had some wearing in to do but that just meant they'd last longer.

When she couldn't walk any more she slept in the scrub. Broke camp early afternoon on the sixth day and got to Kutha two hours later.

*

North of Kutha was Kutha's dump. Plenty of people must have picked through the pile but it seemed like none of them had had a magnet. In under ten minutes she dug out an iron. It was scorched black and the power cord was half melted off but still attached. She stripped the wire for patching supplies. Left the iron on top of the heap for someone who could carry it and kept walking.

More croplands. More greenhouses. Roadside stalls for the passing foot traffic. Close to dusk she came to the bore Rich had told her about, fenced off and guarded by Kutha militia. Trucks had priority. Li joined the foot queue waiting for their turn at the pump. Her waterbag was still almost full from the top-up at Kutha but she drank deep, peeled off the filthy gloves and ran water over her hands, soothing the tight, itchy skin. Rinsed her face carefully, trying not to wet the bandage. Rich had told her to leave it on as long as possible after the blisters cracked, to stop dirt getting in, keep the sun and the flies off. She couldn't afford to let it get infected.

That night was clear and bright again, but she was moving more slowly; it was getting harder to walk through. She rested periodically but didn't let herself fall asleep. Looked into the darkness beyond the fence, trying to picture the wall and all those sheltered people sleeping behind it. What was in their nightmares? People like her?

Footsore, before light on the seventh day, she passed another empty farmhouse. Remnant fencelines and then the hulking ruin of a cattle container. Dry bores and collapsing windmills, a skeleton ute with all the useable parts salvaged. It reminded her of West. She needed to stop but the empty houses didn't tempt her, too much risk of ambush. She made camp. Singed the skin of a sawn-off roo tail and laid it in the ashes of her fire. While it cooked she cleaned her knife and stropped it on her belt. There was plenty of fresh roadkill along the highway at night, feral dogs and rabbits as well as roos. Quicker than trapping. She and Val used to get a feed of roo or wallaby pretty regularly. She hadn't seen a wallaby in a long time.

The sense of time passing intensified when she lay down. There was the work of not imagining what Matti was thinking, whether she thought Li was coming for her. Sooner or later her body's need for sleep would keep her brain quiet, but first she had to run back over everything she'd heard in Kutha, everything that told her she was on the right track, that Matti was safe at the barracks by now. Safer. But even in Kutha there were things to trip her up. *Couldn't swear they did a headcount getting them back on the bus.*

The trick was to slide slideways into other memories. But they didn't always help either. Like the revolving rack outside the newsagent, the other one, in Nerredin. It was chained to a pillar – you didn't leave metal unsecured, not in country towns, not anywhere. Matti had run ahead to look at the picture books. She spun the rack slowly until she found the book she wanted and stood on tiptoe to lift it down. By the time Li caught up she was cross-legged on the footpath, pretending she could read. Li was late for work, still had to drop Matti off on the way. When she pulled her to her feet, Matti grabbed the rack with one hand and hung on. Four and a half and so skinny it was hard to believe the strength of her.

She looked at Li in triumph. You can't make me let go.

In the second after it happened they were both silent, Matti still holding onto the rack and Li holding her other arm like a separate thing. Then Matti's mouth opened and the sound that came out brought Faysal running from the shop, stopped people across the road. But all Li heard, and kept hearing, was the deep, private click as Matti's shoulder came out of its socket.

Frank met them on their way out of the clinic. He was still wearing his knee pads and workboots. Matti turned her back on Li and showed him the sling. He lifted her carefully and carried her out to where Carl was waiting with the ute. That meant Angie knew what had happened too. Carl was polite with her, reserved. She wondered if he was counting the times Robbie had been alone in her care.

When Matti had cried herself to sleep at home, Frank said, What the fuck, Li? She tried to tell him but he stopped her. I don't need to know what happened. I need to know why you dislocated our daughter's shoulder.

She wouldn't come.

He stared at her like he was trying to remember how he knew her. You're not the child. You know that, don't you?

She did know that, how it sounded. How it was, maybe. She was thick with guilt and grief. But she's so goddamn stubborn.

Frank breathed out slowly, rubbed his eyes with the heel of his hand. She's stubborn, yeah. You don't recognise it?

Walking again, at dusk on the seventh day, she could feel the eastern drift of the highway in her body, how it pulled even closer to the fence. Fifty metres, thirty, nearer. An armoured four-wheel drive on the other side turned and accelerated bumpily across the No Go towards her. Too late to do anything except keep walking, look straight ahead. When the vehicle reached the fence, it slowed and kept pace with her. She waited for an order, an interrogation by megaphone. Her whole body was rigid with the effort of not looking. When she finally turned her head she saw two XB Force in blue body armour through the open passenger window. Their eyes were hidden behind reflective visors that had earpieces attached. They gave no instructions, made no demands, just watched her. She knew they carried precision rifles and batons, limb restraints and handcuffs. Studded gloves that they put on first.

She looked away and kept moving. What were they waiting for? Did they want her to show fear? Aggression? Something that might justify a response, justify these endless kays of wire and spikes and military hardware? And then she thought, No, they're just bored. But, bored, they could still stop her, question her, detain her somewhere, come between her and Matti just to pass the time.

The vehicle swung away, back towards the foothills. She watched the headlights until she was sure they weren't coming back.

When she was eight or nine Val had shown her how to tell the uniforms apart. Kahki was the old army, what he called real soldiers. XB Force was sky blue. The precincts' own armed forces used to be grey or black but at some point one of the companies started supplying all the uniforms. Mostly, now, they all looked like XB Force.

Through the night, the blacktop started fading in and out of unsealed corrugation. She slept for a couple of hours in some bushes and then made herself keep moving, but slowly. She couldn't keep walking so many hours, night after night. Her feet ached, her back ached. The pack weighed her down even though it weighed less. The sky lightened on the eighth day over flat, sandy country with fewer and fewer trees. Emu bush and buffel grass and prickly wattle. Stretches of salt flats. She picked samphire and tried to eat it raw but it made her too thirsty.

Up ahead in the scrub there was a circle of vehicles and caravans around a campfire. Rusted but not abandoned. Rich had said there was a waterhole somewhere around here. She approached slowly, but without trying to be quiet. A dog barked and figures moved out from behind the vehicles. Someone started bashing something, wood against metal, in a slow rhythm.

She called out, Is there water? I just want to refill.

The barking became frenzied and a rock thudded past her into the dirt. She turned back to the road.

Sometimes she had a sense of afterlife – that everyone but her had walked away from an unspeakable disaster. All they'd left was their rubbish. She pushed thoughts like that away. What was happening here was still playing out, slowly slowly like a car crash, and there was nowhere for anyone to go.

Before she slept a different memory came, and kept coming, until she stopped fighting it. Just lay there and listened to Matti calling for water, saw her face, flushed and turning in sleep. Flu had gone through makecamp like a truck. Headache, bone ache, sweats, then a fever. By the time Li understood what was happening and tried to quarantine Matti from the other kids, it was too late. For the first twenty-four hours she thrashed in her sleeping bag, panting and crying out. She held onto the horse and made high whimpering sounds. Li gave her the last of the antivirals, tried to regulate her temperature, make her drink. Matti cried out that the fire was coming and Goldie was on fire. She asked for ice blocks and watermelon. For Frank. Frank.

People left Li food, refilled the water bottles she left outside the tent – Sanaa and Amin, Abraham, a few others she'd shared kill with or patched for on the quiet, building up credit against exactly this kind of contingency.

Sanaa stayed to give her news through the nylon shell – her family had survived the flu already. She said bodies had been removed from the camp and burned within sight in the No Go. The people who did it weren't relief, they were outsiders in hazard suits and masks. They agreed that wasn't good. It meant makecamp was on someone's radar, Sumud or Port Howell authorities getting nervous about an epidemic on their doorstep.

The Med Tent had run out of antivirals and disposable masks, they were waiting on a new aid dump. Li breathed Matti's air and willed herself not to get sick until Matti got through it.

Now her daughter lay still and glassy, and Li watched the work of her breathing. Counted through the pauses to the restarts, held her own breath, watching that thin chest as if the act of witness alone could keep Matti's lungs working. The first time Li knew she was pregnant what she'd thought was, I'm going to fuck it up. And she did, her body did, over and over. The surprising part came later. Inside her another heart started pumping fluid, exchanges were made across the border between her blood and the blood of this creature taking form. She churned and swelled up again, aching to the touch. Lead in her bones. But this time it kept happening instead of tearing up and bleeding out of her piece by piece. And she didn't know if she wanted it, she just knew that Frank did. Week after week, she watched his happiness as a kind of certainty settled on this thing she hadn't decided not to do. Carefully, then recklessly, Frank expanded.

Matti's hair was even shorter since the last outbreak of lice, and streaky with sweat, making her unfamiliar. She'd lost another tooth and a big one was already coming, it had changed her face again. She kept changing. Li saw how beautiful she was. She looked and looked. It was so easy to love Matti when she was still like this, when the furious concentration of her self made no demands, resisted nothing, insisted on nothing.

On the third morning she cooled and her breathing became easier. She drank, then slept again but quietly. The heaviness Li felt was barely recognisable as relief. She let it pull her down beside her child and slept with her.

Late in the day, Matti sat up and asked for food. There was almost nothing left. Whatever Li had caught would be rotting in the snares – she needed to get out there to empty and reset them, so they would have something to trade in the coming days. If she left now she could be back soon after dark.

She explained this to Matti while she lined up the water bottles and the two cans of beans within reach.

Matti said, Don't go tonight, Mum.

I won't be long. You just need to drink water and go to sleep. I'll ask Sanaa to check on you.

What if you are long?

Then you wait for me at the Kids' Tent.

Matti kept shaking her head. Li could feel a kind of lethargy coming on that would make it too hard to do anything but lie down beside her, and so she was hard on Matti. Her strong child who had survived. She thought it would make her angry and the anger would make her turn away, make leaving easy. But Matti followed her all the way to the fence.

The duster came up fast, late afternoon of the eight day. Li had only just started walking. She'd seen dust inland in West but nothing like this. Wasn't prepared for the ferocity, the sting, the way it snuck into her lungs. She tied the thermal leggings around her nose and mouth, pulled her cap down low, but there was nothing she could do about her eyes. Dust masked the sun and shrank the world to a swirling red mass that she moved through as good as blind.

Within minutes she'd lost the road. She blundered through choking, whistling air with her arms out in front of her. Her eyes wept and burned. Then she was on her hands and knees, with the idea of finding some bushes to shelter in, turning her back to the wind until this passed. But already she was losing the idea of time.

The railing reared up so suddenly she almost crashed into it. Ran her hands along the rough, gappy wood and stood up. It was a porch. She felt her way over missing planks to the door. The effort of breathing made her desperate, uncaring of the risks.

She pulled it shut behind her and got her back to it, knife in one hand, fumbling for the gun with the other. In the dim light she saw a hall with doorways either side and another one at the end. A layout like hundreds of farmhouses she'd been in, except in this one all the doors had been salvaged, along with some of the floorboards in the hall. She pulled the leggings from her face to breathe more easily, listened, heard nothing.

Li moved through the house, stepping over gaps, checking the rooms. All empty and stripped bare, but someone had been in the middle bedroom recently; the air felt disturbed and there were scuffmarks on the dusty floor. It was the room she would have chosen, midway between the front and back doors. The window was boarded up and stuffed with plastic, like all the others, but light and dustmotes seeped through the cracks.

Listening to the the duster beating gently at the walls, she felt the desire to fall asleep in a house, in a room where people had been, where she could trick herself, in the moment before she fell, that her own breathing was multiplied by three.

She went out to the hallway and brushed the dust from herself and her pack as best she could. Back in the bedroom, she pulled off her rust-coloured gloves and bathed her eyes with gauze dipped in a capful of water. Rolled out the mat and sleeping bag on a solid patch of floor under the window and lay down with her boots on, with the gun and the knife and the torch at her side. She closed and opened her swollen eyes, her tearducts working to expel the grit. After a while she noticed a patch of wallpaper. Great tangled cups of flowers, creamy and tentacled. Magnolias. A flower of temperate climates. Did they still grow anywhere? There had been a painting of the same flowers in a pub where she and Val had stayed for a night somewhere on the circuit. Val had told her their name. He said they grew on trees in the place across the oceans where he grew up. Told her about their sweet cloudy smell and how the flowers would drop and bruise on the ground.

She remembered the pub because they almost never stayed in them. Val was still dry then. A room above the bar with two small squeaky beds and green bedspreads with tiny lumps that she ran under her fingers. The painting was on the wall facing her bed. In the drawer where the Bible should have been she found a paperback with an angry man holding a woman, her dress coming off her shoulders.

Romance, Val said when she showed him. You want to stay well clear of that shite, young one.

A deep verandah ran the length of the upstairs rooms. They could climb out onto it through their window. Val smoked out there and she watched the trucks appear as grey specks of dust that grew into shapes and noise.

She and Val didn't eat dinner at the pub, they went to the cafe down the road, even though it cost more, but they did eat the free breakfast in the room for guests downstairs. Three kinds of cereal in plastic containers, and milk, and a big curving staircase that she went up and down, holding the bannister like a queen.

But the night before, the shouting and laughter from downstairs kept waking her up and Val was awake every time. She didn't mind, it wasn't that different from the circuit camps, but Val minded somehow. When a fight started and spilled out onto the road, he got up and stood at the window. After a while he sang to her, slow and tenderly in his smoker's voice, a song called 'The Parting Glass', and she looked at the magnolia in the moonlight and heard his longing but didn't understand it, and fell asleep.

Li opened her eyes into darkness. Someone was there. She swung up the torch and the gun in one movement and saw a woman in the doorway, holding an axe. Li got to her feet fast. They stood and watched each other.

There's just three of us, the woman said.

That sound again, the one that had woken her. She looked past the woman and saw a man holding a baby in the doorway across the hall. It started crying properly, an aggrieved sound that carried. The man lifted it up to his shoulder, keeping his eyes on Li. His palm made circles on its back.

Li lowered the pistol. I don't have bullets.

The woman said, He has colic. Or reflux. Something.

Her skin and clothes were shrouded in red, the man's too.

You were in here before, Li said.

The man nodded. We heard you on the porch, so we got out the back way. I had him under my clothes, but we couldn't stay out there.

Li saw how young they were, how afraid. The baby's crying was like spoor, it tracked right to them, and an axe wasn't much. You can have this room, she said.

She took the room opposite, rolled out her sleeping bag just inside the doorway and lay listening for a creak of the floor-boards, a rusty hinge, a tear in the blanketed silence of dust. The baby woke and cried through the night and each time she heard the woman shift instantly awake to pat, shush and feed.

In the first fifteen months of Matti's life Li had sung her every song she knew. Every song Val had taught her, every walking song and shearing song, the fire songs and patching songs. Every song for picking, or waiting by the road, every lullaby. Nothing made Matti sleep but certain melodies calmed her into a listening state. As she got older, she listened intently to the stories in the songs. She wanted to know where they all came from.

One night she said, Sing me one you've never sung me.

Li didn't think she had anything left, but then a fragment came to her from before. She thought maybe her own mother had sung it to her.

Guardian angels
watch beside me
all through the night

And what else? Matti asked.

All through the night. The family in the other room, nothing could harm them. She knew that when she left tomorrow, she would leave the gun behind. She closed her eyes and listened to them breathing.

The duster passed by morning, leaving a silence like earplugs. When Li opened the front door the country was shrouded and the road buried. Dust still hung in the air, fine red particles that sieved down in the dim light.

She changed her filthy bandage for the first time. She bled a little taking it off and her uncovered skin felt raw in the air, but the couple told her it looked clean enough. Then they shared food and water while the woman fed the baby.

His name's Billy, the man said.

Li hadn't asked, but she understood the hunger to say your child's name. They came from a town called Lawrence, nearly two hundred and fifty k north-east. A highway service hub that had no one to service anymore. His mother had helped them pre-register for the precincts the year they finished school, when it was already clear there would be no work in Lawrence, and pretty soon no town either. The baby was coming by then. They hadn't planned to have their One Child allowance so early, but his mum said with the way Wars were going, government might change back to Replacement in a few years anyway, so maybe they could have another one later. His mother was dead now – some kind of lung disease.

The dusters get pretty bad at home, the woman told her. We thought it might be better further south.

There was no advance on their pre-registration but they'd heard Sumud might be opening a quota so they decided they were just going to try. They paid for a ride as far as they could because they were worried about Billy's lungs. Their money had run out three days ago and they'd been walking since then. They hadn't heard about makecamp yet. Li organised her pack while they absorbed the disappointment. They told her they had a friend of a friend in Kutha who'd put them up while they figured out what to do next.

Li said, Maybe there'll be a new makecamp soon.

They wanted to know why she was going north. She kept it short to ward off pity, but with enough detail to trigger any useful response. And their reaction, the quick glance they shared, was a small, painful adrenaline shot.

What? You saw something?

The woman said, We talked to a guy the day before yesterday who'd seen a whole mob of children going that way.

He saw the bus?

She shook her head and unlatched the baby. No bus, she said. Just children. Walking.

Li held very still. Walking where?

The man took the baby and settled him against his chest. That was weird, eh, he said. The kids told him they were going up to Lake Ero to camp – you know the big salt lake? They were all kitted out with tents and sleeping bags. He tried to talk them out of it, but they said if they went back Army would get them. He said none of them looked old enough for the ballot but he couldn't change their minds.

There was a buzzing in Li's ears, getting in the way of thought. No adults with them?

The woman shook her head again. That's why he was still worrying about it. They were dressed for the cold, he said, and he checked they had food and water. He gave them some more, what he could spare. He was going to report it to Agency when he got to the next Source booth.

Li remembered how long the bus had been stopped in Kutha. How the newsagent owner had talked about engine trouble. She started repacking, fast, trying to keep her hands steady. When did he see them?

The man glanced over at the woman for confirmation. Guy said two days before, right? So that's what? Three and a half, four days ago?

And how far to the lake?

They told her the south-western edge was two hundred and fifty k north of Kutha, give or take. That was past the turnoff to the base.

Three nights since she left Kutha. She'd lost last night to the duster, but kids got tired. If she pushed it now, cut down on sleep, she could be there in another three, maybe even overtake them. She could feel understanding pressing in and she needed to be walking when it came.

She hefted up her pack. Said goodbye and left them in the house, pulling the leggings up over her nose and mouth again as she stepped through the door. She didn't leave the gun.

The dust settled slowly through the ninth day and into the night. All that time, Li walked. The access road wasn't much more than two hours' drive out of Kutha. If the bus had broken down near the town someone would have walked back in for help. It must have been closer to the barracks. But a bus was too valuable to walk away from. One of them would have stayed with the kids, wouldn't they? Set up camp. Not just let them wander off.

She didn't know how it had happened, but if they were on their own then she understood why they hadn't gone to the barracks. Knew what being taken to an army base would have meant to kids who'd watched recruiters sniffing around their older friends in makecamp, who'd have no good reason to believe that being under-age would protect them. There would have been kids on the bus who'd grown up out here. Maybe they'd camped at the lake with their parents. Maybe it felt safe there.

The trucks kept passing, churning up the dust, but there weren't many people on the road here. When she drank, she thought of Matti up ahead, dry-mouthed, hungry, walking to nothing. She barely ate. She still had a few readies but she needed to save them. She imagined Matti in the back of one of those trucks. Unable to call out, unable to scream. *He'll reach down and grab you up and take you away.*

She was glad Frank wasn't here.

When she came to the next house, some time before midnight, she waited and watched before she went in. It was set well back from the road and she was about thirty metres away in a clump of emu bush, but visibility was good. Open ground, a clear sky now, the moon making clean-edged shadows.

Her head was okay, her head told to keep going, but her body was giving her warning signals. She needed to sleep for a couple of hours.

She moved carefully around the house, staying wide, counting exits. There was a back door, six windows on the ground floor, four upstairs. All boarded up. She didn't have time to set up the tarp and build a fire, prepare food. Walking through the day meant she hadn't collected water either, and that would be a problem soon but she couldn't think about it right now. She needed to lie down under shelter. Sleep.

She dug a hole under the bushes for her pack and ground mat but she kept the torch and the pistol. The knife was in her belt. She went into the house steadily, holding the torch over the gun.

All the rooms on the ground floor were empty. She would sleep down there, near the back door, once she'd checked the upper rooms.

She was almost at the top of the stairs when a man came out of darkness onto the landing. When she turned around there were two more down below, blocking the exit, she didn't know where they'd come from. Turned back and lined up her pistol on the man upstairs and kept going, onto the landing, her hands shaking hard. He paused long enough for her to reach the window but then she had to turn her back on him again to kick at the boards, blind and violent, and she heard him coming, not hurrying now he'd guessed the gun was a bluff, that there was no way out. Li felt the same inevitability, something essential draining away inside her. But as she dropped the gun and reached for the knife, she felt something start to give under her boot. A rotten plank. He ran at her as it splintered, shouting to the others, feet on the stairs, and she dropped the torch and turned and steadied the knife with both hands, aiming for his heart in the dark as he ran right up against her, right onto it. The point of entry cleaved muscle and sinew, not his heart but his shoulder, up into the armpit. They fell back against the boards together and the boards gave way, she could feel his heart beating but then he let go, sucking air, and she wrenched the knife out of him and forced her way through the window without looking.

The roof of the porch broke her fall but it threw her balance, too. She rolled, fell again and landed on the hard dirt below with her ankle bent under her. A burst of pain. She tried to get up, couldn't. No time anyway – she could hear the others coming, couldn't think, pressed against the edge of the porch and felt a gap in the planks low down that shouldn't have been big enough but she forced herself backwards through it.

The door banged open and they ran out onto the porch, directly above her. The high beam of a hunting torch stabbed the dark. One of them shouted a question to the man upstairs and he yelled something back, enraged with pain. Her hand closed around some small stones in the sand and she threw them low and hard into the dark. They made a scattering sound out in the scrub, and the torchlight twitched that way.

A rustling behind her. There was something else under the porch. Probably a snake, dormant in the cold until she'd disturbed it. She held still until the rustling moved away, further under the house, and the fear of the snake became the fear of them hearing the snake and she realised she'd pissed herself and soon they would smell it. She wouldn't let them drag her out they'd have to come in and get her in this confined space with her knife she could kill one of them at least if they didn't have a gun but she couldn't keep going like this it wasn't possible it had to end tonight now trapped or poisoned under this trap house or dragged back inside by men who were too angry to remember some use they might have had for her tomorrow or next week.

She lay in her piss with her ankle swelling up, while the man upstairs suffered and raged and the other two hunted her in the scrub. One of them always stayed close to the house. It would be dark for a few minutes and then torchlight would flick across the dirt in front of her. Hours passed. Her body shook uncontrollably and her mind refused to save her. Her mind told her they wouldn't keep looking this long unless they had a reason. Something worth their time. Her mind dug things up and unspooled them for her in the dark. Whispers and rumours from the road, the boat, makecamp. Things that might end with you inside the XB but maybe not whole. She tried to force them out and a clear memory surfaced, of playing spotlight with Matti and Robbie and Frank in the olive grove. Dark early but not too cold yet, the air smelling of woodsmoke. Matti wanted to hide on her own but then she'd come racing to Li, between sweeps, and Li pulled her in close against the trunk and felt her heart beating and they stayed there, still, as the torch got closer. And then Matti screamed and gave them away.

*

She fought sleep but it took her anyway. Every time she woke they were still out there. Matti said, The Takeaway was chasing me and he was going to steal my eyes, the colour of my eyes, and my voice and make a cardboard of me and throw me in the sea. She said, Mum, can the Takeaway steal grown-ups?

It was still dark when they came back from hunting. She waited for the torchlight to find her point of entry but it passed over the porch without stopping. Maybe the gap looked too small, or they were too fixated on her being out in the scrub. Maybe they were just tired.

One of them went inside, to the man she'd knifed, who was quiet now. The other one sat down on the porch, and she heard him light a cigarette. At intervals, he raked the torch across the scrubline. She waited, counted, but she couldn't predict his timing. Once she thought he must have fallen asleep, and she was flexing her cramped muscles to move when the torch stabbed on again.

She felt the passage of seconds, minutes, hours. Felt Matti moving further out of range, into the unmapped world. Pain came in waves from her ankle. Her body had seized up with cold but she couldn't risk any movement with him on top of her, listening. These men didn't feel cold, or fear. They didn't need to sleep. What they traded in was worth cigarettes. The smell slipped down through the floorboards, sharp and grey, the way Val's first smoke of the day would reach her in the tent and when she crawled out he'd be crouching beside the ashes of the night's fire or standing away at the end of the camp, watching the sky. But Val had rolled his own.

Then a bird called from the scrub. The piece of night she could see through the gap was thinning, separating from the land. It would be light soon, and this man or the other one would step down off the porch and see the gap clearly. There would be no crawling away from here.

Before Matti screamed. Before that. Huddled against her, breathing together in the cold, with the torchlight closing in. Her body warm and shivering, her rabbit heart.

Maybe we're too big.

Shhh.

But maybe I should go over there behind that tree? Mum? Just until he goes past. And then you'll come and get me, okay?

A magpie sang, a wet sound through the dry, and she realised he hadn't used the torch after those other noises in the scrub. Because the sky was lightening or because he was asleep? She couldn't smell smoke anymore, or feel the vibration of his knee through the boards. From the porch there was only a deep stillness.

Her body was unresponsive but she forced it, edging forward in tiny movements. Her ankle hurt like hell and she bit her lip till she tasted blood. When she reached the opening, she lost control of her breathing and the fear nearly kept her down in her hole, but he was asleep or he was awake. She was done waiting.

She crawled out. No sound from behind her. A dark half of her believed he was watching, silent, his finger on the torch or the trigger, giving her a headstart. Fuck him, she wasn't going to look back. Halfway across the open space between the house and the bush where she'd buried her stuff, she tried to get up and run but she fell back down at the first pressure of her left foot on the ground. Shoved her fist in her mouth, nearly passed out. Just had to keep crawling, dragging the pain behind her.

Even when she was digging up her pack she still half believed he was playing with her, pretending to sleep until she started hoping. But she got the pack on and crawled away. Kept crawling. She only stopped once, when the need to empty her bowels came on so fast she barely got her pants down in time. Cleaned herself with leaves and then started crawling again through sand and scrub, her ankle dragging and jarring, hands and knees cut up by prickly wattle. All through the grey arrival of the tenth morning, through the dust that came and went, hour after hour, heading north, north-east.

When the sun was high, she let herself believe they weren't coming. The man she'd knifed wouldn't be travelling this far and if the others were willing to leave him, they would have caught her by now. Or maybe the dust had covered her tracks. Something good from Weather.

She stopped to rest under a couple of mallee trees, took two sips from her three-quarter empty bag and unlaced her boot. She screamed getting her foot out. It was swollen fat, the outer ankle bone obscured. Yellow and purple. The pain when she probed it was wrenching. She took off her vest and wrapped it around a wide piece of bark to make a strap for her ankle. There was no way her foot was going back in her boot, so she tied the boot onto her pack. She ate a couple of ready biscuits, had three more sips of water, then she pulled herself up on the tree and broke off a branch that was V-shaped at the top. It took a couple of goes to cut it down to the right size but after that she could walk, leaning her full weight on the stick.

There were still other people on the road, but not many. When they passed her she felt invisible to them, each sealed up in their private feat of endurance. Her body was a catalogue of things wrong: thirst, pain, lack of sleep, hunger. Her pants had dried and the piss was just another smell but her thighs chafed and stung. Her throat and lips were dry and the burnt side of her face stretched and throbbed under the bandage. Her head ached and she kept having to stop and wait for the dizzy surges to pass. She knew she was dehydrated but what she had left in the bag wasn't going to make a difference. Walking with the stick hurt her wrist, her shoulders – the whole right side of her felt strained and off-balance.

Li tried not to look at the fence because when she did she saw Matti holding onto the wire, face pinched clean by fever. *Mum. Look!* But when she finally did look up, she saw something beyond the fence, distantly across the No Go, that made her stop walking. It was the wall. The XB. The first time she'd ever seen it. People in makecamp had said it was ten metres tall, or twelve or fifteen. They said it was made of steel-reinforced concrete, two metres thick, topped with razor-ribbon wire and cameras and floodlights and machine guns. That the body-heat detection systems started fifty metres away, triggering lights and sirens. Some people said there was another wall inside, an internal border with a concrete No Go, or an airlock that could be flooded with gas before you got to the checkpoint. That was why people risked everything on the trucks.

There was no way to judge how much of that was true. All she could see from here was a grey immensity. She checked herself for a response to the physical presence of this wall, this thing that took up so much space in the imagination of the unsheltered. Looked away and felt no gravitational pull. Frank had always found it strange how uncurious she was about the other side, about the people living there. Don't you wonder what it's like?

he'd asked. She'd only ever wondered about three of them and she was pretty sure her parents were dead now.

I would hate to live inside the wall, Matti had said in their tent, somewhere into the second week on the road to Valiant. It was after midnight, Frank sleeping steadily on the other side of her.

Why? Li asked.

Well, because how do you breathe?

Oh, right. It doesn't mean inside the actual wall – it just means the other side. Like going into a house. This, where we are, is outside and the other side is inside.

But why is that side inside?

Because it's safer, I guess. And they get looked after. There are things on that side that we don't have out here.

She waited, tiredly, for Matti to ask what things but Matti was quiet. Maybe she'd gone back to sleep. A mosquito whined and she slapped it away, held her watch up to her face. Before dawn and after sunset were the times when walking was easy, without the heat pressing down from the sky and up from the road, making the air shake. In two hours they would have to get up and start walking again.

I still don't want to live there, Matti said. It's not the Best Place.

What would it have meant to her to see the XB, finally, know it was real? Not just a story they told kids. What had Agency told them before they drove them out here to the middle of nowhere because no precinct would take that many minors? Where did she think she was going now?

Is the Best Place real? She had asked Frank, prone and sweating under the tarp in the middle of the day. Can we actually go there?

I told you already, beansprout, Frank said. We're going to the best place we can find.

There wasn't much left of the bus when she got to it. Pulled off roadside. No mistaking its shape from a distance, the trademark government yellow, but as she got closer she saw that it had been picked clean. Doors, windows, tyres and wheels. A gouge in the back where the engine and transmission had been. Windshield gone, bumper bars, tail- and headlights. Every removable piece of metal and plastic. A man and a woman approaching from the other direction barely glanced at it as they passed.

Out of habit, Li looked through the space where the back door had been. The inside had been stripped too, including the seats. Six, seven days? Apart from the lack of rust, it could have been abandoned years ago. She limped a slow circuit around it and saw how the sand and gibber were churned up on all sides. Looked pointlessly for signs of camp, for something dropped or discarded, for a message with directions scratched with a stick. What she saw was footprints, drag marks, tyre marks, signs of scuffle. You could do a lot with a jack and a socket wrench but you'd need a vehicle, too, something with a tray. This had the look of a dedicated salvage crew.

It was only a few more kays to the start of the old army access road but it took her an hour to walk them. She stood at the turnoff and studied the gibber. No trample of feet, nothing but old tyre tracks. No barriers or warning signs anymore, nothing to stop her limping all the way to the barracks, just in case. *But they said if they went back, Army would get them.* She walked past the turnoff and kept going up the highway.

*

90

What happened at school? Frank asked Matti. Valiant. Dinner-time around the small kitchen table in Teresa and Navid's flat.

Nothing. She mashed her beans with a fork and scooped them up with her fingers. Oh. Soldiers came. After literacy.

Li kept her voice neutral. What kind of soldiers?

Matti shrugged. They had those grey-y-green uniforms? Like the ones when we were coming into Valiant.

Li hadn't known they would send recruiters into the school — not this soon. She should have known that.

Don't they have to send a note home? Teresa asked.

Hani said, Handsup! Bangbang! And started coughing.

Into your elbow, mate. Navid gave him water in his sippy cup.

Matti looked at Frank. I don't have to go to Wars till I'm fifteen.

No. Frank said. No you don't.

But then if I get picked I have to go. The soldiers said we have to keep our promise.

Jesus, Teresa said softly.

Frank was still. Li couldn't tell what he was thinking. He said, That isn't something you have to worry about now, sprout.

Matti kept looking at him for a second and then nodded. You don't have to worry, Hani, mate, she told her cousin, cos you won't have to go to Wars for ages.

She took a couple of sips every hour, feeling the waterbag light-ening. She should be drinking morning and night, holding off while she walked so she didn't sweat it out, but she didn't have enough water left to hydrate properly in the cold hours. Her throat was dust dry and the shifting of the remaining liquid as she walked tormented her. She tried to focus on the lake where she was going but her mind took her away. Sometimes she was back on the stairs with the men coming out of the dark, crawling away and hearing their breathing behind her, and then it wasn't her crawling away, it was Matti. Or they were back on the highway from Nerredin and Matti was saying, I'm *sick* of walking, and Frank said, Tell us a story, and Matti started. My heart pants as I cuddle in beside my ten-year-old cousin. I'm only five, so you can see how frightened I am. This story isn't happening right now, the girl is remembering, so it's back the time. In the green meadow, no home to sleep in, wolves about. And no Mum or Dad.

Li put the stick down wrong, jolted her foot and cried out. She knew she couldn't walk much longer without water but she didn't have time to stop and harvest it, she'd lost too much time already. The dizziness and the pressure behind her eyes made it hard to think. How long before her body stopped working, started shutting down? If she finished the water then she wouldn't have to keep feeling it sloshing against her back. And maybe it would keep her going for a few more hours but she wouldn't be able walk through the night, whether she drank it or not.

In the end she couldn't stand knowing it was there. She tried to sip it and she did feel a bit better afterwards but it was very hard to start walking again, and as soon as she did, the emptiness of the bag began to weigh on her. That was it now. Even if she stopped, it was too late in the day for condensation to help her. Now it was just her and her failing body. And if she kept walking, if she made it to the lake and found Matti there, what would she have to offer her? How would she save her? Matti didn't know she was coming, she wouldn't wait. Even now her child was leaving the lake, or was too thirsty, too hungry.

Matti was dying, afraid. Matti was dragged into a truck and disappearing in dust. *The Takeaway wears a black coat.* She saw herself tiny and crawling across a space made for giants. For things with wings and wheels.

At dusk, still the tenth day, a Homegrown truck went past. Just another truck. Except this one stopped up ahead of her. When she drew level, the cab door opened and the driver climbed down. An older man, sun-creased and balding, wearing tiny shorts. Val's age. No, Val would be older. This man was holding a bottle.

She watched him cross the road towards her, knowing she couldn't run. It was only her hands that gave her away.

He held the bottle out. Go on, it's clean.

She didn't take it.

Don't be a hero. You look like you could murder a drink.

I don't have any trade, she said. But she took it. Felt the cool liquid through the metal.

Spose you'll have to owe me, then.

She unscrewed the lid carefully, sniffed it. Tilted the bottle. The water was cold and heavy in her mouth and it tasted of nothing. She drank and drank. Gulped it – felt it running down her throat, branching through her body, making things possible again.

You got a container? the truckie asked.

She hesitated, the waterbag wasn't something she could lose, but the water in her belly made her reckless. He took it back to the truck and pushed his door open wider so she could see his co-driver sitting up in the cab with a rifle. Company supply trucks were always double-crewed now, and the crew was always armed. He said something to the co-driver and she reached back and passed him down a jerry can without taking her eyes off the scrub. One of her knees jiggled nonstop, keeping time to some too-fast rhythm.

Li watched the truckie fill her waterbag without letting a drop spill. She understood this was his personal supply. When he brought the bag back it was full for the first time in days. The heft of it made her lightheaded.

He looked at her foot. What is that, sprained?

I think so. Maybe a ligament.

The other thing he'd brought back from the truck was a first-aid kit. He unzipped it, resting it open on one knee while he sorted through it. I've got anti-inflam in here somewhere. Here you go. He threw her a small green tube, kept hunting. And a whadayou call it, compression bandage.

Why? she said, holding the cream.

He shrugged. Company issue – no skin off my nose. Half this stuff's past its use-by anyway.

It came to Li that maybe he didn't want anything. The woman called down to him through the open driver's side door to hurry up.

He said, Yeah, yeah, and pulled out the bandage. You're going the opposite way to everyone else, he told Li. Where you headed?

Lake Ero.

On that ankle? It's still about forty k to the lake turnoff. You know it's dry, right?

I'm meeting someone there.

Hell of a spot for a date.

Yeah. It's my daughter. We got split up.

How d'you know she's there?

She took the bandage from him and stuffed it in her pocket. I heard she was with a big bunch of kids, heading that way to camp. Maybe they thought there'd be water. Have you seen anything like that? Just children walking on their own?

I haven't been up this way in a couple of weeks, he said. They had me on the Gulf run.

What about other drivers? Anything you heard?

He shook his head. You see people all the time. Can't always stop. If I saw a bunch of kids on their own, but.

Li saw him thinking about the limits of what he could do. She imagined, for the first time, someone like this stopping to pick up her child from the side of the road. Because she was a child, not for what he could get because she was a child. She looked past him at the truck, the size of the wheels, the distance it could cover while she crawled. If Matti had got into a truck, Li would never reach her walking. If she hadn't, if she was still there camped on the lakebed? Forty k. Li could be at the turnoff in half an hour.

Can I get a lift? The truckie was already shaking his head. She said, Just as far as you're going that way.

You know I can't do that.

Fucksake, Stu. The woman had moved over into the driver's seat, eyes still on the scrub through the open door. I am not getting docked again because of your bullshit.

I can patch, Li told him. You need anything fixed, I can fix it. She looked at him straight, knowing she was filthy and stinking, blistered and cracked-lipped and lame. Or. Whatever you need.

He took in her meaning and his face twitched and then went stern. No passengers, love. Company policy.

She'd insulted him, she saw that, injured his sense of himself as a good man who did good things. If he didn't want to trade, she didn't know how to fix it. She said, Who's going to know?

He jerked his head back towards the cab.

Is she the boss, then? She the one I need to talk to?

Bloody hell, woman. He was angry, finally. Company's the boss. Everyone's just looking out for themselves.

But she was already limping past him onto the road, her stick sliding out on the gibber.

Christ, the truckie said behind her. Stay where you are, you're no sweet-talker.

He crossed in front of her and said something to the woman up in the cab. Li watched her jaw working, saw her shake her head. He tried again and she reached for the CB handset on the dash and held it out to him.

You wanna call it in? she said loudly. Knock yourself out.

The man held up his hands in defeat but Li stepped forward on a hot wave of urgency. She knew if she could just lay her hands on the steel of the truck she would be lifted. The co-driver jerked the rifle up and fired past her into the ground.

Li threw herself sideways, away from the explosion of sand and gibber, landed on her sprained ankle. Shouted and balled up reflexively, knees to chest, shielding her head, her skin stretched so tight over the pain she hardly felt the stones.

When she raised her head, the woman had the rifle trained on her through the open door. She said, In case you were wondering we had bullets. She was somewhere in her twenties, freckled and red eyed. The rifle was a .308, the kind Carl had used for pig hunting. Li had never been shot at before, no one had done that.

Jesus, Ellie, the man said, you need to lay off the wakey. She look like a hijacker to you?

She looks like a decoy. And your bleeding heart's gunna get us both killed.

Li stayed down. Without the truck, suddenly, she didn't know what to do. Get up, she figured, but the stick was two metres away and she couldn't think how to close the distance. Pain preoccupied her. The woman got down from the cab with the rifle, walked past her to the edge of the road and started looking for the spent casing.

Then the man was beside Li with an armful of readies, some brand she hadn't seen before. He put them at her feet, said, This stuff tastes like cardboard but it's loaded with sugar and protein. He held out his hand, and when she didn't take it he went and got her stick and laid it down beside the packets. You should go back, file a report, maybe try the relief groups. Someone lied to you. Pack of kids wouldn't last five minutes up here.

The co-driver was digging in the dirt with her boot. She said, I heard about that.

The man didn't look up. What'd you hear about, Ellie?

Couple of drivers on this run called in a big group of minors heading north.

When? Li said. How long ago?

The woman picked up the casing with a satisfied grunt. You didn't hear about it? she asked the man. Last time was Habib, bout three days ago. Wanted permission to pull over.

What'd Control say?

She shrugged, wiped the casing on her jeans.

He was staring at her now. They told him not to stop?

Course they did. He had to clear customs.

Three days, Li thought. More than one sighting. A slow buzz of elation. She took the compression bandage out of her pocket and started unwrapping the vest around her ankle. It hurt like hell going on but her ankle felt stronger inside it. The man had gone round to the back of the truck and she heard metal on metal as he opened the doors. The woman swore under her breath, went back to the cab and swung herself up. Li got out one protein bar and shoved the rest in her pack.

The man resealed the doors and came back to Li. The highway keeps going east, he said, but you're looking for a turnoff north. It's a sand track. Head up there and when you see the dunes, you're getting close. He took a blister pack out of his top pocket, popped two pills and held them out. Truckies' special. They'll keep you moving and won't feel anything that'd slow you down. The truck horn blared. He jerked his head back at the cab. She doesn't.

Li took the wakey, swallowed it dry, waited for him to leave.

This stuff we freight, he said, they grow this stuff under the sea now. Plenty of water, no Weather. He shook his head. Move there myself if they needed drivers.

Why was he still talking to her? Maybe he was waiting to be thanked. The pills were a hard mass in her gullet – she made spit and swallowed again, forcing them down. The co-driver started the engine.

The man took a step back and spoke under the noise. I left something else for you back there. I hope you find your kid.

She watched the truck pull away, the acceleration of it. When it was gone and the dust had settled she saw the melon on the road. Small and perfect, the size of a rain globe. She limped over and picked it up and it fit in her hand like it had grown there.

*

She walked into the dark and through the dark. There was enough moon and the pills cleaned out the pain and cold and exhaustion and everything else she didn't need. Her brain buzzed and cut with precise instructions for each nerve and muscle. North. She was a wave that wouldn't break. A fine thread floated free inside her brain, high enough to observe with clarity and detachment how she surged across the night. She felt the full waterbag moving like blood against her back, the perfect weight of the melon. She ground her teeth and covered the distance. When morning came she was still walking through a country that had fallen away in the night and seemed to be still falling, redder, barer, flatter, wider, with the sky expanding into the space between. Dry-mouthed, dry-eyed, jaw clamping, her stomach in knots but she was close. And the thing driving her had shifted gear again. Not fear now. Hope. That this was where her child had walked, what her child had seen. That they would look at the world together again.

On the morning of the eleventh day she reached the lake.

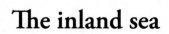

The inland sea

Matti wasn't there. No one was there.

The whole expanse of the lakebed was empty, all the way to the horizon. But the track she'd come in on was a beaten mess of footprints and there were fresh signs of a camp on the shore. A big one. Tent holes and flattened patches, dead remnants of fires, more footprints all around them and out onto the salt. Small bones and bits of ready packaging and plastic bottles. She shouted Matti's name until her voice cracked and then she went down on her knees. She'd missed them by a couple of days at the most.

She crawled a few metres alongside one set of prints that led out onto the salt pan. A child's feet, not much longer than her hand. The same drive that had got her here told her to get up now and go, keep going. That Matti was still in reach. But when she tried to stand the pain was so intense that she couldn't believe she'd walked for more than twenty-four hours on that ankle. Her stick was useless, she couldn't get up.

Li smelled mud beneath the salt. Cracked the crust with her fingers. Whatever the truckie had given her, she was paying for it now. Her head rang. She was parched, her vision was blurring and her chest was tight. A long way down there was the pulsing of her swollen ankle. She worked her pack off and fumbled inside for the melon, laid it beside those small footprints. She said Matti's name again and then she let her body go down all the way onto the dry lake and rocked herself and cried, a ragged circular noise.

It was late in the day when Li woke, in pain and cold and thirsty. The wind had picked up and layers of sand and salt had crusted on her skin while she slept. Now her eyes filled with the same grit. The sun's heat had thinned and the night was coming behind it.

Mechanically, she registered the danger. Put her thermal layers and her jacket and cap back on and drank four capfuls of water. Her ankle throbbed. Under the compression bandage the swelling had spread in a dark purple mess along the side of her foot. She rubbed in more anti-inflam and put the bandage back on. Then she got on her hands and knees and dug a solar still. She should have done it earlier, but at least this way it would start working as soon as the sun came up. There was moisture not far below the crust. She cupped an empty ready pack into a hollow at the base and covered the hole with one of her smaller plastic sheets. Heaped salt around the edges to seal it and weighted down the centre with another handful. Cut down a discarded water bottle for the second still. Three would be better but two was all she could manage. The temperature was dropping. She needed shelter now.

In the dunes, out of the wind, she got out her torch and started to dig another hole, longer and shallower this time, banking the sand up on each side to maximise the windbreak. She was warmer when she finished but her ankle hurt worse. After she'd unrolled her big plastic sheet she realised there was nothing to raise it up on, to keep the condensation off her. Closed her eyes and felt a weight pulling her down, heard Angie say, *Everything's a decision now. Nothing just happens.*

Then Li remembered the stick. She crawled back onto the salt crust to get it and stuck it upright in the sand at one end of her hole, twisting and forcing it down as deep as she could manage on her knees and then building up sand around the base. Draped the sheeting over it and weighted down the corners on both sides. Then she dragged her pack inside and laid down more plastic and the mat and the sleeping bag. Thought again and heaped up the sand under one end of the mat for her ankle. Sat in her shelter and chewed slowly through two protein bars. What she needed was a fire but, apart from her stick, there was nothing here to burn. She felt a million stars pressing on her but she didn't look up. Wasn't interested in where she was. The salt got into her dry throat and she thought about her stills, waiting for the day's heat to draw up saltwater out of the lakebed and purify it, drop by drop. Then she eased off the bandage and rubbed in the cream, and put on her balaclava and got into the sleeping bag and zipped it all the way up.

It wasn't enough. Hour after hour the cold deepened and sharpened, pushing up through the earth and down from the stars to inhabit her fully. It made the throbbing in her ankle worse, then better, then she couldn't feel it. Started to shiver and couldn't stop. She rubbed herself, pumped her arms, trying to catch the heat as it left her body. Thirst tormented her. Matti ran away. Matti was always running away. As soon as she could walk, she ran. Out of Li's arms and down the long stony driveway, onto the road. When Li caught up with her, she screamed. She thrashed and kicked and bit, eyes on the horizon. Ran further next time, into the bush, into town. People brought her back from everywhere. She hates me, Li told Frank, with bruises on her neck. Don't take it so personally, Frank said. She's a kid. Kids run away. Li said, She doesn't run away from you.

Cold. She reached for Frank, for the warmth of him. Cried out. Got up on her knees in the sleeping bag and licked condensation off the plastic. Above her the stars burned and blurred and ran. Stars so thick they made smoke. Lumps of galaxies like slow burning wood. She was standing in the dark, away from the camp, with Val. Val was naming the stars for her, the ones for direction and the ones for stories, the dead stars and the mechanical ones, patched together from kevlar and alloys, wearing out and failing to bounce their signals, drifting off course and malfunctioning.

Frank, she thought, she's getting too far away. But Frank was gone.

Navid had called the salvage depot and Li's shift manager had found her and passed on the message that she had to come. When she got to the desal plant, Frank's shift had finished two hours ago. Navid wasn't where he'd said he would be and no one would tell her anything. Finally one of the men left what he was doing and led her to a container where the workers slept between shifts. As he turned to leave he put his hand briefly on her shoulder.

Navid was sitting on a bench outside the container, leaning forward with his head resting in his hands. He sat up slowly when she said his name. Then he told her there had been an accident. A sling had snapped.

He was on a camp bed inside. A sheet over him and plastic sheeting under him so the blood wouldn't ruin the mattress. When she lifted the sheet she couldn't decipher his face.

It's him, Navid said. I don't want you to hope for that.

It hadn't occurred to her to hope for that. She had known she would lose him when they met, and when they lay down in the paddock, when he asked her to stay and she said yes she would stay, when Matti was born, when they went out dancing after they sold two seasons' harvest in advance and they couldn't stop talking about the future, when they were on the road together and the future was still there. She just hadn't been ready today.

Navid pushed her down gently into a chair and let go, like she burned. She couldn't take her eyes off his body. This was their last time together, soon he would be gone completely, and she was watching for some essential detail – some proof or sign. She heard gulls outside and something landed heavily on the wharf. There was the static hum from the lightstrip above her. There was the clock and Navid breathing behind her. A smell of skin and iron. There was nothing of Frank here. She knew it was him, she didn't delude herself, but the crushed body in bloody pants and workboots could have been any man out there.

The shift manager knocked and came in, wiping his boots. He stood behind her and spoke quietly to Navid about human error and risk ownership, the terms of independent contracting. He said it was unfortunate. He asked what they planned to do with the remains and offered more plastic sheeting. He made it clear they would need the bed soon. He wiped his feet again as he left.

School would be over in four hours. She would have to go there and tell Matti what had happened. Matti wouldn't believe her, she would want to see, and Li would have to decide if that was right, and she would have to decide without Frank. She would have to make every decision about Matti alone now. But first she had to take her eyes off the body on the bed.

She thought about how she'd never wanted a child, had feared it, feared herself, and how Frank had tried to make her believe she was capable. That there was enough room in the world, that Wars wouldn't last forever. How she had changed her mind, slowly, falteringly. His faith in the essential goodness of people drew it out in others or suspended their disbelief somehow – finally even hers. It was a kind of grace he had and it would be in their child too, she decided. What she knew about parenting she had learned from an alcoholic drifter who had no memory of his own mother. But everything she got wrong, Frank would make right. Everything the world couldn't offer, he would provide. And that's how it had been. All these years he had been teaching Matti his language of grace and she had watched and listened without ever getting closer to learning the words.

Behind her, Navid said, I never should have got him the job. I'll try to get you a payout but he wasn't on the books. So. He shifted painfully. How will you bury him?

She saw that the bed was facing out towards the Gulf. East, where Frank would never go now. Whatever Teresa wants, she said.

He moved towards the door. I'll get some of the boys to help put him in the van.

Li spoke with her back to him. Can you get us on a boat? She heard him release the door handle. Stood up and turned to face him. Navid. You do that, don't you? You and Teresa? That's what you do. Can you do it for me and Matti?

He met her gaze finally and she saw he was angry with her for knowing when to ask this of him, for seeing that he had no choice.

She went back to the salvage depot. Her shift manager had told her that if she walked out there would no job to come back to, but he owed her two weeks' pay and she would need cash where they were going. There were still a few hours before school finished. She thought of those hours as a gift for Matti.

On the bus to the the depot, and while she waited for the manager to see her, and while they argued, and on the two buses from the depot to the school with the money in her jacket, and waiting outside the gates with the others, she kept searching for the right words, shaking them out and stacking and rearranging them, dumb and persistent, looking for the combination that would cut cleanly and not scar.

She watched Matti crossing the playground with a group of other children. Not one of the kids who dragged their back-pack along the ground but one who carried it carefully because she knew exactly what it had cost. When she saw Li waiting she slowed and peeled off from the others. She usually walked back to the flat on her own. Li wanted to take it back, give her another hour another minute, but it was too late.

When she told her, Matti looked at her carefully, not speaking. Li tried to hug her but that was wrong already, shaming, so they just stood there while the crowd dispersed, and then they sat on the school wall.

Matti touched Li's mouth, testing for truth. She said, But he didn't tell me he would go.

Li shuddered. Matti took her hand away and stared at her. A grown-up crying was proof. Li watched the death go into her, this unbelievable thing, saw her pupils soak it up and darken with it. She pulled her in and Matti pushed her face into her neck and a wounded sound came out, muffled against her. Li rocked her like she had rocked her when she was a baby, when her crying protested all the things she hadn't asked for and was helpless against. But when Li was too tired to hold her anymore, when she felt desperation boiling up inside her, then Frank had lifted Matti and carried her through the dark, his body like a boat, a promise, and that low creaking sound he made over and over until she quieted and slept on his chest.

She looked up at Li out of a face that was already remade by loss. And now where is he?

What had Frank said about Robbie? Had he just lied? I think he's in here now. She touched Matti's chest and then her own.

Matti concentrated, face screwed up. I can't feel him.

Li was so tired. What's the last thing you remember?

The last thing of Dad? Matti thought back, lips sifting quietly through the night before. He was late, so he hung me upside down to shake out being late.

Li nodded, seeing them in the crush of bags and shoes by the door, before Frank headed out for the night shift. Did he say goodbye?

Matti's face opened a little. I said, I love you be safe, and he said he loved me and he would be and have fun at school tomorrow.

Can you feel him now?

She hesitated. Yes? But not inside.

Okay, not inside. In Li's mind the ruin of Frank, plastic-wrapped.

*

They were nearly home before Matti had another question. Will he wait for us?

Yes.

Where will he wait? In the Best Place?

She didn't want to keep lying to her. She wanted to pull them both down into sleep and sleep through everything that was coming. She wanted Matti to stop asking. Yes, she said, in the Best Place.

She lived through the night. When she crawled out to pee before dawn, the salt was pink and phosphorescent, a paler crust of stars. She looked north and saw the whole horizon blink.

The sun swelled up molten over the flat edge of the world. She waited for it to reach her, to heat the plastic. Then she slept.

In the thin warmth of the twelfth day Li stood in the abandoned campsite with the dunes at her back and looked out at an immense, low flatness, veined pink and white, a glare off the salt, back and out as far as she could see. The horizon was low and the sky filled all the space with clouds. A long way north there was smoke.

The cold and the rest had eased her ankle and she could walk a little with the stick. She started looking for proof. The campsite wasn't enough; how many big road camps had she passed along the highway? But there were other things. Shallow toilet holes and uncovered shit too close to camp. The distance a kid would be willing to walk away alone in the dark.

And then, a little way out on the salt, she found the remains of someone else's still, half full of parched-looking plant matter. Li got down on her knees and laid her hands flat on either side of it. She had taught Matti how to do this on the road to Valiant, made her practise over and over in the dead resting hours, even though Matti complained that she was hot and sick of digging, that they wouldn't be around to drink the water.

Right there, she made a list of things that would keep Matti alive. She knew ways to get water, knew how to make a snare out of anything you could bend, how to keep a tent dry and watertight, how to share body heat. She had thermals, some food, some safety in numbers. And she knew how to be among people. Robbie, the kids at school, the kids in makecamp – she was always in the middle of things. Like Safia but without the calculation.

It was a choice she was making to believe Matti could survive, she recognised that, but if she stopped believing it she would never get out of here. So she made a deal with Matti. Wait for me, she told her, I'm coming. I just have to get myself right. Give me three days. Stay with the group, remember what you know. Don't get in a truck. Just set up camp and stay there and I'll come.

She widened Matti's still, firmed up the sides and cut down another bottle. Covered it with her last sheet of plastic. When that was done, she checked the other two and drank half the distilled water with absolute attention. Poured the rest into her waterbag and resealed the stills. Then she ate Matti's melon. It was overripe and astonishingly sweet. Matti had eaten melon once. Her fourth birthday. The Nerredin co-op had bought up a bulk-load of bruised and damaged watermelons off a truck heading south. They were selling it frozen by the piece. Frank bought enough to fill a bowl, they stuck in the candles. Matti and Robbie wolfed down the sugary chunks, gnawed the rind, asked for more. They didn't know there were other kinds.

The sugar bolted through Li's blood and left her sick with betrayal. But in a little while she felt hydrated, her brain sharper and her body responsive. There was something missing, something good, and then she realised that she didn't have a headache. For the first time since she got here she could imagine walking out, the physical sensation of it. But as long as she was stuck here, she would use the time, so that when she caught up with Matti she could go back to keeping them both alive.

The dunes around where she'd slept revealed the tracks of small night creatures. She unpacked her dump wire and made and set a handful of snares. The stick was no use in the dunes, it was easier to crawl. There had been trees of some kind here that had been ripped down to stumps for firewood. But it wasn't as barren as she'd thought yesterday; there was saltbush and small mesquite plants, prickly acacia and something that might be rubber vine. Still nothing to burn, but adding plants to her stills would increase the water supply she'd taught Matti that.

The sun was high now, early afternoon. She needed to figure out a way to get off the ground tonight and keep warm.

The four-wheel drive was further into the dunes, about fifty metres from the end of the track and buried up to the bottom of the windows. She found it by the fierce glint off the windscreen. It looked like someone had turned off for shelter, or maybe the track used to come in that far before the dunes had blown over it She shovelled the sand away from driver's door. Saw that the driver was still inside.

The door was rusted stuck. When she got it open the heat of the cab washed over her, and a smell of leather from the body hunched over the steering wheel. It was brown and shrivelled, a brittle blanket of skin tightened in on itself, still clothed in fragments of shorts and T-shirt. A long time dead. When she put her hands on it, it was smooth like the bark of a ghost gum and weighed almost nothing; she dragged it out easily and it stayed rigid and whole. She propped it on the sand against the rear wheel hub and crawled into the cab.

Small fragments of plastic were scattered over the passenger seat and floor – probably the remains of a water bottle. Three empty cans, labels long disintegrated. The dash compartment yielded registration papers, a vehicle maintenance handbook, and a wallet with nothing in it except an old-style driver's licence. Daniel Baker. Date of birth more than seventy years ago. A Saint Anthony medallion hung from the mirror. Reaching under the driver's seat she felt a wad of folded-up paper and drew it out carefully. It was a map, fragile but intact. She put it aside to look at later and hauled herself into the back. Daniel Baker had probably slept here. There was an empty thirty-litre jerry can in the boot, too heavy to carry but still useable. She sat for a minute with her eyes closed, feeling the heat through the glass of this obsolete vehicle that would keep her alive.

Back in the front seat she unscrewed the cover on the steering column, ripped out the wiring and stripped it down for more snares.

When she went back to the lakebed to check her stills, there was something new; a shine to the north. She stood a long time looking at it, shielding her eyes against the glare off the salt. Water. She hadn't seen it this morning but she didn't think she was imagining.

Val had a mate he used to talk about, Eddie, who coughed himself to death before Li was born. He was from North, before, got compulsory redistribution south like everyone else when it was declared a sacrifice zone. Val had stories from Eddie about river systems fed by seasonal deluges, rivers that channelled all the way down into the dry heart, feeding it, bringing life. This had always happened but in the years before he had to leave the rain had started becoming less predictable, more cyclonic.

Val had learned how to trap and snare from his father, before he came across the oceans, but Eddie taught him about pods and seeds and grasses, bush fruit. On the circuit, Val would go out from camp and bring back different plants from different places. Some he ground up and cooked, some they ate raw, plants that looked leathery and inedible but could taste like anything from fruit to game.

You just gotta know where to look, Li-Li, he told her.

She didn't have the patience to learn. Snares were different. That was making something, that was using her hands. But because of Eddie, they never went hungry. If Val was here now, he could show her what there was to eat that she was missing.

There was a sound above her, faint and high up. She squinted and made out black shapes moving across the sky like flecks of dust on her pupils. They dropped lower and landed and settled on the shine. Desalinating a ready supply of water would be a lot quicker than what she was doing now, and if there were birds, that meant fish. But it was too far away.

She drank from her stills. Added handfuls of saltbush leaves and then squatted awkwardly, leg extended, to pee on the plants. Then she took her stuff back to the four-wheel drive in two trips. Draped the vehicle with the biggest plastic sheet, weighting it down with sand, and positioned the jerry can to catch the runoff. Then she got back into the front seat and unfolded the map carefully. The lake took up most of the top third. The highway ran east through the bigger towns like Lawrence and Tarnackie, Curr and Graceville and Brunt, and then there were all the roads branching off it to smaller inland places that were gone to salt or dust now. At the eastern edge were the foothills of the Dividing Range. Fengdu wasn't on the map, it was on the other side of the range. Might as well be across the oceans.

There were no XB markings. Strange to look at this part of the continent with only the old token borderlines, the ones Val said you could cross without even knowing. And something else was missing. The sacrifice zone. This map had been made before she was born, when North was still just north. Not an off-limits, government-and-Company experiment derailed by Weather – just a place where people lived.

It was a kind of ghost map, she thought. Still, it was valuable. She found Yara's pen and sketched in the course of Sumud's XB, as far as she knew it. She was patchy on where Sumud finished and New Flinders started, on the size of the gap between precincts. But the kids would stick to the highway, stick to the fence. The fence was what they knew.

She tried to imagine what they were thinking. Somewhere east of here was another checkpoint in the fence that led to another gate into Sumud. But she'd heard makecamps never got established there – the environment was too harsh, too isolated, and XB Force was too aggressive. Did the kids think someone would let them in? Or maybe they weren't that stupid, maybe they had another plan. She remembered crouching in the No Go with Matti to watch the jumpers run for the truck. *I'm going for the kids because they're faster.*

The sun was dropping, the cold coming in through the glass. Outside, the driver's body lay exposed. Frank would have buried it but she didn't have the energy to spare. And he would have hated what he was becoming in her mind: a moral compass, unsullied, barely human at all. You used to cheat at cards, she thought. You knew exactly how good-looking you were. When Matti came into our room at night, too scared to go out to the toilet, you always pretended you were asleep.

She put on her extra layers and climbed into the back seat, into her sleeping bag.

There was growling and panting. Howling. Something scraped and circled the walls, testing for a way in. She tried to drag herself up, weak with fear. She lay in its grip and waited to be consumed.

Please, Mum, just can you stay?

I'll be back soon.

What if you're not?

I will be. Why do you keep asking me that?

Because I have to be ready for the worst thing.

I'm only checking three.

But please.

Stop it. Go back to the tent and lie down.

I *hate* you. You don't care about me. You're just a bad mother.

That's right. That's why I'm doing this.

Silence. Li turned away from the fence and started walking. Her vision narrowing, the ache already at the base of her skull.

Mum! Matti's voice at her back. Done with pleading – something else in her voice. Mum, look!

But Li didn't look, didn't turn back, wouldn't play the delay game. She could feel the fever coming. Her mind was on the snares, the distance between each one, how many she could check and reset and still get back before it took hold.

So. That was the last thing. The thing she carried, the place she came unstuck every time. *Mum, look!* What where you trying to show me? What did you see? She was turning all the time now, looking back fast to catch it. A flicker of light or shape of cloud, a wobbly tooth, a new trick, something small with wings. A clue.

In the morning the sun came in sharp through the windscreen. Her breath was visible in the car but the core of her was warm. The thirteenth day. Her ankle felt better and the swelling had gone down. She would try walking a bit further today – not just to take care of water and food.

She rubbed in cream, eased the compression bandage back on, tried to remember when her body hadn't hurt. Her hands were good, she barely felt them now, but the side of her face was tight and itchy all the time. Parts of the dressing were stuck to her cheek with salt and grit; it took dead skin away coming off. She touched the lumps and scales of healing underneath. No pus. She got out the first aid-kit, cleaned the area and left it uncovered so the salt could do its work. The rear-view mirror was there but she had no desire to look.

When she crawled out, the driver's body was gone. There were drag marks on the sand. Paw prints. Not foxes. She followed them a little way into the dunes, something tugging at her memory from the night. If there were feral dogs around, she needed to be in the vehicle before dark.

But the jerry can had collected ten centimetres of water overnight. It was like winning a jackpot. She drank it all, slowly, and felt a profound sense of wellbeing that cut through the taking of the body. She came down out of the dunes and squatted to pee around the still again, scanning the salt pan. Every morning she was wary, expecting to find other people here. With the numbers on the road, she figured some of them would come up the track to the lake. But maybe people had heard it was dry.

Birds again. They wheeled above her, heading north. More than yesterday. And the shine up there looked closer. Close enough to walk to.

There was a rabbit in one of her snares. It was bloody from struggling but it went still to watch her. Only when she crouched down she could see it trembling. She killed it fast and skinned it, cut out the entrails and the bladder, checked the heart. She thought about the paw prints and took the kill back to the four-wheel drive and put it inside. Dogs weren't the only scavengers. If she didn't find firewood out there she'd have to eat it raw.

It took three hours to reach the water. Li followed the footprints she had seen the first day, out over the salt pan. She carried a folded plastic sheet and three plastic bottles, one with still water in it. The crust broke under her with every step. Walking jarred her ankle and the stick hurt her whole arm, wrist to shoulder, but she moved quickly enough. Just not quickly enough yet to walk out of here.

The small footprints led her on and on. Narrow, the heel lightly indented, the toes pushing off strongly. Seventh months pregnant, Li had felt a kick and looked down and seen the underside of a whole foot pressing out against the skin high on her belly: heel, toes, everything. Thought, What are you so ready for?

Matti would have got on the bus in the one-size-too-big green and purple trainers they'd scored from a relief dump at makecamp after her old ones wore through. It was hard to think about her on the road with shoes that didn't fit but Li thought about it, talked to Matti as she walked. I'm coming I'm still coming, don't do anything stupid. Hold on.

She looked up sometimes to check the shine ahead of her. It widened slowly from a bright line to something that held the sky. She saw the distant shapes of birds and heard them calling.

The southern shore of the lakebed had been picked clean of firewood, but out here there were branches carried down by northern rivers in flood and stranded on the salt pan. Her stick sent warnings through the ground. Lizards got out of her way, and once a snake. She gathered up wood into small heaps to collect on the way back. There were colonies of ants and grubs and beetles, whole ecosystems in the wood. Maybe she could eat some of them or use them for bait. Val would have known. Then she thought about fish traps.

For the last part of the walk she watched the shine coming to meet her. Beyond it, a long way north, black smoke funnelling up to the sky. Grassfires in the sacrifice zone or burning toxic waste, or whatever the fuck they still did up there.

At the edge of the water the footprints kept going, walked right in. Li eased herself down on the salt and stared at the place where they disappeared. All the way here she had felt Matti beside her but her child's feet had not made those prints. Matti hadn't walked into the water. Matti couldn't swim.

It took a few moments to really see the lake, the flat pink skin of it, the small shivers, the way it contained the clouds. She lay down and put her face close to it, breathing the wet silty smell under the salt, like the rivers that flowed in West when she was a child. It wasn't drinkable yet but there was so much of it. Movement in the water, birds calling from further north. A place like this, you could live.

She dug a muddy saltwater still right there at the edge. Cut the top off one of her bottles and put it in, weighted it down with stones and sealed the hole. When it was done she got reckless and drank the last of her water, then got up slowly, sorely, and started gathering driftwood to make a fish trap.

It was half built when she saw the first fish. Dead, floating. She pulled it in with her stick. There was no smell or bloat and when she touched a wet finger to the scales and put it on her tongue it only tasted of salt. She limped around the edge of the lake and found more dead fish, a lot more. The water must have been too salty for them; she could desalinate it but it wasn't going to feed her, not unless the birds came a hell of a lot closer. There was no point thinking about the other possibility – that the rivers had carried poison down from North. She had to drink. Had to hope evaporation would filter out whatever was killing the fish.

It wasn't even disappointment she felt, not really. There was still the rabbit and her snares. She was just tired. What had she thought – that she'd bring Matti back here? Build a shelter? Hide or trade when people came through, trek two hundred k to the nearest Source booth once a month for a status update? She was an idiot. This place would be unimaginable in the hot season, worse than Nerredin.

She ate two crackers and checked the seals on the still – the plastic had already steamed up. Might as well rest her ankle while the bottle filled. She moved back from the water's edge to where it was dry, loosened the compression bandage and lay down. Eyes closed, faced turned up to the sun. Then she remembered Rich telling her that healing skin would burn easily, and she pulled her cap down. Thought about Eddie's northern rivers flooding down to make an oasis in the dry. People said the sacrifice zones were mostly dumps now, that there was nothing left to dig up and everything was contaminated, and Weather was too extreme up there for Company investment anyway. It was just an uninhabitable Old Testament wasteland. But the stories Eddie told Val had never been about poison, they were all about how fast life came back.

It's about to start in five seconds!

They came running, Li from the woodpile, Frank from the pressing shed. Li was thinking this better not be another false alarm, with everything they had to do before dinner. Matti had lined up three chairs under the jam tree, one each for Frank and Li and one for her rag horse, Goldie. She came out from behind the tree and they clapped and she stood behind the card table. This is a *magic* show, she said.

She was wearing an old black singlet of Frank's, dishwashing gloves that were too big for her and a newspaper cape with a hole cut out for her head. She had three tins and she put a stone under one of them and shuffled the tins and then asked someone to guess where it was now. Frank guessed and she got a stubborn look and told them to shut their eyes.

125

Hoka poka! And when they opened them she lifted the tin and the stone wasn't there. They whoo-hooed and clapped.

Matti said she was going to make one of the tins disappear as well.

Close your eyes! There was a clang of metal rolling away on the hard ground. Da-da! Now I need a volunteer.

Frank waved Goldie's foreleg in the air.

Okay Goldie, you can come up. And I need my disappearing chambler. She dragged a cardboard box out from behind the tree. Frank passed up Goldie. Matti swished her cape around, said the magic words and threw the horse into the box. Da-da! She stood there with her hands on her hips, daring them to doubt her. Frank's shoulders started shaking. Matti looked at him hard to make sure she wasn't being mocked, and then, satisfied, threw herself in sideways after Goldie, almost toppling the box. And now *I'm* gone! she yelled from inside.

Li couldn't stop laughing. It was so easy to love her child at this moment. So basic and uncomplicated, even someone like her could get it right.

Okay, now I'm the teacher and I'm going to go through the roll. But hang on, where is it? Un*fort*unately the roll is missing. Matti ran for the kitchen, yelling over her shoulder, Sorry about this, I just need to be doing stuff in a rush, so you'll just have to wait.

The screen door banged behind her. Frank picked up the discarded parts of the newspaper neither of them had had a chance to read yet and started piecing them together. Li listened to Matti inside slamming drawers and telling off invisible children. Frank dipped the paper to show her a headline: *Lance extends north west sacrifice zone.*

She looked at the dotted lines and skull icons on the map. The redrawn southern border was a thousand k north of where they sat, give or take.

That's getting close.

He squinted at her. You reckon?

You know what I mean. There'll be more people coming down.

They won't stop here. They'll take the redistribution money and keep moving south.

Okay, right, ready to go. Matti was back with a piece of paper and a pencil. Where have all the kids gone? She started calling the roll.

Li thought about the wood waiting to be split and felt a slow burn of frustration. Frank kept reading his salvaged newspaper, glancing up now and then to play his part. He was just better at this. His appreciation was real but he had no qualms about cheating, and at a certain point he would find a way to end Matti's endless show without crushing or enraging her. Whereas Li would just sit there nursing her boredom and irritation until all the pleasure had dried up, and then she'd roll her eyes or raise her voice and the whole thing would be ruined.

You know I went to high school with him, down in Warrick?

With Peter Lance? Li had never heard this. He grew up in West? Bet he keeps that quiet.

I don't know, Frank said. He got inside the XB, didn't he? Got into government. I'd put that on my CV.

Quiet, children! Matti yelled. You're not *listening*.

Sorry, beansprout.

My *name* is Ms Twinkle.

Hang on a minute, Li told her. Then, to Frank, Were you mates?

He shrugged. Yeah, we were. We hung out after school, went to parties. He looked back down at the paper, at the conviction politician in his suit and hard hat, the drilling rigs, the straggling exodus, the map with its old and new demarcation lines. I painted houses with him and his dad after we finished high school. Before he moved to Valiant.

Matti came to lean over his shoulder, studying the pictures. Is he a bad man? She could switch mode just like that.

I haven't seen him in a long time, sprout. I couldn't say what kind of man he is.

But did he do a bad thing?

Frank sighed. Yeah. Yeah, I think he did.

Li watched him figuring the right amount of truth to give her. She said what she knew he believed but wasn't sure she did. Matti, people can do bad things without being bad people.

Can they really?

Really.

How many things?

She watched the clouds, which were also in the water. Clouds that rolled and crashed, reefs of gold and orange with the sun moving through them, clouds that flared and spent themselves like smoke. She ran from the fire, she crossed the sea. She found herself back here on the salt, alone.

If Val was here now, he could tell her what was wrong with the fish. He'd like it here. It wasn't North, but it was closer. He used to tell her that one day when she didn't need him anymore, he was going to save up a whole season, two seasons, and just go, head all the way up. See for himself. One night at a circuit camp she lay in her blankets by the fire and listened to him swapping stories about people who'd been to the sacrifice zone, or tried. No one had a story about anyone coming back, but Val said that didn't prove anything. He reckoned it wasn't as bad up there as government wanted them to believe.

Li said, What about your check-ups?

Thought you were asleep, young one.

I bet they don't have the hospital up there.

Val had a thyroid condition and his liver was shot. Once every season, a free hospital set up camp on the circuit.

True enough, Val said. I wouldn't be much good without my pills.

I bet it's not even like that anymore, Li told him, like what Eddie said.

Val nodded and fished a thread of tobacco off his tongue. Nobody's home is what it used to be, Li-Li.

The sun's heat thinner again. Time to start back. Nerredin was flat country too, big fast sky. Matti liked cumulus clouds the best; they lay on their backs on the dirt behind the house and she said the sky looked like a pop-up book. The memory felt dusty and generalised. Li tried to imagine Matti seeing this sky, these clouds, but she couldn't, she couldn't do it. She couldn't do it anymore.

The bottle was full. And the hole had filled with saltwater again – the edge of the lake had moved a metre south while she slept. She drank and decanted and then packed up the still. It'd be under water soon.

Before she put the compression bandage back on, she tried moving her foot a little, testing her weight carefully. It felt better. She should leave tomorrow, even if she couldn't get far. She had some water now, some food, and there were towns east of here where she could resupply. But there was a heaviness on her. She was barely going through the motions in her head.

Walking back, she kept her eyes on the ground and concentrated on each step, on the new effort of carrying wood under one arm, because that seemed to be about all she was good for. When her stick knocked against a small piece of wood, she stood staring at it for a long time. Knew she was seeing something that wasn't there, and knew that was dangerous. The smooth surface, all that compressed movement, the wild grain in the wood. Matti's horse.

Li got down clumsily and caught it up in both hands. Brushed salt from the creases of its limbs and mane, put it to her lips and traced Matti's scowl, Frank's promise. The fastest horse in the West. She shuddered with tenderness. Couldn't believe it but she held it, and it fit neatly in her palm, all action, mane flying back, legs a blur somehow. It was real. Real. She wiped snot and tears, tasted the salt on her arm. Remembered Frank at the bar with that long-distance look as he worked the horse out of the wood. She missed him so much. They should be doing this together. I promise you, she told him. I swear.

She drank again when she got back, drank her fill and there was still water. Leaving felt real now. Tomorrow.

The four-wheel drive's bonnet had rusted through in places. The engine was gone but the bonnet prop was still there. She dug a fire pit and roasted the rabbit on the prop. The smell made her weak, carnivorous. Her stomach growled and her mouth filled up with spit, but when the meat was ready, it was too rich for her to eat more than a few mouthfuls.

Dark fell down all over the lakebed. She stayed by the fire, with the heat easing deep into her bones. Somewhere out there, the sound of howling. She unbuttoned her pocket and held the horse, remembering Matti asleep in the tent, gripping its wooden head. For the first time she let herself see the fragility of the thread she'd been following – rumours and reported sightings, maybes. But the horse was real. Impossible but real. Out there, in all that salt, Matti had led her right to it. So, it was true. Sooner or later anyone could roll a six.

Tomorrow she would walk back to the highway with both feet on the ground. And there would be another truck, a driver who was persuadable. She would sit up in the cab and watch the road going under the wheels until they were there, right there ahead of her on the roadside. And Matti would turn around and see that she had come.

Gulls woke her. She lay in the four-wheel drive, disoriented for a minute. Then she remembered: this was the day she was leaving.

It was barely light but somehow the light was different – softer, more diffuse. Had she dreamed the birds? The sound pulled her back to Valiant and the enormous blue of the Gulf and Frank in the container and the seabirds curling and crying way above it all.

But when she opened her eyes again, she could still hear them. What were they doing here?

Li cracked the door and the smell hit her. Fresh and salty, and wet like the beaches where she and Val had camped for a couple of summers, back when the west coast was still on the circuit and there was work on the kelp farms. She breathed it in and caught something rotten underneath. The air was thick with bird cries now. She didn't understand until she limped out of the dunes and saw the water. It lapped twenty metres from where she stood, reaching back and out beyond the edges of her sight.

Through the night those northern rivers had kept running down, flooding the lakebed. And while she slept, life had come back, too. The water was livid with birds. Gulls, herons, ducks, black swans, birds she'd never seen and couldn't name, all calling and landing and jostling and taking off in spurts across the water, reaching down and pulling up fish. The stink of dead fish along the shoreline rose to meet her, but the birds ignored them because the water was heaving with life. Reeds shivered and flowers bloomed pale and wide-cut on the surface. On the shore and even in the dunes, life showed green through the sand. What she thought of was Matti's Best Place.

Li left her stick on the shore and walked into the water to convince herself that it was real. It was cold and shallow, deepening to a metre when she waded out. A pod of pelicans announced their descent with low honks – astonishing in their grace and power until they hit the water in a series of lumbering jolts.

She sank into the water up to her neck, shivering, feeling it touch her everywhere. The plenty of it. Scooped it up and let it run over her face, soothing the itch. She stripped, threw her clothes back on the shore, and rolled naked. Let the salt lift and hold her, taking the heaviness from her legs, her ankle. She scrubbed her skin with mud. Waded back to the edge and washed her filthy clothes and her stiff sour underwear. Stood up under the first thin heat of the sun and looked down at her cleaner self, muscle and sinew, the sharp angles of ribs and hips, her breasts gone slack, everything reduced.

It jolted her into a decision. She wouldn't leave today, she would take this gift and carry it out with her tomorrow.

Naked, she dug out a large still at the water's edge, deep enough to hold the thirty-litre jerry can. By the time she finished digging she wasn't cold anymore. Then she made fish traps. On her hands and knees, scooping up the wet mud, it was a childhood feeling. She had always meant to take Matti to the beach in Valiant.

By the time she was done, her clothes were salt-stiff and dry enough to put back on, and the first trap was already full of yellow and silver fish. She worked in a steady frenzy, cleaning and filleting the fish, rubbing salt in and covering them in saltbush leaves. Skewered other fish whole and roasted them on the bonnet prop. She dug another, deeper fire pit, roped driftwood into a rough tripod and hung the salted fish in the smoke, hoping her wood supply would last long enough to do the job.

By midmorning the flies were coming, drawn to the rotting fish. There had hardly been any flies before now. She worked to keep them off the drying meat but gave up trying to keep them off her face. There were toads, too, a kind she'd never seen in West. Bloated and yellow, emitting a stop-start engine rumble under all the other noises. They were slow but she wasn't tempted to catch them. Most of the birds ignored them too but the gulls dive-bombed them along the water's edge, flipping them onto their backs and ripping their bellies open to feed.

All day the birds kept coming, preening, feeding, jostling on the water. The sky was solid with them, their shrieks and their shit and feathers falling. Where were they coming from? She hadn't known there were this many birds anywhere. All day grasses and small plants grew up and covered the shore and the dunes, and smaller flowers emerged from them. It made her feel like a child.

When Li turned nine, Val bought her a magic garden. They set it up in the tent; the small tricky cardboard landscape on its plastic base, and poured the liquid into the channels that fed it, and then waited. She had fallen asleep waiting and missed the first bloom of colour on a fir tree, the first snow on the mountain. This was like that. She had fallen asleep with the outline of life and woken to life itself exploding around her, the chemical transformation so rapid it clambered over itself, multiplying at fantastic speed.

She tasted the flowers and they were sweet and nutty, so she picked armfuls, leaving some to dry on the roof of the four-wheel drive. Ate and ate, feeding herself up for the walk ahead. Her new still was working so fast that she could fill her waterbag and what extra bottles she could carry, and have plenty left to drink.

When feral pigs came in the afternoon, they ignored her and she kept her distance. There was enough here for everyone, more than enough.

After Nerredin's school closed, when they were running classes in their kitchens and sheds and paddocks, Li made Matti her own magic garden. Not from a packet – Wars had put an end to the flow of cheap goods. She and Angie had done it as a science experiment with the kids. It turned out the main ingredient was salt.

One by one the kids had got bored and drifted off but Matti stayed, hardly blinking while the liquid soaked into the crystals because she wanted to be the first one to see it. But it had taken too long, or they got the ratio wrong, or the temperature. In the end even Matti ran off. Then Angie said, casually, like it was nothing, Why don't you hang onto it? Take it home, just in case.

And in the morning there was a green crystal forest in the fridge. Matti wrapped her arms around the bowl and hung over it, staring. Touch it, Frank said. But she shook her head. I don't want to wreck it.

People arrived at the end of the day. Three adults and two kids. They were pushing bikes with panniers and hauling a small, heavily loaded trailer. Their faces, hair and clothes, the bikes, everything was caked in red dust. They stood, staring, taking it all in. Then they whooped and hollered and ran down to the water. Li looked away, went back to her drying fish.

When she looked again, the woman and the two men were setting up tents at the foot of the dunes about a hundred metres down the beach, while the kids hauled up water in collapsible containers. Then they all sat down to eat. Later, the kids chased birds, making shrill sounds as they explored the shoreline. They stared over at her from time to time, but they didn't approach. Li stopped paying attention when one of the men waded in with some kind of speargun.

There were so many things she might have got wrong with her fish. Not enough salt, not enough drying time, too many flies. The strips she'd left to dry had a brittle jerky texture that seemed right but the smoked fish needed longer. She couldn't afford to get sick. She would keep the fire going tonight as long as her wood lasted.

She did a stocktake. There was food to last a week, a little more if she was careful, and all the water she could carry. She envied the shop family their wheels.

What are you doing?

The older boy was standing behind her. She hadn't heard him come. Her pulse sped up with the shock of proximity, of speech.

Smoking fish, she said.

He pointed downshore at her still, the jerry can sitting beside it. What's that for?

So I can drink the water.

He looked sceptical. We use pills.

Huh. You got many of them left?

Yep. We got everything. We had the shop in Lawrence but there were too many dusters and then everyone went away.

Lawrence. She thought briefly of the couple with the baby. A breeze came up off the water, shifting the direction of the smoke. She made adjustments. The boy was still there, staring.

Are you on your own? he asked.

Yeah.

Why?

Nalanjin! The woman was walking fast down the beach towards them. Get back here!

The boy said, You could camp with us. That's my mum and my dad and my uncle and my cousin Laz. His mum's dead. He said this with the ease of a child who knew themselves personally immune to loss. We're going down to the big camp. Mum says we can stay there till they let us in.

Did he mean makecamp? She cleared her throat. You see any other kids on the way here?

He looked at her blankly.

Maybe a group of them? Without any grown-ups?

The boy shook his head, backing away a little at her tone. His mother called again, getting closer. Nalanjin! Leave the woman alone! Li heard her fear and felt no answering tug of feeling. She would get her child back.

His face cleared suddenly. There was this one boy, just with his dad? They tried to steal our bikes at night but my dad shot at them and they ran away. He paused, satisfied. My dad says people like that are how come there are walls.

She didn't want this boy with two parents and a bicycle. Didn't want his voice, his skinny child's body, his dumb certainty anywhere near her.

Here. She scooped up four fish she'd left salting. You want to rinse these and cook them straight away.

I don't really like fish.

137

She stared at him. Don't eat them, then. Give them to your parents. And tell them they can have whatever water's left in that jerry can.

He stood back, unwilling. The same look on Matti's face when she was, how old? In the highchair, still. They'd collected the eggs together, laughing at the weird places the chooks hid them, and Li was flush with good parenting. But in the kitchen Matti scowled and pushed her plate away.

You need to eat your dinner.

No. Yuk.

Come on, Matti, just try it.

Matti picked up the egg by its oily fringe and dropped it onto the ground. Li scooped it up and put it back on the plate. Yolk seeped out. You're not getting down till you eat it, she said.

Matti sat in the chair until it was dark. Halfway through, she wet herself. She didn't cry and she didn't eat the egg. Li was trapped in the kitchen, unable to leave her alone in the chair, hostage to the lesson of not wasting food. Matti watched her and her eyes were murderous. They held their breath, waiting for Frank to come home and break the spell.

Will they still be so smelly when they're cooked? the boy asked.

No. She was desperate for him to be gone. You got wood, right?

We got pellets. They burn better than wood.

Okay then.

He took the fish reluctantly, kept staring. Then his mother was there. These four fish are for you, he said, and started gabbling Li's instructions. The woman put her hand on his head and her face softened into security. She nodded her thanks.

Li said, If you're going to Port Howard, the makecamp got cleared out two weeks ago.

138

The woman stared at her. Are you sure? There's a lot of people heading down that way.

Li shrugged. There's Source in Kutha. Check for yourself.

The woman looked stunned. She nodded again and turned back, tugging the boy with her. Li couldn't work out how they hadn't heard yet, the way people talked on the road.

Mum, she heard the boy saying, what's wrong with her face?

She went and got out the ghost map from the four-wheel drive. Lawrence was about eighty k north-east. It had been a decent-sized town when the map was made and the highway went right through it. There was no way the family would have missed the kids unless the kids were further ahead than she'd figured. Then she remembered the bikes. Travelling like that they would have covered the distance in less than half the time, probably only camped one night. Matti could have been well past Lawrence before they even left.

Not long after sunset, Li banked up the firepit and bedded down beside it. She lurched awake in the dark to snarling and birds screaming. Reached for her knife. A child cried out in fear and there were shouts from the beach, then gunshots. She got into the four-wheel drive, ripped the Saint Anthony medallion from its rusted chain and held it in her fist but the child cried on and on, a thin, jarring sound. Matti had cried like that all through the first year of her life, cried until Li was drowning, until she wanted only to be lifted clear of this devastating error. Threw the chair across the room, smashed the bowl. Ange found her shaking Matti, shouting at her to stop. Said she wouldn't tell Frank if Li swore never to do it again.

She didn't have the thing you had to have to do this, didn't even know what it was. Wanted to walk away from it to somewhere quiet, but she couldn't because they existed – both of them. And she couldn't give them up.

In the morning, the beach was a killing field of blood and feathers. Streams of birds flew in to replace the dead.

The family left while Li was still cooling the last of her smoked fish. The older boy stared as they passed and the adults nodded soberly. She understood that he must have relayed her question from the way the woman caught him by the hand in some kind of demonstration of how not to lose your child. As if it might be contagious.

One of the men dropped back and laid something on the sand ten metres from her. Thanks for the water and the fish, he said.

Li waited till he'd almost caught up with the others before she went to look. It was a dust mask. She brushed off the salt and held it, dangling by its elastic. Wondered where they would go when they found out she was right. Not back where they'd come from. Anyway, with all the unsheltered heading south, there would be another makecamp soon enough.

Three days east, Li came to what was left of Lawrence. The town was shuttered and shrouded in dust and people walking through picked over the buildings for anything they could use. The general store was locked up tight – either Nalanjin's family had planned to come back, or they didn't want to give away what they couldn't carry – but the boards had already been pulled off one of the windows, and the glass salvaged. The shelves were bare but she found a can of peas that had rolled under the counter.

There had been four road camps between the lake and Lawrence, some just a couple of families, some big enough that she had to walk in and ask. Every kid she'd seen was accounted for.

She slept in the shop and walked out on the nineteenth day into a low-level duster that cleared to make way for other dusters. A dim and bloody sun. The daytime warmth was gone, days behind her. The dust deadened sound so that people loomed out of it dreamlike. Even engines were muffled, the trucks sounding distant until they were almost on top of her.

Between dusters, she saw spinifex and buffel grassland, mulga scrub. Behind the fence, to the south, were low tussocky hills and the XB came and went. Here and there were derelict houses and what remained of fencelines. Sometimes smoke rising from a chimney. Once, someone came out of a shed, their face hidden under a beekeeping helmet and veil, and stood watching till she passed.

The highway was sealed again now but dust lay so thick on it that it could have been a dirt track. Dust blew in eddies, lifted with every step, particles filling the air, coating her clothes and skin and eyelashes. The dust mask made it almost bearable. She experimented with wrapping a strip of clear plastic around her eyes and tying it behind her head. It helped for a little while but the plastic sweated against her skin and the dust worked its way in until her eyes were raw and weeping again. In the end she made a bandana out of her thermal leggings and pulled it down most of the way.

These dusters weren't fierce like the one north of Kutha, but they were persistent enough to make her feel a bit like she was choking all the time. And when a truck went past it boiled up an explosion so intense that she had to crouch down at the roadside and bury her head in her arms until the dust subsided. The highway would be quieter at night, easier walking, but she couldn't risk passing Matti in the dark.

The foot traffic wasn't thick but it kept coming. Everyone was caked in dust. People carried their lives on their backs, their mouths and noses covered with masks or rags. They wore goggles or sunglasses or welding visors, scarves or veils, hats with gauze hanging down. Some of them were accompanied by underfed dogs, watchful and dust-coloured. There were people on bicycles and occasionally horses, cloth-muzzled, dust streaming back from their shoulders like red wings. Once, a camel loomed out of a red cloud, a man swaying on top, holding a crossbow, everything he still owned stacked behind him.

There had been no bores yet along this stretch of highway but sometimes there was Trade set up out of the back of vans at the roadside, selling water by the litre or by the scoop, and readies, masks, sunglasses. Their mark-ups were huge but they were still getting customers.

Li moved as fast as she could. She'd managed twenty-five, sometimes thirty k each day since leaving the lake, resting a few minutes every hour or so with her foot up on her pack and her eyes shut against the dust. She'd given up on the fantasy of a lift almost as soon as she got back on the highway. A bicycle was her preoccupation now. She was on the lookout for someone desperate enough to trade one away, even though she wasn't sure she'd be able to pedal. There was another town coming up on her map, about two more days' walking, bigger than Lawrence – maybe there'd be something there. What could she trade, though, that would be worth a bicycle? Every single thing she had left that was keeping her alive? It wasn't much more realistic than a ride in a truck, but it kept her mind off the dust.

Her ankle hurt but it was holding. She'd been afraid the stick would mark her out as easy prey but plenty of people had them, because of injury or age or just to pace themselves.

She asked everyone. People had heard about the children walking but no one could say for sure that they'd seen them. The stories were elastic and contradictory, delivered with the conviction of retelling. There were ten kids or fifty, more; there were babies among them, they were barely minors; they were hungry and ragged and well-provisioned.

143

No one could tell her where they might be going. A few people talked about a Company camp somewhere between Sumud and New Flinders. All they knew was that it wasn't a place you would take children to, and it wasn't a camp that would get you inside. The only other place after that was Permacamp. She'd heard about it back in makecamp. Permacamp was an official Agency camp outside Fengdu, had been there for years, but it was all the way east, across the Range.

Some of the stories sounded more like paranoia than rumour. One woman had heard that trucks had stopped for the children, the drivers offloading food and water out of pity. Someone else described an organised child-begging operation with adult ring-leaders, leeching off other unsheltered.

It didn't make sense. They were all on the same highway, people gravitated to each other in the roadcamps at night. Why was it so hard to pin down an actual sighting? A bunch of kids on their own, walking or camped, wasn't something you would miss. Why was their existence so provisional? The children in these stories emerged out of some collective dust and faded back into it again, untouched and untouchable.

Li unbuttoned her pocket and closed her hand around the horse, fit her thumb into one bent foreleg.

The road swung towards to the fence or away, the No Go came in and out of view through the dust. She hadn't seen a patrol in there since before the lake. What there was, now, was dogs. Feral and hungry, they lay low in the scrub or slunk across open ground; they fought and fucked. Sometimes a pack converged on the fence-line, all dust and matted hair and drool, snapping and snarling at anyone who strayed too close, working themselves into a frenzy. Maybe they were an accident or maybe they were a part of XB Force's defence system. Cheaper than landmines, cheaper than vehicles and guns and uniforms. The weaker ones would die of thirst or starve but there would always be more.

There were the dogs and the unsheltered. The road. The trucks. The dust above them, enclosing them all. Li wondered if there was anything still up there watching, still capable of recording all these small pulses of radiant heat that moved distantly parallel with the wall, moved and stopped and moved again. It might register the thermal energy of the wall itself as a long continuous flickering that the small pulses could never breach. It might be high up enough to see the wall for what it really was, to see the dust on both sides.

Late in the afternoon she met a man who said he'd seen them. He was walking alone, pulling a dusty tartan shopping trolley. A parrot hunched, hooded, on his shoulder. Hundreds of kids, he told her, camped roadside north-east of here the morning before last.

She didn't trust his willingness, but she couldn't resist hearing him out. Did you talk to them?

He pulled down the rag that covered his nose and mouth and spat red into the dust. Flung his arm out at the trolley, an all-encompassing gesture. I offered them everything I had. They wouldn't take it. Girl says to me, scrap of a thing, not more than thirteen, says God gives them what they need. The bird clicked its beak under the hood and shuffled irritably. I said, Girlie, from the look of you lot, he isn't up to the job. You know what she says?

The road shook under a truck and they pulled to the side and hunkered down. The man shoved the parrot, squirming, under his coat and coughed into her face. Shouted through the roaring.

She says, God looks after us because we're walking for God. I said, How's that? And she says, People made Weather but only God can take it back. She says they're walking to show God they're sorry. He waved an arm at the road. For everything. All the war, waste, stuffing up the climate, these goddam walls. It wasn't their fault but they're sorry anyway.

The truck passed and they stood up, facing each other. His eyes were wide and locked on hers. He was mad, she realised. It was all in his head.

She says, this is exactly what she says, God'll save us when God's ready. Until then God keeps us safe. He nodded at Li, eyes wide. So I said.

Li shouldered past him and kept walking.

I'm telling you, he called after her. They wouldn't take food, nothing. I *tried*.

She wouldn't ask anyone else. It was all bullshit. Fearmongers and rumour-mongers. Madmen invoking God to feed their own fantasies. What did these kids represent – what threat, what need – that nobody asked where they'd come from and who might be looking for them, or where they thought they were going? Matti walked through the lizard brains of the unsheltered like an aberration, like a talisman of a world gone to hell. Li found she was crying and smudged the tears angrily into her dust mask. There had never been hundreds. She should have spat in his face.

Then that feeling passed. People would make the children into whatever they needed, it didn't change anything. This was between her and Matti. They had made a deal that Matti would stay put and wait. But then she remembered that Matti never agreed to the deal. When had she ever done what Li told her? Matti hadn't wanted to stay in Valiant or makecamp and she wouldn't want to stay here, choking on the dust at the side of the highway. She wanted to get to the Best Place.

All those rumours had started from something. Something further along this road, where everyone else had come from. If the kids had left the lake a day or two before she got there, and they'd been walking ever since, they might be a week ahead of her, but they couldn't be covering more ground in a day than she was now. If she could get a bike she would close the distance faster. If she couldn't, then she just had to keep walking.

The dusters eased off at sunset. Li cracked the mask and breathed deep. She rinsed her eyes and her scabbed cheek with a capful of water, dug a toilet hole behind some bushes. After another hour's walking she came to the fringes of a road camp that stretched most of the way back to the fence. She didn't avoid them now. Joining meant she could search the camp at first light. And with this many people in the dark, it was safer to stay in close than take her chances being followed away from the crowd.

She set up her bed a little way back in the scrub but near enough to catch the talk. People were sharing water and readies, contributing roadkill to be cooked over the fire. The camps were about more than safety in numbers, they fed some need for community that people put away in daylight. It reminded her, painfully, of the road from Nerredin but if she pushed back past that, it took her back to Val, to the feeling of childhood.

Listening·in, sifting through languages, she heard that Sumud might have to open a skill quota soon, or drop the buy-in price, because of some kind of epidemic. Someone's cousin had called from inside New Flinders to say he'd made it through the gate under a truck. But trucks didn't slow down along flat road like this – they just fanged through. Your only chance was a road-house. More urgently than getting inside, people talked about water. Who had it, how much they'd paid or traded, where the next bore was supposed to be.

The kids fell asleep in swags or tents or on their parents' laps. Li looked at every one of them, would walk the camp at first light, but she knew Matti wasn't here, safe by the fire.

Someone asked about the children walking and Li listened harder but it was just the same stories she'd already heard. Ghost stories.

Then a woman said, But where are they walking *to*?

And a man barked a laugh. Where are any of us walking to? To where someone might let us in.

A rush of talk, people translating to each other. Li lost the thread. Then the first woman spoke again. But why east? New Flinders hasn't opened quota – all that's up there is Transit.

Li thought, Transit must be the Company camp. The one people had said to stay clear of.

There's Permacamp. Eventually.

But the woman dismissed this. No one's walking across the range in the cold season, let alone kids. All the talk now is Sumud, right? I mean, that's where we're all heading. Right?

A new voice. Maybe they're not trying to get in. Maybe they're trying to get somewhere else.

Silence while this was considered.

Like where?

Maybe one of the Deep Islands.

Li opened her eyes.

All those islands went under.

Bullshit. That was just a couple of them.

You can grow stuff there, I heard. Weather's not so bad, plenty of water. And they don't have the ballot.

Who says they don't? Ballot's everywhere – even inside the XB.

Think about it. Would it be worth the time and money for government to ship people over from there?

It was so strange to hear other people talk about the best place like it wasn't just a private game. Li couldn't get her bearings. Around the fire the talk went on and she didn't know anymore if it was real or if she was just arguing it out in her head.

Deep south though. It's too far, too hard to get there.

Everywhere's hard.

Not that hard. You know how bad the howlers get offshore? Even if they made it to the range and then across the range and then all the way round the XB to the east coast, how's a bunch of kids going to pay their way onto a boat that'll handle those seas?

That made sense. Everyone knew about ballot ships going missing on the long haul across the oceans to wherever the Front was now. And, here, the refugee problem had gone away years ago. The boats just stopped arriving.

Inshallah, they'll just let them on, someone said.

Yeah, and maybe Allah will carry them over the range in the dead of the cold season and fly them to the islands. Those kids aren't going anywhere the rest of us can't go.

The Agency office in Valiant registered new claims on Saturdays. Li had to work so Frank took Matti. The first Saturday, they had left in the dark and came back in the dark. Matti was holding a piece of paper tightly, swaying on her feet.

I played with some kids, she said, and there was a fight and soldiers took some men away and we got this ticket, so when we go next time we can start from there.

Frank met her eyes over Matti's head.

Matti said, When it's our turn, we're going to pick the Best Place. Aren't we, Dad?

Later, in bed, her told her, There was a woman with three kids in front of us. She said once you get pre-registered, you can nominate a preferred destination.

Bullshit. Sheltered isn't a choice, it's geography.

You know that's not true, not always. People get in. Anyway, I'm not even talking about the XB now. He half sat up to explain it right. That woman, she has a cousin who was a horticulturalist. He got status for one of the Deep Islands eight years ago. There's no ballot there, Li. I mean, officially, yeah, but she said government hasn't enforced it in years. The islands are just too small, too scattered, too far off the mainland. He waited for that to sink in. There's good growing land too. She reckons their water comes from aquifers and they never sold it off. Her cousin thinks they're going to open up quota again, but very specific, mostly food security. If she can get pre-registered, he'll sponsor her and her kids. She said maybe he could help us too.

Why do you think people will help us? Why do you still think that? She lined up the evidence against him. The way government kept Nerredin's water supply at a trickle while the town slowly dried up. How no one sent aid after the howlers or the fire. The trucks that passed them without stopping, day and night, on the highway to Valiant. West was dying and it was being left to die. One day government would declare the whole state a sacrifice zone and the XB precincts were tensing for it, but Frank still talked like someone, somewhere was going to do the right thing.

He was quiet for a while, lying with his back to her. Angry, or maybe asleep. He had to be up at four. Then he said, What do you want us to do, Li? What's your plan?

Winning the lottery isn't a plan.

You think I don't know they're afraid of us? She could hear how tired he was, how battered. They're afraid if they let us in they'll become us. I know. I don't know what else to do. I don't want Matti running from Weather her whole life. I don't want her to get shipped off to Wars. I want her to believe people will help, and not be wrong about that. He rolled over to face her. What we can do except get in the system and wait for our turn? But if everyone else is trying for on of the precincts, maybe we can get to the Deep Islands instead. If they need agricultural workers, why not us?

He was wrong, he was wrong. But she listened to him in the dark and loved him for believing in a place where water flowed out of the rocks and children didn't go to war, believing they could make it real for Matti. For believing in the future.

Okay, she said. Why not us?

The operator had set up on the road through Tarnackie. The bold print on Li's map had suggested a truckstop and a general store, farming supplies, a pub. It was mid-morning when she walked in. At first it looked like another ghost town, but when she got past the Wars memorial she saw four crates, all occupied, near the skeleton of the old phone box. More people straggled along the roadside, waiting their turn.

Company had given up maintaining pay phones outside the cities four or five years ago, but the boxes still caught the eye, still signalled communication. It was a smart place for an operator to set up trade.

Li went closer to see what was on offer. The operator was a young woman with a folder of Cnekt cards clipped to her belt: solid build, safety glasses sitting on top of her dreadlocks. She was red-dusted and looked like she hadn't slept inside in a while, same as her customers.

A mini satellite dish and solar-powered battery pack were set up on a folding card table. Four handheld sat phones, all in use.

That meant she could patch, or she worked with someone who could, and she had good access to tech. The whole set-up was lightweight, portable, well put together. Li couldn't figure how a sole female operator had managed to keep it this long.

She scanned the street for backup. A feral-looking young guy sat on the porch of the boarded-up feed supply store, lazily watching the queue. One guy. She wondered if there were others round the back.

The operator was adjusting the antenna on a phone for a customer. She glanced up at Li. Two thousand for a ten-slot, she said. Cash or trade.

Twice the going rate in makecamp, Li thought.

People were looking at her sideways, hostile. A bearded man said, Hey. No jumping.

Yeah, yeah, everyone knows the drill. The operator glanced at Li again and jerked her head towards the queue.

Li stepped back and watched her taking payment in advance. Most people offered trade. Waterpure tabs or readies, half a dozen eggs, a wrinkled bag of apples, a good length of copper wiring, a torch. One woman had high-thermal wear, still in the plastic.

Li needed to use a phone but she resented being suckered like this. Didn't have enough trade to be suckered anyway. She itemised her supplies. Less than two days' water. Enough dried fish for three more days, her camping gear, the plastic, the high-thermals, her tools. Nothing she could spare. But she had to call Agency. Just because the Port Howell branch had lost Matti didn't mean her claim wasn't being run through some other branch's database right now. You never knew with government. That's what kept people hoping.

She wasn't queuing anyway, fuck that. Went to wait in the dead phone box.

Someone got up off a crate and the queue shuffled forward, dust clouding and settling again. There was none of the sociability of the road camps. These people were barely making eye contact with each other. Everyone looked hungry and beaten and older than they probably were. A woman with a young child halfway down the line had a bony, dust-coloured nanny goat on a lead. There was a man somewhere in his twenties with a missing arm and purple scars all over his face.

Li turned her attention to the phone box, not expecting much. The handset had been broken apart and stripped of receiver, carbon transmitter, steel conduit. But the phone itself looked more promising. The outer armour had been comprehensively removed but the housing was basically intact. The lightning-bolt icons gave fair warning: try to pick the lock and you'd hit a breaker switch connected to the grounding terminal. That would trigger an electrical current upward of a hundred milliamps, shutting down the whole system. Shutting down whoever was messing with it, too.

From the scorch marks, it looked like someone had triggered the kill switch on this unit. That's what happened when amateurs tried salvage. Li had bypassed the kill switch on this exact model in Nerredin and a dozen other towns in West. Val had probably done hundreds, but pickings were a lot thinner now – most people didn't even bother checking boxes anymore. Especially the young ones, like this woman, busy sharking her customers and missing what was under her nose. Because if the kill switch had already been triggered then this phone was easy tech.

The four-pin angle was rusty. It took Li nearly a minute to pick with a tension wrench and a short hook, but the housing came off cleanly. Underneath it was the security layer – the trigger mechanism a burnt-out mess of wiring. Whoever died in this box had taken the risk for her but she was still slow and careful unscrewing this layer.

Hey Stokes, the operator yelled. We taking goat?

Li glanced over. The goat woman's child was trying to pull the animal away.

No, the guy on the porch called back. We are not takin fucken goat. Jesus.

She's a good milker, the woman insisted. I'd get two thousand for her easy at market.

Then find a market, the operator said. We're not running a farm.

If you can't carry livestock, butcher her.

Mum, no! The boy was trying to wrestle the lead away. She slapped him and he crouched down with his arms around the goat.

Please, she said to the operator. I need to call my husband – he went ahead.

Can't do it. You got a complaint, take it to Stokes over there.

Li got back to work. She was through to the circuit board now. It was intact. The circuitry was fried but there was plenty here she could use – the terminal block alone should buy her two phone slots, minimum. Couldn't believe her luck. She glanced at the operator again, who was talking to an older man on one of the crates. No one was looking Li's way. She worked fast with the screwdriver and needle-nose pliers. Nearly there.

You're done, the operator told the man. You want more time, you pay again.

He fended her off, the phone still to his ear. No, please. I am second in the queue.

Not my problem.

They tussled over the phone and the queue stood watching, weirdly compliant but on edge. A wiry, middle-aged man near the front caught Li's attention – the way his eyes were moving between the scene in front of him and the porch. He would be the first one to blow. The feral, Stokes, eased himself off the porch and lifted a sawn-off shotgun but he didn't look worried enough. If he didn't shut this down now there was going to be a free-for-all and then Li could forget about making her call.

The operator got hold of the phone and pushed the man hard in the chest, knocking him off the crate. Stood over him as she cut the connection.

No! He got up, shaking. You cannot! I paid good dollars.

Back the fuck off. The operator had something in her free hand now, it looked like a water pistol.

You know Agency is not a ten-minute call, the man said. You know this. But you take my money for nothing. For hold music and Company ads. He spat. Bloodsucker.

The operator lowered her safety glasses, stepped back and sprayed him full in the face. He jerked as the liquid hit him and she stepped in close and sprayed again. This time he went down, clawing at his eyes.

The people watching swayed, a mutter coming off them. Stokes fired a single shot straight up into the air. There were screams and the queue began to unravel.

Li lifted the circuit board out. She wouldn't be trading today – she just needed to get away from this mess before anyone saw what she had. She stepped out of the box, shielding her salvage awkwardly with her pack, and started moving away. Slowly, nothing attention-grabbing. Now four people from the queue had weapons turned on the rest. An older woman with a handgun, a man with curly hair and a meat cleaver. The bearded guy who'd told her not to jump the queue had a knife to the throat of the middle-aged man and was twisting one of his arms up hard behind his back. A girl in a beanie stood clear, aiming a hammer-grip slingshot.

The rest of the queue scattered down the street. Li was dissolving with them, she was almost at the first abandoned shopfront when she heard Stokes' voice behind her.

Oi. Stick woman. Not you.

She stopped.

Come on back here and show us what you got.

Li thought, Goddammit. Went back slowly. Stokes watched her come.

The older man was still on his hands and knees, wheezing, spit coming out of his mouth. A woman came forward and knelt beside him, dabbing at his eyes with her scarf. Please, she said, will he be blind?

The operator, glanced down from packing her gear into a duffel bag. He'll be fine, just keep flushing his eyes.

The woman helped him up, led him away.

I saw you working away in there, all low-key, Stokes said to Li. Let's see it then. She brought out the terminal block. Let *her* see it, he said.

Li passed it to the operator who turned it over in her hands and shrugged. Didn't give it back. I can get us that kind of scrap with one call, she said.

And? Stokes looked at Li. She gave up the circuit board. Well, I'm not, like, an *expert* or anything, he said, but this looks like a decent bit of tech. Looks like the sort of thing you should have spotted, Jas.

The operator put her hands on her hips. Hey, Stokes, you think this crew'd do better without me, you just let me know.

Stokes looked at her for a minute. The bearded guy was folding up the card table, the girl was keeping lookout for something at the point where the road opened out to the highway again. The other two had wandered over.

I bet you can patch too, Stokes said to Li. So what do you think? Would we do better with you?

Did he expect her to weigh in on this little power struggle? She just wanted to be gone from here, if not with her salvage then with the rest of her stuff. If they took her pack she would die of cold before thirst or hunger got a look in. So it was important to answer right.

Serious question, Stokes said. Are you a better patcher than Jasmine?

A stillness in the group, the operator's expression unreadable. Li was tired of it suddenly. They would do what they were going to do.

She said, I don't know what she patches like. She can't salvage for shit.

Stokes started laughing quietly.

Abruptly, Jasmine laughed too. Gutsy move, she said, and dropped the terminal block at Li's feet in a soft explosion of dust.

From up the road the girl whistled. The operator shouldered her bag and walked towards her, ignoring the crates and the table. The others collected them as they followed, like picking up after her was routine.

Just Stokes left now, but he had the sawn-off and enough ammo to waste shots. Which way you headed?

She thought about lying, jerked her head east.

Going against the flow. I like it. You should come with us.

Li stiffened.

I'm not *telling* you. It's an invitation. We could use you.

I'm not interested.

He nodded. But you want to get somewhere, right? She followed his gaze out to the highway and saw a ball of dust barrelling towards them. Stokes grinned at her. We've got wheels.

Then she was lifted, flying, and the road was not an endless obstacle ahead of her but a means to cover distance. To raise dust instead of choking on it.

She didn't ride up front like she'd imagined but in the tray of the ute with the canvas top pulled down over the frame. Her and Stokes and the other four, plus swags and packs and strapped-down fifty-litre water containers. She watched the highway through the dusty plastic windows in the canvas, scanning and discounting the groups that blurred past on foot. She wasn't expecting to see them this soon but she looked anyway. She would know her just by her walking.

They sat with their backs to the sides of the tray, like on a taxi, their personal gear stowed between their legs. The curly-haired guy was Lucas, the older woman was Eileen, the girl in the beanie was Mira, and the one with the beard was Dev. A dusty kelpie curled between them with its head on Mira's feet. The operator, Jasmine, rode shotgun with the driver, a baby-faced man in his thirties called Shaun. No one talked much after Stokes did the introductions – the ride was too loud and the dust worked its way in through the canvas seams, so it was better to keep your mouth shut. Li figured there'd be time to ask about the children walking later. Right now, this was enough.

Mira's head lolled onto Dev's shoulder. In sleep she looked even younger – not more than fifteen. Dev handed round a bottle. It came to Li, too, and she drank. The water had a stored taste but it was clean. Lucas griped quietly to Stokes about Jasmine but Stokes' attention was always on the road. Like hers.

Eileen rested a folded newspaper on her pack, doing the crosswords between bumps. She was greying but it was hard to pick her age. Older than the others, Li thought, and carrying her damage deeper. Once she banged on the cab window for Shaun to pull over and they all piled out, dispersed into the scrub. Li too, her bladder tight with the unexpected water.

They stopped again late in the afternoon when Stokes spotted a roo flung back from the side of the highway and so camou-flaged with dust that Li had missed it. It was a boomer, a big one. She and Dev helped him haul the carcass onto the bonnet and tie it down. Lucas swapped the front seat with Jasmine, who chose the spot beside Li, facing Stokes. She sat braced with her legs apart, dismantling one of the phones for no good reason Li could see, except to demonstrate that she had plenty of kit in a metal toolbox bolted to the tray. Stokes started whistling some three-note tune and kept it up until Dev elbowed him quiet.

Halfway through putting the phone back together, Jasmine dropped a screwdriver. She hunted cursorily among the bags and legs and then turned to Li. You got a Phillips eight-mil?

Li considered denying it but to stay in the ute she had to be useful. She picked out the screwdriver by feel – no need to show Jasmine what else she had. Waited for her to hand it back. Then she turned away and watched the road and the scrub and the fence and the sky running together. The faces on the roadside were easy to account for now because there were so few of them and they were all going the wrong way. She felt speed, acceleration. No ache in her ankle. Played it over and over, the moment she caught up to Matti, how she wouldn't be empty-handed. Twenty-one days. She opened her mouth and swallowed the road.

They'd been driving about two hours when a tyre blew out. The ute swerved and skidded into the dirt, Shaun fighting for control. He jacked it up and they examined the tyre in the fading light.

Well, shit, he said.

Stokes and Eileen went to look for a place to camp. Li saw that the ute had been modified to fit truck wheels, suspension raised and the rims ground out to fit the oversized hubs. She'd learned to do this in Teresa and Navid's garage. She wondered if Shaun had done it, and where he'd got a welder.

Where's your spare?

Shaun pointed at the right front wheel. He sent Mira to hack off armfuls of spinifex and they packed the busted tyre tight. Stokes came back and said they'd found a place near a dry riverbed on the inland side of the highway. Shaun drove there slowly across the tussock and sand. It was a good spot, well into the scrub and with tree shelter.

The group set up efficiently. They rigged up a big tarp between the trees and unrolled their swags under it, and no one objected when Li made her bed on the fringes. Mostly they acted like she wasn't there. When Stokes asked her for a hand with the roo she helped him to rope the carcass over a branch and slit the throat and skin and gut it. It was good not to be sitting around.

The phone gig, back in the town, Stokes said. You think we're just ripping people off, right?

She concentrated on where to make the cuts. You're charging what the market allows.

We're providing a service people need. And we pay market for phone credit too. Bulk price, but still market. We have to make a margin.

Why don't you buy straight from Cnekt?

We look like an approved provider to you? He shrugged. Okay, Jas lets it go to her head sometimes but we have to control the exchange, otherwise we're just going to get overrun.

Li thought someone like Jasmine would always find a reason to control the exchange. But Val had taught her a version of the same thing. If you couldn't command respect, you might as well hand over your tools and do it for free.

They worked in silence for a bit. She needed to ask about Matti, she would soon. It was just that she'd already heard so much bullshit on the road.

You been much further north? Stokes asked. There's some good salvage up there. Inland settlements off the main drag, not even on the map, most of em. Not as picked over.

Li shook her head. I get by with the roadside dumps. People don't know what to look for.

True. But you need towns for dumps though. Tarnackie was the last highway town between here and the range. It's mostly industrial and military from here.

She should have guessed that. Her map was fifty years old at least. So, what, there's nothing?

There's a roadhouse about eighty k east, he said. And then there's Transit. We tend to steer clear. They have a bit of an aggressive recruitment policy.

So that's what Matti was walking into – a Company labour camp or a military zone. She tried not to let the fear in. There was no point. All she could do was follow.

Why are you still going east then?

Dev got a tip-off, so we're checking it out. We're just careful. Stokes whistled and the dog left Mira and came over expectantly. He threw down the offal. Not keen to stray from the highway, are you? I saw you watching out. Something you don't want to miss?

She told him.

That's shithouse, he said. Genuinely, as far as she could tell.

Maybe you've seen something?

He thought about it. Not anywhere we've stopped. On the road – harder to say. People are kind of a blur, you know. He helped her with the rump, where the skin clung hard. Shaun does most of the driving. Reccies and stuff. And Dev talks to people, sets stuff up. One of them might know something.

When she asked Shaun at dinner, he thought he remembered passing a big group on the way back from a fuel run two days earlier. They looked young, you know? And they were heading east, which nobody else is. He scooped up his meat with the damper Lucas had cooked in the ashes. But I was mostly looking out for trouble. They didn't look like trouble, so I didn't look too close.

After they'd eaten, Shaun and Stokes took off alone in the dark, driving gingerly on the stuffed wheel. No one commented. Li found a good river stone and sharpened her knife. Thought about the group Shaun thought he'd seen, adding up the days, trying to make it fit. She was about to get up and go to bed when Jasmine came and sat beside her. She was drinking some kind of turps out of a tin mug. Li hadn't seen water to spare for making alcohol since makecamp.

Sorry about your kid, she said. The words came out like she'd run them in her head a couple of times. And. She shrugged. I was a bit of a dick. Before. She leaned in and her breath stung the inside of Li's nose. Everyone here's got a *thing*, you know? Shaun keeps the ute running, Stokes is food and water, organisation. Dev's ex-Company, so he's connected. Fuck knows what Mira brings but she's Dev's kid so, you know, not optional. Lucas is kind of new but he's good with weapons. Another shrug. I'm the operator. No one taught me to patch but I get by. If you can do it too.

She was backlit against the fire and Li couldn't see her expression. Probably she was full of shit but it made sense to protect your advantage in a group. Maybe Jasmine had worked out it was better not to alienate her too far – not give her a reason to muscle in.

Jasmine said, That call you wanted to make, back in town. That was about your kid, right?

I can pay for the call, Li told her. You saw my trade.

Jasmine opened her mouth, shut it again, shook her head. Drank. Li watched her trying to remember if she'd already made her big gesture. She pulled a phone out of her jacket. You don't have to pay. You're part of the crew now.

How many hours since this woman pepper-sprayed an unarmed man on his knees and tried to take Li's salvage? But she needed this call. Her mind itched with it. If Jasmine wanted to build up some obligation in her head, that wasn't Li's problem. So she took the phone, waited until Jasmine said, I'll give you some privacy.

She called the Agency hotline. Punched in language selection, her status number, the missing-minor claim number, their change-of-status claim number. Got comfortable in the dirt, left leg extended to take the pressure off. Shifted slowly through queues, tuning out the hold music, the ads, the official advice to call back in working hours or find a Source outlet. After twenty-five minutes she got a toneless notification that there was no update. She hung up, checked the battery and looked over at the fire, where Jasmine was talking to Mira, re-filling Lucas's mug. Her generous streak holding.

He picked up on the second ring.

She said, I put you on the claim, said you were family. You'll get the call.

Someone asking in the background. He covered the phone, said something and the other voice retreated. When he spoke to Li, he kept his voice low. I told you, they're not going to call.

Then you call them. Let them know someone with sheltered status is looking for her. Or call the relief groups.

Li —

Goddammit, Chris. How many people you think I know inside?

He said, I have my own kid. I can't claim another one, that's the rules.

You have a kid?

Yeah. Aaron. He's nine.

Pride in his voice, or softening. It was a crappy connection and she was wasting time being thrown by this – that Chris was a parent too, that they'd had kids so close together. Matti always pretended Robbie was her big brother, big cousin. She said, I'm not asking you to claim her. Just keep her safe till I can get there. We already have a change-of-status claim in the system – you're not on that. I don't need you to sponsor us.

You won't get in if I sponsor you or not. Quota's bullshit, there's only buy-in. You got that kind of money?

Li pushed the phone against her ear, so hard it hurt. She tried to listen past the static, to make his life inside audible.

Where's her dad?

Was this the first time anyone had asked directly? She had a sudden hunger to talk about Frank. He wanted to claim for the Deep Islands, she said.

Deep Islands aren't in the XB.

I know that. You don't get to choose but you can nominate a preference. He put the Deep Islands first, then any precinct.

Chris made a sound that could have meant anything.

That's what he and Matti wanted.

Nobody tries that anymore, he said. Deep Islands haven't opened quota for years – they hardly even deal with the Agency now.

You looked into it?

Yeah, I looked into it. His voice had got even quieter. You think Suyin and I want Aaron to grow up here?

Of course Li thought that. They were inside the wall. Well then, she said. I guess we'll have to take our chances getting in.

Jasmine was standing up with her back to the fire, looking over at her. Calling time.

She heard the way Chris breathed down the phone, not impatient anymore, just trying to slow it down so she'd get it. You won't. Listen, Li, *you* won't. Your kid turns up, she might have a shot. What is she, seven? Eight? Probably got a better shot without you. But the life she'd have in here as an unaccompanied minor – I don't think you want that for her.

She couldn't keep her voice steady. Do you have any idea what it's like out here? Chris? How fucking sheltered you are?

And what do you think it's like in here? Walled up, waiting to get overrun or short-strawed for buy-in? What do you think happens when things run out? I promise you, Li, this is no place for a kid on their own.

But nowhere was. She was exhausted suddenly, like some part of her had believed in Matti's Best Place after all. Look, she said. Just, if they call you, just claim her. Temporary. I'll give you a number you can call me on, okay? Soon.

I'm not going to call, he said. I already told you I can't help you.

Then I'll call you. I'll keep calling.

Okay Li, you do that. The voice in the background again, insistent. Chris sounded as weary as her.

Li said, She's your family too.

No. I don't owe you anything. It wasn't my fault.

When he disconnected the call it was very quiet. She had a sense of the continent around her, how it went on and on, and she was so far away from the fire. She listened to them. Jasmine asserting something, Dev disputing it but turning it into a joke, Eileen's laugh, like something shaking loose. She didn't want to be alone in the dark. So she went over and Lucas made room for her on his rolled-up swag and she sat down between him and Eileen, and the heat was good.

Anything? Jasmine asked.

Li shook her head, passed the phone back.

Lucas offered her the bottle he was holding but she shook her head again. They left it alone, picked up some argument about Wars – where the Front was now. She noticed how Dev and Mira stayed out of this, talking quietly between themselves.

Her number came up, Eileen said, beside her. Last year. That's why they're out here.

Li watched Dev watching his daughter, who should be at the Front now, the child he was trying to save. She remembered Frank in Valiant, looking across the kitchen table at Matti. His unreadable expression. *That isn't something you have to worry about now, sprout.*

Eileen said, I lost my kids. Long time ago.

Li turned, stared. Do you know?

I know they didn't come back.

Li tried to read it in her steady face, how long it had taken her to give up.

Eileen said, Don't you start crying.

Here. Jasmine pushed a mug into Li's hand. Bush tea.

The smell was pure alcohol. Li thought about that and found she didn't care. She held the mug in both hands and drank, absorbing the burn and the after-scum of leaves. The sugar tasted real. The shock of it hit her system as hard as the spirits.

Eileen said, They were proper good kids.

Jasmine leaned over and poured more into the dregs and Li drank again. She drank steadily and with purpose, like Val. After a while she looked up and Eileen was watching.

Why are you here? Li asked her.

That's a big bloody question.

I mean. Jasmine said you all had a thing.

Jasmine refilled Li's mug again. Auntie Eileen's from North, she said. We couldn't get by up there without her. Wouldn't even get there without her.

Where north? Li asked.

Huh?

How far north do you go?

The others had gone quiet.

Oh, you know. Jasmine indicated the general direction, spilling her drink. A bit.

Dev farted forcefully, elbowed his daughter. Mira! Is that how I raised you?

Good one, Dad. Mira leaned away and started coughing. Oh, that is so rotten.

Lucas said calmly, You animal.

Not my fault, Dev said. You all know what roo does to my guts.

Jasmine caught up. You'll be sleeping *waaay* over there.

I'll be sleeping under the tarp, he said. Right in between the two sharp thinkers who turned down a perfectly nice goat.

Li said, North's bullshit.

Eileen said, You'd know, would you?

It's just another place with Weather. Li looked around the faces and shrugged. There's no way off, there's nowhere else. There's just the wall.

She drank into the dark parts of her brain and the drink made a path between them, step by step. They couldn't let them in. Not her and Matti, not Safia, or Rich, or the two with the baby. Not the family with the shop that sold everything, or the dusty unsheltered walking to camps that didn't exist anymore. And not these ones around the fire who thought they were beating the system. Because if they got in, if they all got in, then the whole continent would tip and go under and they'd all drown together. So fuck Chris, she didn't need him. She'd find Matti herself and then they'd make whatever life they could wherever they were. Not the best place, just any place. And when they couldn't stay there they'd go to the next place. They wouldn't waste the time they had running to some bullshit poison paradise or walking around the wall trying to roll a six. She realised she was saying these things out loud, taking up all the air, and she bit down on the rim of the mug.

Check it out, Lucas said. Jas's new mate can't hold her piss either.

*

171

Val taught Li to patch, like he taught her everything else. Pretty soon she was helping him. He said she had the knack for it. Told her she'd inherit his tools and his customers one day, when he got too old for the circuit, but it had happened sooner than that.

On her twelfth birthday, he took her into a bar for the first time. Some inland town, in the lull between lunchtime drinking and night-time drinking. He ordered her a lemonade and a packet of cheese and onion chips, and a half-pint of dark for himself.

This is a special occasion, he said, and she watched the tender way his hand closed around the glass. All those dry years couldn't cure him of the need to fall.

After that, he drank sporadically, convulsively, in great all-night inhalations. Mostly in the shearers' camps along the circuit, where the alcohol was cheaper and more lethal. He would set their tent up a little way from the action and hurry her into bed, and later she would crawl out and watch him laughing, head back, loose-kneed. Like the other men but different. She watched him rant and slur and lose his balance. He wasn't a tall man but he seemed to go down from a great height.

Afterwards he would be pained and shy with her, struggling to meet her eye. He would make promises. Tell her how he'd given it up years before she came to him, and that he would again.

She started going with him when he got paid for a patch. Men he knew in the towns saw them coming and laughed at him. Couldn't give your missus the slip, Val?

When it was just the two of them and he brought bottles back to camp, she took her bedding out into the scrub. He would shout for her but she kept her distance until he was past noticing, and then came in closer to make sure he was okay. One night she watched while he burned the fingers of his left hand slowly, methodically, with his lighter. His drinking hand. It didn't help – it

172

just meant she had to take on his patching jobs for two weeks. That was when she started carrying his toolkit, in case he lost it when he fell down somewhere. His hand healed, but bit by bit he got too shaky for fine work. Within a year she was the patcher and he was the one who trailed her round the circuit, fronting up for the jobs to make it look more legitimate. Customers stopped caring pretty fast though. Like Val said, she had the knack for it.

He was going to leave her, she saw it in his eyes. The guilt he couldn't carry. He would leave her somewhere and go north and she would be alone, circling in the dark. She watched him every minute, would have left any place to go with him, but she couldn't make him stay.

For a while he fell back on shearing, or cooking for shearers, or fencing. He'd always been able to turn his hand to anything, but in the end all he could do was shake and drink.

She was fifteen when he died in the free hospital. After that she just kept going, town to town, the way they always had. Nerredin was just another stop on the circuit for almost ten years, and then one day it was something else.

Sometime in the dark, she was shaken awake. Li, time to go.

It was Stokes talking. She sat up and her brain contracted.

Come on, get your shit together. You got five minutes.

A thumping behind her eyes. Big, slow tongue. She heard movement around her, the ute doors slamming. We breaking camp?

Stokes flicked torchlight into her face, making her wince. This is what we came for. There's a convoy coming through, big one. They'll refuel at the roadhouse.

And?

And, so we're gunna resupply too.

Her stomach clenched. I don't want to do that.

Sure. But you don't really have a choice, do you? We don't carry passengers.

Li made it clear of the bedding before she threw up.

Jesus, what are you – cut? I need you to be up for this. That was the deal.

She'll be all right. Jasmine's voice behind him. She can match with me. You're okay, right, Li?

Li got up slowly, turned to face them both. Jasmine didn't seem to be suffering. She seemed sharp, focused, almost pumped. She held out Li's waterbag and Li drank carefully.

I'm okay, she said. I'll be ready in five.

How was it possible that she could smell the water runners before she heard them? First the top notes of fuel and rubber, and then something deeper, a heavy and expansive smell that made her throat ache. Then the dust and the roaring, like a howler with lights.

From the scrub Li counted the Quench tankers pulling up in front of the roadhouse. The others crouched around her, watching, as the tankers filled the truckstop and overflowed into the rest area, out of the light.

Twenty-seven, Jasmine said quietly, at her elbow. It checks out.

When did my info not check out? Dev asked. Name a time.

He and Eileen were on her right, with water containers, Lucas and Stokes behind them with the wheel brace. No torches. Shaun and Mira had the ute ready two hundred metres back, on ground that was too soft to hold a heavier vehicle.

The drivers were climbing down stiffly, leaving the headlights on while they started fuelling up, or heading inside to wait their turn. The security guards took up positions, guns at the ready, but there weren't enough of them and they were getting distracted by the smells of fried food and koffee from the roadhouse. No way a convoy this size could cover all the angles. It occurred to Li that maybe the crew she was with could highjack a tanker after all. One tanker. If there were more of them and they all had guns, if they shot out most of the headlights, and if there wasn't a CB radio in every cab to call for Company backup. No. Hijacking convoys was just another bullshit story people told each other in a place like makecamp, so they could feel like someone, somewhere was winning. Stokes had a different name for what his crew did. He said they were mosquitoes. They didn't take Company on, they just fed off it.

On the way there, the mood in the tray had been keyed up but not tense. Stokes said they were just going for water and spare tyres this time; Quench ran its fleet on biofuel and they needed diesel. Fifteen, twenty minutes' quiet work. The convoy would go on, barely lighter and none the wiser, and she would be in the back of the ute again, closing the gap. All she had to do was make her contribution. So now she watched the scene outside the roadhouse, looking for the spots with the least light and the biggest gaps between security. She felt dried out and queasy. Felt like shit. There was a delay on every thought and the smell from the roadhouse kitchen wasn't helping.

Jasmine put her mouth against Li's ear and pointed at the rest area. There, on the edge, she said. Close to the road – not too much ground to cover. She touched her steel-capped boot lightly to Li's ankle. Can you run? If you have to?

Bit fucking late to ask now, Li thought. She'd left her stick in the tray when she saw she'd have her hands full, but her ankle felt solid so far.

Run, yes, she said. Drag fifty litres, maybe.

I'll stay on your left. We just have to get halfway and then Shaun and Mira can take over.

Li wrapped the plastic tubing of the siphon tighter around one hand and felt for the empty container with the other. She was wearing a harness made of bicycle-tube inners and rope, crossed over her chest and around her hips, to drag the water back to the ute. She had her toolkit and her knife and Matti's horse in her pocket. Everything else she owned was in the ute.

Most of the weight'll be on your hips, Jasmine said. Just lean. She hesitated. You'll be right, we do this all the time.

Li felt an unexpected flash of gratitude. The drivers were moving inside.

Right. Stokes kept it just above a whisper. Me and Shaun'll go first – get us a spare.

Shaun said, Two tyres is better than one.

Let's see how we go, eh? Stokes shuffled forward. Jas, Dev, check the time. See you at the ute in twenty.

They came out of the scrub and ran forward in a crouch, almost touching, keeping the containers off the ground. Crossed the highway. Only security left now, black cutouts of bodies and guns in the headlights. They were aiming for a tanker on the near side of the rest area. No guard around that she could see, dozens of other vehicles blocking the view from the roadhouse. They moved through the gaps between headlights, hip to hip, like they'd been doing this for years. Li blocked out all the peripherals: her throbbing head and churning gut, the location of Eileen and Stokes and the others, the music and voices leaking through the glass doors of the roadhouse, the smell of asphalt and cigarettes. It was just the two of them closing on the tanker they'd picked out. They were in the rest area now, on the hard dirt. Jas caught her foot on something and Li steadied her on the run.

Her ankle was holding. She felt quietly amazed that they were a good match.

They reached the side of the tanker and flattened themselves against it in the dark. Jas was readying the drill. Li put her container down and moved her hands along the metal, feeling for rivets, then guided Jas to the weak point directly alongside the seam. The warmth of her hand was unexpected. Li shifted forward to keep watch, offering Jas her back, and Jas braced against her and positioned the drill.

The noise was muffled by layers of padding and tape but Li kept scanning, listening for guards. She had a sense that the darkness around the rest area was fuller now than it had been a minute ago, kept hearing tiny sounds out there that she couldn't account for. Stokes and Dev should have a spare off by now. They'd be rolling it away or going for the second. Jas braced harder against her back, Li felt the last brief resistance in both their spines and then the drill was through. Now she turned around and let Jas guide her hand to keep pressure on the hole while she changed up to a fatter drill bit. That cool, taunting smell came through the metal and she felt the immensity of the pressure inside.

Jas leaned in again and in ten seconds the hole was wide enough. They swapped places and Li uncoiled the tubing and worked one end into the hole, keeping the other end bent over on itself to make a seal. Fed the tube deep into her container so it would fill quietly. When she released the seal the flow started almost immediately but it was too slow. *One thousand, two thousand, three thousand.* She adjusted the angle, felt a gush of water. Some sound, not too much. She felt Jas tense but she was calm, focused.

The container was half full when Jas nudged her and pointed. Two figures ran past them to the truckstop, bent over, carrying something between them. But not their crew. *Three-quarters.* Jas blew out between closed teeth, a tiny sound. *Hurry.* Were there other mosquitoes descending on the convoy? What were the chances of none of them fucking it up?

Full. Li sealed off the tube and eased it out. Jas screwed the lid on and positioned her empty container. Started unwinding her harness. Li hooked up, unsealed, adjusted the flow. More sounds on the periphery now, too many and not quiet enough. Somewhere on the other side of the tanker a guard swore and there was the double click of a gun being cocked. Hard to tell how close. She tied Jas's harness to the handle of the full container. Turned back. The second one was only half full.

Fryer? someone called from the truckstop, waddaya got?

Close it off, Jas breathed in her ear.

A single shot. A guard yelled, Got one!

Almost full. Someone shouted, Mozzies! and there was more gunfire, less controlled this time. She sealed the tube, screwed on the lid. Heard people run out of the roadhouse, feet pounding in the dust and darkness.

Watch your aim! someone shouted. Keep clear of the fucking trucks.

People were coming out of the dark, closing on the convoy like it was a carcass. A guard yelled, Keep the fuck back! Screams, gunshot. The tubing was caught in the hole.

Leave it, Jas hissed. Just rope up.

But Jas's own harness was dangling loose. Hadn't Li done that? She let go of the tube and fumbled for the end of her rope, looped it round the handle and knotted it. When the pain came it was annihilating. Her leg gave way and she fell down screaming. Answering shots in their direction and Jasmine stood over her and stomped on her ankle again.

Li retched, tried to twist away out of range but she was tethered to fifty litres of water. Jasmine grabbed the rope and dragged her back. Li gouged up a handful of dirt and threw it in her face – she yelped and dropped the rope. Steel caps hammered into Li's shins, sides, belly, jaw. There was no room for these smaller pains through the agony of her ankle but when she tried to take Jasmine's legs out and bring her down where she could fight, her body wouldn't do the work. *Knife*, she thought. A word like mountain. Like fly. Jasmine got on top of her, pinning her arms, banging her head back on the ground and unleashing the tube in her face. She was choking, drowning. The skin flayed back from her bones, couldn't get her head up. Somewhere outside the water there were hands wrenching at her waist. Then she could breathe and Jasmine's weight was off her and she rolled over and vomited liquid.

When she sat up, the siphon tube was whipping around near her head and her toolkit was gone. Was that what this had been for? All of it? Li wanted to kill her with her hands. She started crawling after her but there were bodies everywhere in the head-lights. Where the fuck had they all come from? They ran towards her and past her, carrying bottles and cups and bags and tins.

She thought she saw a figure hauling a container, right at the edge of the light. Tried to get up but something in her ankle ripped and give way. For a few seconds she hung on the edge of blacking out and when she opened her eyes the figure was gone. Looked back and saw that people had reached the tankers. Two were wrestling over the siphon tube. It came free and water arced up thinly from the hole, catching in the headlights. The crowd made a gutteral sound. A guard fired into their backs and kept firing. Li started crawling away again, just trying to get to the road now, get out of range, but it hurt so much to move.

All around her people were running and shooting and shouting and falling.

And then it hit her that Matti could be here, trapped somewhere in this mob. Li turned back, looking for smaller shapes, yelling Matti's name. In front of the nearest tanker, a man got the gun off the guard and smashed the butt into the side of her head, then he stepped back and fired straight at the tanker. Panic, chaos, bodies falling. But they were just in the way. And now the tanker sprang new leaks and people held up their containers or their cupped hands until they were pushed aside. The smell of blood and water.

That was when she heard helicopter blades, saw the lights in the sky and knew she should have got away sooner.

Transit

Li started work in Serkel's salvage facility two weeks after they brought her in. Any sooner would have been unproductive. She had broken bones in her ankle, torn ligaments and tendon damage. The medic had put her lower leg in a cast but assessed her as otherwise fit. She gave her a bunch of shots and some crutches, and then confined her to Charlie compound for fourteen days. Her status number was printed on a band around her wrist.

The first day, she walked around the fence on her crutches. There was a thick, sweet stink in the air and she saw that Matti was truly out of reach now.

When she was done looking, a couple of Essos had to carry her back to the sleepbox. She lay on a cot, breathing sweat and mould and old blood, and looked at the metal grid on the metal ceiling, at the damp and rust. Someone coughed persistently in a corner. The woman in the next cot lay looking at her out of dark, exhausted eyes. This part is hard, she said. You won't feel it as much when you're working.

Her name was Camila. She'd been in Transit for a month. Li turned away and gripped the Saint Anthony medallion. They'd missed it somehow when they processed and tagged her. It was flat and warm, it held her warmth. She traced the ceiling grid with her eyes, working inwards until she got to the smallest box and then starting from the outside again.

Charlie compound was a concrete toilet and shower block, two twelve-metre shipping containers for sleeping in, and a patch of dirt out the front where the women queued for the shift vans. It was surrounded by other fenced compounds, each one separated by concrete paths and linked by two gates. There was a central compound with a cracked runway down the middle and a concrete hangar where they got fed. Cameras on the fences. Essos, always in pairs. The whole lot enclosed by a rigid mesh outer fence, at least five metres high, angled in and topped with razor wire. Unclimbable.

This was Transit. And Transit was in the No Go. Now it was the highway that was out of bounds – she couldn't see it from Charlie compound, couldn't see the perimeter fence either, couldn't even see the industrial complex north of Transit, where Camila said Li would be working soon. All she could see was fences and all she could hear outside them was dogs.

The horse was gone, fallen out of her pocket somewhere in the chaos at the roadhouse.

By the time the medic said she was work-ready she'd figured it out. She couldn't break out of Transit. Every link gate had an individual lockcode. There was nothing in here she could cut the fence with and even if she could dig under it, there were all the other fences outside Charlie. She would never get the chance, anyway; there were always Essos around, the cameras, lights at night.

But the shift vans took labour out of Transit to the complex facilities. The women who worked shift said you could see the highway from the complex, and that trucks and water tankers came and went regularly through Serkel's own gate in the perimeter fence.

Li believed the stories about jumpers getting inside the XB under trucks. Some kind of harness would help, but if she couldn't get rope then she needed a truck with tandem axles. She could use the crutches to brace herself across them. Her leg was the problem. In the black fug of the sleepbox she closed her eyes and traced undercarriages, counting non-moving parts, looking for handholds, places she could hook her leg over.

She worked a week in the complex before she had a chance. The van dropped the women off and picked them up in the loading bay but she was never outside long enough to time the coming and going of the transports. And after her first shift she gave up the idea of hiding a piece of rope in her clothes – the bodychecks were too thorough. All she could do was count wheels, notice where the drivers stood and the Essos stood.

Then, at the end of her eighth shift, while the women were walking in single file to the van, two guard dogs got into a fight. In the brief interval before the Essos had them back under control, she stepped out of the line and lowered herself awkwardly under the nearest truck.

They sent a dog after her. It lunged at her in the confined space, snarling and spraying spit, teeth taking lumps out of the air in front of her face. Hitting out at it with her crutch only increased its fury.

You got ten seconds, an Esso yelled, then I'm dropping the leash.

The drivers stood around while she crawled out, dragging her crutches. Some of them were laughing.

The Essos cable-tied her and sent her back in the van with the others. Management had a procedure for non-compliance.

Onebox was cut down much smaller than the sleepboxes, with a hatch in the door. It had a mattress and a blanket. A bottle of water. A bucket. When they put her in there, Li shouted, screamed, beat the walls and the floor till her skin split and her knuckles swelled. Three weeks since they'd brought her into Transit, the days moving away in a straight line and Matti receding.

Once a day she got food and water through the hatch. The ceiling had the same grid as the sleepbox but it was only light enough to see it for a couple of hours. She huddled in the blanket trying to think her way out of here, and then through every gate between here and maingate, think of a way to get the maingate code, get past the dogs, get back to the highway.

An Esso banged on the hatch, passed in food and refilled her bottle. Stayed there on the other side of the door for a moment.

Can you hear me? You gotta give this up. Hey. Say something if you can hear me.

Li thought she recognised the voice. It was Megan, one of the ones who'd carried her back to the sleepbox the first day. She tried to speak but she had no voice left.

Megan said, You only get boxed one time, that's procedure. They're short on labour now but once we do another intake you won't be worth it for them, even with skills. You been in there three days already, you need to give this up. Show em you've learned your lesson. Hey. Whatever you think is out there, it's not. Not for you. It's just Transit now.

They let her out after six days. She went back on shift, showered when they told her to, slept when they told her, went to Medical, waited at the link gates, waited in the food queue. She kept count of the days and waited for something to change, for some disruption or breakdown that would give her a way out, but everything was the same, over and over.

And then finally she understood. Matti was lost to her. Not dead, not yet. She could still feel her in the world, still waiting for Li to come and find her. But Li would never come. That was what Megan had tried to tell her. There was no leaving here.

Serkel's logo was everywhere in the complex and on the trucks. A green arrow circling round on itself. Sometimes the words *Renewing excellence* stencilled undeneath. Li saw it in the camp, too, rebranded over the old airbase signs or printed on discarded packaging. Serkel was Company, like Quench and Homegrown and XB Force were Company. Serkel bought waste by the shipping container from the global tech companies and military, and salvaged the gold and silver, copper, aluminium, plastic, glass and steel. Government waived the import charges and Company wore the cost of the ships that didn't make it. It sold back the metals and minerals or used them on its own production lines. Dumped the rest up in North, or at least north of the XB. It was a good set-up, she thought. The transport overheads would be high but labour costs were minimal: everyone in Transit was on the points system, even the Essos. Making target covered your food and accommodation, basic medical, transport. Beating target earned you bonus points for readybars, soap, pads, koffee, sweetener, gum. Li had spent points before she had any, gone deep into debt for her medical, and she couldn't see herself breaking even.

Some of the metals and plastics from salvage went to the other facilities in the complex where Serkel manufactured medical supplies and ammunition. Megan said they were helping the Wars effort. In the salvage facility, Li mostly worked with hand tools, indifferent to their easy availability and range and quality. The crates of cell phones held no more interest than the ancient television units. She just took them apart, sorted the reusable components. There was wakey for the double shifts, or something like wakey. It didn't even cost points.

The Essos bodychecked them after every shift. There were things you could pick up in the complex – sharp edges, poisons – but Management had procedures to limit opportunities for self-harm.

Twenty-six women shared Li's sleepbox. It had ventilation grilles but no insulation or heating. Stank of feet and mould. The women worked different shifts and brought their different stinks back with them in their hair and skin and camp-issue jackets. Dump stink or chemical stink or gunpowder stink. They slept in shifts too, one woman got up off the cot and another woman lay down on it. You were never alone. It didn't matter to Li. It would have mattered once but it didn't now. Not the noise or the smell, not the skin diseases they picked up in the shower block, the respiratory sicknesses they passed, one to the other, or the way her ankle itched and festered inside the cast. Not the rank shitbox. Not the snarling out in the dark. Not the fights or the shaming or freezing out – the pack closing against one woman until it was another woman's turn. The dripping ceiling and the icy burn of the walls didn't matter. The snoring and crying and fucking and heads banging against metal at night. It didn't matter when her period came back and half the women in the box were bleeding at the same time, scavenging cloth and paper, leaking and staining their shared bedding. As the cold season closed around them, they pushed the cots together and slept piled up like dogs, sharing heat. It didn't matter to Li because her privacy didn't matter now, her mind didn't matter.

And because there was consolation too. They told their stories in the dark. Li didn't talk much but she listened to each precise accounting of loss. Anna and her sister had run for a truck and Anna didn't make it. She stood on the road and watched her sister slip and go under the wheels. Lumena had two children under Replacement. The ballot claimed them both – one was on the Front, the other had been on a ship that didn't get there. Kathy's father died of prostate cancer, slowly, in a makecamp. Jun had been separated from her whole family in a gate riot outside Fengdu. Susanna's girlfriend was beaten to death. Camila paid her way onto a boat and when it started sinking she dropped her baby into the outstretched arms of a man in the water but a wave broke over him and her baby went down without a sound.

Azzi cried, listening. She said, My boy was terrified of the sea. He read books about sharks. I gave him sedatives to get him on the boat, but when we were in the water, he couldn't stay awake. I tried to hold him up but he was too heavy.

Before Transit, Li had been alone with her grief, hauling it around like combat gear. Out there no loss could approach hers. Who had she thought she was? In here, their losses rubbed against each other, blunting the edges and smoothing into one thing. The lost were dead or they were alive, they were status unknown. They belonged to no one in particular, and spread out like that, they were easier to bear. What had she thought she wanted? She didn't want to be alone.

Rest day was the hardest. There were so many hours. She had to concentrate on keeping her thoughts small, they slipped the fence and got out where the dogs were.

A man called her name through the fence. It was early morning and she had just got off the van at the end of her shift, was walking back to the sleepbox with the others, single-file along Charlie fence, and it took her a minute to lift her head. He was standing up against Delta fence, holding onto the wire with both hands. Rich. All that separated them were the two fences and a metre of concrete. He said her name again but she didn't want to remember him, all her work now was not remembering. She walked into the sleepbox and lay down on a cot that was still warm and she looked up and started counting the grids, but she saw his face again outside the fence at makecamp, heard him laugh and call her wild woman. *If you get caught you can't help her.* She hunched over, hit her head against the wall. She tried to beat back the memory but it was right there, all of it, all the time, waiting to steal her oxygen.

She counted until she slept. And while she slept, Matti called to her, I just don't want to be in the other room without you

Mum, because it's dark. And when she woke and passed through the gates and stood in the food queue and rode the van and worked shift, all the memories came ripping, the flashes of her voice and face, her smell. And it stayed like that, day after day after day. It couldn't be lived with but Li was still alive.

You don't talk too much.

Megan stood with Li by the fence in the weak sun, smoking. Rest day. The gale had beaten itself out overnight and now the tussock was still and silver in the afternoon light. Megan's hand shook a bit when she passed the cigarette and Li knew she was still thinking about the dogs. A couple of hours earlier, Megan and some other Essos had been repairing a damaged section of the outer fence, near maingate, when a pack of dogs had come at them through the gap. They'd shot a couple and the rest of them got busy fighting over the carcasses while the Essos closed up the fence.

Cigarettes were on the points system, some kind of cheap knock-offs. It was mostly just the Essos who could afford them. Li had never been a smoker but she understood Megan was sharing something that had cost her. The chemical hit to her lungs was thin and harsh. It made her jittery and then calm, dulling her headache. The smell had none of the richness of tobacco she remembered – it didn't remind her of anything much. What it did was mask the stench from the dump. Megan said Sumud and New Flinders both used it, so it kept expanding across the No Go between the precincts. She said in the hot season you could pass out from the smell.

Megan knew all kinds of things. She'd been Transit security for three years and she got on with people. Supervisors, drivers, even management. Some of the labour treated her like she was the enemy and that made it harder for her to do her job.

I knew you weren't going to be one of them, she told Li.

Some of the other Essos had come to Transit looking for work. Megan had been picked up off the highway, same as Li. People got assigned according to their history, their abilities. Megan had done security before, for a container farm that went under. She carried herself right, had some combat and weapons training.

That doesn't make me an arsehole, she said. I didn't put my hand up.

A lot of Essos were like Megan. They remembered people's names, they joked around with them, went as easy as they could on the searches. Vouched for people when they were too sick to work. The Essos had their own compound, better food, hot water, but some of them had people they cared about in the labour compounds too. Megan's younger brother worked in the medical-supply facility. She'd been trying to get him upgraded to security for two years. She didn't see him much because women didn't guard the men's compounds.

Li liked listening to her. Maybe that was what Megan got out of it. She didn't want sex, or at least she hadn't asked. It wouldn't have mattered much but Li preferred this.

Megan was quiet for a while and Li focused on a scavenger bird circling outside the fence. A bird was good. There were so many of them around Transit because of the dump. Too many at once reminded her of the lake, but she only had to look at one.

Sometimes she worked the smelter, or on the crushing machine, feeding in CRTs and monitor glass to be shattered in a grey cloud and then carting the debris to the skips for dump transport. Sometimes the glass dust was too thick to see the woman next to her. Sometimes she tasted blood. Her eyes and throat stung from the PVC and the flame-retardant but she couldn't smell the lead, couldn't feel it quietly accruing in her soft tissue, settling in her bones.

The medic had said she might not walk easily again. The damage was too sustained – the tearing and breaking on top of the sprain that she'd walked on for so many days. But she didn't have to walk far now. Just from the sleepbox to the van, the compound to the food shed. The medic said her blood lead level was up and asked if she was following procedure. Li thought about the decontamination block where they hung their overalls and showered at the end of their shift. The water was heated on the complex's power supply because hot water was more effective. She liked the warmth, the feeling that the shift ran off her and went down somewhere below ground with the other shifts. Except the water was recycled like everything else. They all went round and round.

When she thought about Matti's horse now, her certainty was gone. Had she ever looked at it again, after the first time? She could only remember touching it. Why hadn't she looked?

She tried to hold the horse in her mind, there on the salt pan, the hot belief of it, but all she could see was a piece of wood.

Scheduled break. Li, Camila, Susanna and Trish were out in the loading bay, sharing gum. They got one meal on shift, usually readybars, so the gum helped. They got counted off before and after break and there were two Essos out there with them but mostly they left them alone. Li and Trish lay on their jackets on the concrete with their legs up on the bench – Trish had varicose veins.

When there wasn't a wall of trucks in the way, they could look north from here and see the No Go's perimeter fence and the highway outside it. Today they looked back the other way instead, beyond Transit, to the dump. On a cold, still day like this they hardly noticed the smell.

Camila said, Tammy says you could walk to Sumud in four hours.

The women on the dump shift had a clear view of both precincts' walls from the southern face of the dump. They said if you were working up high enough on a clear day, you could see the tops of buildings inside Sumud.

Trish said, You wouldn't make it. Dogs'd get you.

Or you would, Susanna said, and they'd shoot you from the top of the wall. There's no gate anyway.

Li put another quarter of gum in her mouth to bring the taste back. She closed her eyes to ease her headache and listened to Trish chewing. Most of Trish's points went on gum. She'd found God and given up smoking years ago, back when you could still get cigarettes without any special kind of trade. Still missed it. She'd told Li that every time she lit a match she tasted nicotine.

What do you reckon it's like? Camila asked. Inside?

Better than outside, Susanna said. Better than here.

Trish stopped chewing for a second. Tammy says a lot of the rubbish is the same stuff we would have chucked out. Really munted stuff.

Not all of it, but, Susanna said.

Camila said, What d'you think, Li?

Li didn't open her eyes. Company wouldn't have the contract unless there was money in it.

I bet you can still get anything in there, Susanna said. Look at the trucks.

The buzzer went. Trish eased her legs down, making a huffing sound. Susanna helped her up. Li got up on her own but Camila waited, held her crutches ready.

In the shower block, Camila asked Li if she believed in the children walking.

I heard about them, Li said. People had stories. But nobody ever saw them.

It was the lightning storms that battered the camp. It was when the rain came in violent dumps that washed away topsoil, carving rivers through the mud and flooding containers. It was the burning cold in her hands and feet at night and the ice on the ground in the morning, it was the hail that smashed the van's windscreen and killed half the dogs. It was the crying from Family compound because another child had coughed them-selves to death. The signs kept accumulating until Li couldn't turn away from them anymore, had to face the truth.

She stopped counting the days, then, counted the lost things instead. The baby she never wanted, who had stolen a year of her sleep, who Frank had rocked and she had shaken. The one who said *Dadda* first, the one she had wished away, who ran away and ran away but was always with them. Who bounced on the sofa naked, flexing her muscles, and ran wild with Robbie, who was stung by bees and loved a rag horse. Who swung on the high monkey bars, face shining, calling, *Mum! I don't need you!* Who kissed the radio when the Mynas scored and wrestled with Frank and made herself sick laughing. The kid who made up the Best Place on the road to Valiant. Who cried because she missed walking. The one who said, *I hate you* and, *Just can you stay?* Who said, *Mum, look!*

Li held her close, rubbed her worn. Never told the others. Matti was dead now. She would never find the place where it happened, never know for certain, but she felt the truth of it in her body. Lightning and flood told her, freeze and hail and weeping. There was no way for a child to survive the cold season out there. And this, in here, this wasn't life, it was something else, something that couldn't be added up.

The Essos wore surgical masks now, when they came close. Gloves when they body-checked. Li submitted to the handling, opened her mouth obediently, keeping her tongue flat, but she could have told them it wasn't necessary. She wasn't going to kill herself. What she thought was that she would get one of the sicknesses, something you couldn't be vaxxed for. Or eventually the lead would do it. She just had to wait.

*

Sometimes they prayed at night. Not all of them. They took turns to lead the prayer and they prayed in different ways and languages. Li never led but she liked the call and response, the murmur or drone, the silence. She felt closer to Matti and Frank at those times, closer to Nerredin. And something else that she thought she remembered when she listened to them praying with Saint Anthony in her fist. She thought maybe it was her mother.

Often Camila was beside her. Li had never had a friend before Angie, only Frank. Camila was nothing like Angie but there was a warmth in her, some quality that hadn't been extinguished, that was good to be near.

Trish led the most. She still had a smoker's voice and she was older than Li, too old, really, for the work. She'd been a minister once, and then, after her town was gone, an itinerant preacher. She lost her husband and her grandchild in a forced evacuation, didn't know if they were together or dead. Trish could recite whole passages from the New Testament, if that's what they wanted, or she could just talk. She asked them to think of someone who had wronged them, and forgive. Li thought about Jasmine's warm hand at the side of the truck, heard her saying, We do this all the time. She thought about how they could have done her over on the road in Tarnackie but they'd strung her along instead, had waited until they knew what she had to lose so they could take it from her.

Something raw and violent opened up in her but she turned away from it.

That's what I like about you, Megan said. We can just have a smoke and I don't have to worry what you're going to come out with.

They stood further apart at the fence now and they didn't pass the cigarette back and forth anymore, but Megan still gave her the last few drags when she was done. She looked over at the sleepboxes. I don't get some of them. Always going on about what's out there for them. It's just noise, you know? They know it's not gunna happen.

Li said, Could you leave? If you wanted to?

Megan shrugged. This isn't bad. I get food, I get smokes, I know where I'm sleeping, I know what I'm doing every day. And I can keep an eye on Benj. It's just a job, you don't want to think about it too hard. She passed the butt to Li. Nobody out there's looking out for me, you know? And you and me, we're not getting inside. So maybe this is as good as it gets.

Li finished the cigarette. She said, I've got no reason to be out there.

Get up, Tammy said. This one's mine.

Li rolled over slowly to the edge of the cot and groped for her crutches. There were about a dozen women in the sleepbox, not long off shift.

I see you by the fence with your little screw, Tammy said. What're you giving up for the smokes?

Nothing, Li said. We just talk.

We just talk. Don't you have any fucking self-respect?

Li shrugged. She was on her feet now and Tammy faced her across the cot, reeking of dump. Li kept her eyes down. She'd worked fourteen hours and she was lurching with tiredness but it was too soon to move away to an empty mattress. Tammy wanted to hit people, mostly that was what she wanted.

You're wasting your time there, Trish said.

Tammy turned on Trish. You telling me what to do?

I'm just saying. What are you going to do that hasn't already happened to her?

The box was quiet with listening. Then Tammy sat down heavily on the cot and settled onto her back with her arms folded behind her head. Looked up at Li with her jaw working. Yeah, she said. Too easy.

Sometimes there were fights in the food queue but mostly people were too tired. And mostly there was enough food. Sometimes when there were fights, Li lost hold of where she was and mixed this queue up with the queue at makecamp, but then one of the others would talk loudly in her ear or shove her forwards, and she would take her bowl and sit and raise and lower the spoon until the bowl was empty. She felt like a child then, and felt a tenderness that she didn't know where to direct.

One day she was leaving the food shed as another women's compound was waiting to go in. In the queue she saw a face she knew. She stopped walking and stared until the woman behind Angie nudged her and Angie looked up and saw her too. It was the strangest thing, like looking through time. She hadn't seen Angie since she and Carl left Nerredin without saying goodbye, more than two years ago.

Angie had more grey in her hair now, and the face of an older woman, more than two years older. From the stain on her fingers, she worked ammo. She just looked at her, why didn't she speak? The women around her shuffled or stood blankly or leaned into the cooking smell. Li wanted to tell her everything. She wanted to tell someone who'd known Frank since primary school how he had died and she wanted to ask about Carl – if he was alive, if he was here too. She wanted to say Matti's name.

The woman behind Angie was watching Li, curious and hostile, protective. Li saw that this was Angie's friend now, and felt the loss of Angie like she never had since Nerredin. She had let her go. She had turned away from the pain of Robbie and left them to carry it, as if two people could carry it. Angie looked away and then back again, like she couldn't help it. Li saw what was in her eyes and she felt it too. That it was unbearable to show themselves to each other like this.

The queue moved and Angie's friend shoved her and she went into the food shed. Li stayed where she was until all the things that had threatened to spill out of her were quiet again, and then she went back to the sleepbox and counted the grids from the outside in. She remembered how this had happened before, when Rich called her name at the Delta fence. But it was different now – she wasn't poisoning herself with hope anymore.

In the sleepbox they talked about the children walking, what they'd heard and what might be true. The women who'd lost kids approached this idea like a cliff edge. But when it was too hard to speak the names of their own children, then they prayed for the children walking.

Susanna said, Why would God leave them out there alone?

Maybe we brought it on ourselves, Azzi said. We knew there was no future and we went and had them anyway.

Li tasted metal. Beside her, Camila made a small sound that wasn't meant to be heard.

What about the kids? Tammy said. What are they being punished for?

A shudder ran through the room. But Trish said, The God I know is a merciful God. We're never alone, God always offers a way back. Maybe the children are walking to find the way back.

Camila said, What kind of God would ask something like that from a child?

Li thought about how standing on concrete for twelve hours made Trish's feet swell up, how slowly she climbed into the van at the end of a shift, and the painful way she breathed at night when her veins wouldn't let her sleep. We think we've lost our children, Trish said, and it feels like a punishment, I know that. But what if they're not lost? It's too late for us, but what if there's still a chance for them to be saved?

You believe that? Camila asked.

Trish said, I believe all children belong to God. Her voice shook and steadied. Our children are held in the hand of God. They walk under God's hand and they shall come to no harm but shall be lifted.

The way back from Central compound took her past Family compound. No other way. The kids under twelve roamed the compound while their parents worked shift. Sometimes there was an adult with them, organising activities, portioning out gum. Just like makecamp.

In the beginning she'd stood by the fence through her breaks, searching the compound through the wire, but she'd given that up after Megan had called in a favour and ran Matti's status number through the records.

Now she never looked. Except one time when she went past, there was a kid at the fence on his own, tying long strips of plastic onto the wire. She recognised the packaging. There were grey strips and white strips and Serkel green and the kid was weaving them into a pattern. Tongue out, frowning. The wind caught the plastic and it unfurled like thin arms. Matti held the wire, she didn't ask anymore.

My girl, Li thought, dumbly. And there was nothing she wanted more than to hold the body of her child.

When the Essos came to take Susanna out of Charlie, every woman there fought back. They held onto Susanna and each other. They punched and kicked, shouted. Even the ones who had turned their backs in the showers. Even the ones who said Susanna should never have been let into Charlie – must have given some Esso what he wanted at procesing so he'd look the other way. Even Li. She fought to keep Susanna but she didn't understand why Susanna, or any of them, mattered enough to warrant this. The blind heat of it didn't feel like Essos against labour, it felt like a mob struggling over some resource that had already run out. More Essos came running in from Delta, men she didn't know. They had batons and spray. One of them shoved her against the container wall, bashing her head back on the metal. For a stunned second their eyes met and she saw his uncertainty, that he didn't know why either.

There were women in the sleepbox that night, women with red eyes and bruises, who talked like they hated Susanna more than ever. At the next shift search, Megan told Li she felt sorry for Susanna but it was an oversight that was always going to be picked up.

There's fertile women in Charlie, she said. Management couldn't take the risk.

After that, Li mostly saw Susanna through the fence, looking into their compound from Delta. Same clothes, same hair, just the other side. It had never occurred to her that being a woman was something you might long for.

Trish asked them to count their blessings. Some of the women had men in Delta, partners or sons or brothers. They spent the time between shifts and meals and sleep pressed up against the fence.

But you're lucky too, Camila said, Jun said, Lumena said. You never had a baby.

Yes, Li said. That was lucky. I never wanted to take the risk.

Sometimes she prayed to Frank. Was it praying? She told him she was sorry. And she grieved for him. While Matti had been alive, while she'd hoped for that, there hadn't been room, but now there was so much time.

There were things Li was forgetting – she reached for them and they receded. But she remembered Frank. The way he slept after a twelve-hour shift in Valiant, on his back, palms open. Those strange chess pieces he carved for her their first cold season together in Nerredin, to replace the lost rook and knight in Val's old chess set – the one with stubby little wings and the one with the long tongue. His eyes on her and his hands. He couldn't sing, not at all, but when he was concentrating on something he would whistle in perfect tune.

Trish said they should think of someone they'd wronged and ask to be forgiven.

You were the one who was right, she told him. We just should have stayed.

She saw him the first time at a Weather meeting in the Nerredin school hall. She'd only been in town a couple of days, had picked up some patching at an equipment-hire business and they'd recommended her to the printing press. She was only there to hand out some flyers. Weather meetings were good for trade.

Frank got up and spoke. He wanted the local growers' association to approach the government again about turning up the water supply. It hadn't rained in four years by then and groundwater salinity was off the charts. She liked his voice but she was thinking about how towns like this were a joke. The people who lived in them just couldn't see the punchline yet.

The first time they went to the pub, people kept coming past to say hello. Women. But he had a way of keeping his eyes on her while they talked, laughing silently at the things she said.

You move around, he said, you see a lot of places. You look at a town like this and you reckon it's dying. But there's all kinds of stuff going on here. Stuff you miss if you're just passing through.

Li told him how every year now on her circuit she arrived in dead towns that had been up and running the year before, never saw it coming. She didn't normally talk this much. He listened but she couldn't puncture his optimism. It pissed her off, but something in it pulled at her too. Not blind hope but not blind hopelessness either. And the whole time, she could feel another conversation running underneath, too fluid for her to catch. His hands were long and lean-fingered, capable.

Nerredin's not going anywhere, he said. He nudged the leg of her barstool gently with his boot. You should stick around.

They faced each other in the doorway of his shed, not quite touching. I'm glad you're here, he said. I've got things to show you.

She moved around the space, looking at what he'd made out of lightning-strike wood, out of drought wood. Strange hybrid creatures, work in progress, sweet dust rising from the wood shavings curled across the floor. There was a loft with a mattress and a window that opened out to the olive grove. She kept paying for the room at the pub, though.

He said, I knew her since school. We were gunna get married. Lived in town for a while. But she didn't want to stay here.

Li told him she wasn't interested in marriage. Or a kid. He needed to be clear about that. He nodded, his eyes on her.

The trees were pruned hollow in the centre and the branches hung down in a flickering grey curtain all the way around the trunk. It was like being underwater in there. He pressed her back against the wood, ran his hands over her, knelt in front of her. She pulled him up by his hair, pulled him inside her.

Stay, he said. You can be here. You can live here.

The stillness felt like falling. Nothing had prepared her for it.

*

In the dark, Camila said, You never wanted a kid?

The others listening or asleep. Rain on the roof, coming in through the vents. Li ached. Her head, stomach, muscles, each ligament. Worse at night.

She said, We fought about it. Why you'd do it. Especially after the ballot started.

Everyone wonders why they'd do it, Camila said. They still do it. Otherwise, why do anything?

That's what he said. Li felt Cami's hand against her hand under the blanket and her fingers closed briefly around it. Camila, who had the baby anyway.

Li said, He was so goddamn hopeful about everything.

Salia lay on her back and rocked her head from side to side. She said, Refuse shift starts at 7. Area A van departs 6.45, B van 6.30. Scheduled rest breaks, 11 to 11.15 and 3 to 3.15. Sunset 5.45. Shift finishes at 6, all vans depart by 6.15. Dinner shift 6.30 don't be late or miss out.

Tammy said, Shut up. Shut up shut up shut up.

It was quiet in the container for a moment. Just breathing, coughing, cots squeaking.

Salia said, Don't be late or miss out. Day seven is rest day. Day twenty-eight is Medical.

Li queued for two hours on her crutches and then went into the container and the door was shut behind her from the outside and the medic looked up from a screen and it was him.

Wild woman, he said. I been waiting for you to show up.

Li said, Where's the other medic?

Tropical island. Don't worry, I'm fully qualified.

Li stayed where she was with her back to the door. She didn't want to see him or talk to him, but medical wasn't a choice.

You remember me, right? Rich, from Port Howell?

She nodded. You looked after me. She heard how flat it sounded but she couldn't make it mean more than it did. And she hoped he would leave it there, not bring up other things.

I done a bloody good job, too, and then you tried to break my ribs. He looked tired, and hemmed in by his surgical mask, by the clutter of equipment, the strip lighting. The other medic had always looked tired and sick. Too many patients, too much exposure. Right, he said. You better give me your number.

She went over and held out her wrist, leaning onto the other crutch. Her attention was briefly caught by the bright screen – the novelty of a working computer. He typed her status number in and sat waiting on the timer.

She said, They give you Source access? She didn't care, it was just strange.

Nah, this is all internal. Look. He opened a new window and typed in *explosives/prison break*. Got a pop-up requiring an administrator password. He closed the window, kept waiting. They give me access to three pre-approved medical sites. Otherwise this is basically a filing cabinet. Her record opened and he saw the date at the top. Whistled. Thought I was hard done by. You been in here two months already?

It felt longer but she couldn't think of a reason why they'd lie.

Rich was scanning her record. So, we need to see if your BLL's come down. And I'll have a look at that ankle. What happened there?

Steel-cap boot.

His eyebrows went up. Still pissing people off, yeah?

She sat on the examination table while he took blood. He told her he had a backlog of tests but he should have the results in a week or so.

Press down on that, he said. You get headaches? Or cramps, muscle ache, anything like that?

Li said, So this is your job now.

Yeah. Living the dream. How you going with the crutches? Any shoulder pain, wrist pain?

It's okay.

He lifted her leg onto the table. What about this, how's the pain now?

It's okay.

211

Okay, he said. Well, I'm taking this off, it fucking stinks.

He was quiet while he sawed off the cast. She was used to the smell, but the rotting ditch stench when it cracked open seemed like a separate thing, coming down on both of them from somewhere else. Rich coughed forcefully, then looked up and grinned, sharing his disgust. And Li surprised herself with a half-laugh of apology. The skin on her foot and ankle was deteriorating, like something that had been forced to live underwater. He cleaned it with alcohol wipes, examined it, and then rubbed in a cream and dusted it with antifungal powder. Then he got her to stand on the other foot and place the damaged one lightly on the ground. Her foot angled inwards beyond her control.

It'd heal better if you kept it elevated more.

It doesn't matter, Li said. It's good enough.

He went over and unlocked the supply cupboard, pulled stuff out. Came back with a rigid walking boot and a long sock. He knelt down in front of her. You can take this off to wash and dry your skin. Wash the sock too, I'll get you a spare. Keep it on the rest of the time, you can loosen the straps when you're lying down, but. And don't put weight on it yet.

The other medic hadn't offered this. Li wondered how many points it would set her back but it didn't seem worth arguing about.

Kneeling there, fitting the straps, he said, You didn't find your kid?

She didn't answer.

He said, I am sorry about that. True.

Li had a flash of his eyelashes up close, back in the factory, when he took off the bandages. Then Safia's voice in the dark and that seething mess of panic busting open in her chest. That was far enough.

Hey Li, he said when she was at the door.

She paused, reluctant.

I'm glad you didn't get yourself killed yet.

Outside it was starting to rain, heavy and straight. She went back to the sleepbox. The rain on the metal roof turned the container into a drum. She lay on a cot and let it beat everything down.

There were ways to get through rest day. Sleeping was one. You could do food prep or laundry or cleaning for extra points. Now that the rain had set in, they always needed people on sandbagging, or hosing out the sleepboxes after a gut bug went through. Or you could do the activities. Most of these were in the rec tent in Central compound where the food shed was, too. Rest days were staggered but there were usually thirty or forty people off at the same time, plus the under-twelves. Apart from Family compound, Central was the one place women and men were allowed in the same fenced areas. Sometimes a woman from Charlie got the same rest day as her brother or son or partner, or a man she'd been talking to through the fence. There were male and female Essos in Central, too, monitoring things. Management had zero tolerance for any behaviour that might lead to unnecessary medical procedures.

There was a choir, a dance group, talks, storytelling for the kids. Things that didn't use a lot of materials. Sometimes they organised crafts – colouring in, or weaving with strips of packaging. Management supplied pens and scrap paper. No scissors. If you didn't want to join in, you could watch. Li watched everything except the dogs. The dogs got fed every couple of days, mostly rabbits. Sometimes trappers came to the fence to trade, or security would do a run. At feeding time the dogs ripped each other apart over the carcasses and people bet points for gum, or cigarettes. The dogs reminded Li of every mongrel in every town she'd ever passed through, just hungrier.

There were thirteen books in the rec tent. Most of them were torn picture books, the rest were romances and Serkel catalogues. Li sat at the table and read them all. Sometimes Management gave access to the runway and supplied a football. Some of the Essos played too. She would have joined in if she had two good legs. There was one man who moved like Frank, the same head-up alertness and sudden bursts of speed. Frank could take the ball off another player and score before they knew it was gone. He'd been vice-president of the Nerredin football club and he never gave up on the Mynas making it to Regionals. They went to home games together, kicked a footy with Carl and Angie, but Li didn't have a team – not the Mynas or anyone else. Frank said it was because she'd moved around too much, never got loyal, but it was more than that. She didn't understand why you'd let yourself care so much about something you had no control over.

She liked the talks best. The speaker and topic were set in advance and written on a sign outside the tent. Folding chairs were provided. People talked about anything, about what they knew. Pig hunting, jewellery making, genealogy, astronomy, the Hadith, container farming, old movie stars. Sometimes there were questions or arguments but mostly people were happy to just listen. Sometimes people talked about politics, or Weather, or Wars, or life inside the XB. You could do that as long as you didn't cause a disturbance, but Li felt that these weren't really the things people wanted to hear about. She thought they wanted something close to what she did – stories that took her outside the fence, that filled her head without touching her. Essos came on their breaks, and some of the supervisors did too. Li went to all of them. She'd never been so hungry to hear other people talk.

One rest day she was in the rec tent with Camila and Trish and a handful of other people waiting. The talk was supposed to be about dog breeding, but the speaker hadn't turned up. A coughing sickness was working through the camp and a lot of people were too sick to leave the sleepboxes or nervous about contagion. The people who were there sat apart from each other, and some of them wore rags over their mouths and noses. The ones she recognised looked different, vulnerable, with their heads all freshly shaved from the last lice outbreak. Li knew they would wait the full hour, just in case.

Then she turned around and saw that Angie had come in. She was sitting near the back with her hands folded in her lap, looking down. The stubble on her head was fully grey. Li had never seen her in the rec tent, had only seen her once since the food queue – through a fence on the way back from Medical. Her heart beat faster. She didn't know if Angie had seen her yet, if she would have recognised her from behind with her own head shaved. She wanted to tell her she was sorry. Tell her something. Thought about going back and sitting beside her but she was afraid she wouldn't be able to speak, or say it right.

A man along the row from her coughed into his arm and people stirred and sighed and someone got up and left. Li was gripped with a fear that Angie would leave too, and so before that could happen she got up herself, not making eye contact with Camila or Trish, and walked to the front. She faced them, and the seven other people and the empty seats and Angie, and she didn't know what she was going to say, but then Angie looked up, and she did.

She said, I'm Li. I'm going to talk about dryland farming in West.

A few noises of surprise, relief, Camila's startled attention, people getting comfortable.

Angie saw her now. She was watching Li like something wild that had got out. Li remembered the speech Frank made for Angie's thirtieth, how he'd told the story about her chasing him around the playground with poo on a stick their first day at primary school, and Angie had laughed so hard she knocked her drink over. Frank was good in front of people, knew how to put them at ease. Cup night, Weather meetings, that presentation to the CBP delegation from Sumud that re-secured their import licence. She'd always avoided it. But standing up here now she wasn't talking to people. Just Ange.

We lived in Nerredin, about three hundred and fifty k inland of Valiant. Good-size town, nearly a thousand people when I first got there. Used to be sheep and wheat country. We had an olive grove. A hundred and twenty trees, small-scale production, mostly selling into Sumud. It wasn't a normal crop for the region but they were established trees and they stood up against the drought and the salt. Olive trees have got a really extensive root system so they can tap into deep groundwater. They can tolerate the cold and if it gets too hot they sort of shut down their system in the hottest part of the day. They're really tough trees. They do need some water to fruit but we had an allowance, and we had these plastic skirts around the trunks that trapped condensation and fed it down to the root line, so they got enough. They'll even grow back after a fire. Most of the time it's wildstock, though, it'll bush out but it won't bear fruit.

She paused. Couldn't remember the last time she'd talked that much in one go. She was out of breath but there was more she wanted to say. The audience sat quietly. Camila was watching her, a few people were looking down or away into the distance. Trish had her eyes shut and she was nodding. Angie waited.

Nerredin was a big producer for West. Even bigger once the cereal-cropping country further north got lost to rising salt and the west coast got too unreliable. It wasn't easy growing country though. We had fourteen years of drought, so we relied on the pipe – the Liu-McKenzie pipeline up from the south coast. Salinity got worse and worse but we kept adapting. People grew all kinds of things under glass, mostly whatever there was demand for in Valiant or the XB. Millet was a good one, there were a few millet producers.

Angie swayed slightly in her seat. The man in the third row coughed again, tried to smother it.

People grew sorghum, too, and a lot of warrine, and some of the modified wheat strains. The sheep container didn't work out, but there was a big yabbie farm in the old Bickley dam that did really well once they got the salt levels right. And then Homegrown claimed two hundred acres of abandoned farmland just north of Nerredin for a saltwater greenhouse. The howlers on the west coast were getting worse so they were looking inland and we had the population and the infrastructure and a lot of local experience. We were right on the highway too. They were going to try tomatoes first, see how it went. That would have been close to a hundred jobs once it got up and running.

A couple of people nodded. There was consistent demand for tomatoes inside the XB, everyone knew that because of the trucks.

Li said, They started building a pipeline from their desal plant on the coast, so there was construction work for a while, security work. They were going to build the solar tower next. But there were too many attacks on the pipeline and it got too expensive for them to guard it, so they pulled out.

The man with the cough put his hand up. People weren't supposed to just interrupt. Li looked at him, uncertain.

Did you ever have a howler come through there?

They were well outside the howler zone here and from the way people shuffled and leaned in, Li guessed that most of them had never seen one.

Yeah, she said. We had two in the last two years. Both mid-category.

What was that like?

She cleared her throat, trying to corral her brain in this new direction. Well. Howlers have got a smell to them. You can get a smell of grass before they hit, even when there's no grass, or a sulphur smell, like lighting a match. We weren't ready for the first one. We lost some people. And a lot of people left after that. We lost infrastructure too, had to rebuild with prefabs, but the older buildings stood up okay, mostly just broken windows and roof tiles. It hit the farms north of town pretty hard but people further south were okay. We lost the harvest but we kept most of the trees.

A woman said, I thought howlers wiped out everything. She sounded let-down.

Yeah, but we only got the edge of it. And it was mid-category, like I said.

Li could see the grove, suddenly, from the top of the rise. Not a blackened ruin, but grey and green and flecked with purple, flickering silver. Frank's inheritance. She said, After that, we got re-zoned and we applied for Weather Alert and by the time the second one came, we'd had the two bunkers built for the district. We didn't lose anyone else. The howlers weren't what finished us. She looked down at Angie and remembered. Anyway, I'm not talking about Weather. I'm talking about Nerredin.

She understood suddenly what she was trying to offer. Not an apology. A gift.

Someone in the front row said, Well, get on with it.

Angie leaned forward and Li saw their town suspended in the air between them, fragile and provisional. Bob and Shamila's hardware store. The red dog that slept in the entrance to the takeway. Faysal's newsagent. The farm supply store and the general store, the op shop and the bakery. The pub with the sandwich board on the verandah advertising Ivan's lunch special and the winners of the raffle. She could see taxis waiting on the corner and a driver leaning on her door, talking to the man who loaned his donkey every year for the Nativity play. The Wars memorial in the middle of the park, salmon gums and hard-baked dirt where the old people played bocce. She could smell bread and fertiliser and desiccated coconut and clove cigarettes and hot chips. A child ran across the wide road without looking.

Tears were running down Camila's face. Angie got up quietly and moved along the row of chairs towards the entrance.

Li said, to her back, When we walked out, there was just the school and the pub still standing. I don't know if there's anything left now. But people lived there. We lived there. It was a good town.

Afterwards, the man with the cough came over and thanked her. He said, I won't get too close.

It's okay, Li said. Don't worry about it.

Camila and Trish were waiting for her near the entrance.

The man said, I enjoyed that. I was looking forward to the dog breeding, but I enjoyed it. I didn't know much about West. Very interesting. You could have been talking about my town.

He turned away and started coughing again, and he coughed gently for a long time, bent over. Li looked past him at the empty entranceway where the grey light came in.

Rich said, Why aren't you wearing the gear? He'd just shot Li up with a new viral vax Management was trialling against the coughing sickness.

I'm wearing the gear. She was shaky from exhaustion and whatever he'd pumped into her system. She'd been sent to Medical from the food shed, along with everyone else from Charlie who wasn't already sick. Come straight off the back of one and a half shifts, covering for absent labour. It was dark before she started queueing.

Like hell you are. He swivelled the monitor round and she focused on the screen briefly. It took her a minute to even remember last month's bloods.

He said, Your lead levels are tracking twice as high as last month. You're not using the protective gear. Why?

Because it doesn't matter.

The fuck it doesn't. Maybe you don't feel sick but you are sick – you're gunna be.

It doesn't matter.

Have you got a death wish, Li? Cos people in here are dying fast enough. He looked worse than last time, bruises under his eyes like he'd been double-punched. He was masked but his beard had been shaved as well as his hair and it made him look more exposed. She knew he hadn't volunteered for medic and she knew what he was up against. Half the women in Charlie had the cough now. Security had regrouped the sleepboxes into sick and not sick yet.

She said, I'm not wishing for anything.

Look, he said. I'm sorry you lost your kid. True to God, I am. But that is bullshit.

Okay. Is that all? Cos I'm back on in five hours.

No, it's not all. I got you something.

It was a knee crutch. Top of the line. She stared at it as he brought it over to the exam table.

I don't have the points for that. How'd you get that?

People like me, Li. I'm a nice fella. No, wait, don't get up yet. He checked his watch, checked the injection site and her pulse. He asked about tingling, numbness, nausea. Then he helped her step into the crutch, with her lower leg resting on the platform in a kneeling position, and tightened the straps around her calf and thigh. She let him take the other crutches and cautiously tried a step. Another step. Remembering how to place her leg instead of swinging it.

Keeps that ankle elevated, see? And it'll give your shoulders a break. He readjusted the height for her and made her practise walking the length of the container without looking down. It was so good to have her hands back, not to have her shoulders and armpits and wrists hurt with every step.

She turned to face him, getting the hang of it. I don't understand how I can have this.

He grinned at her. Relax, Li. I told you, people like me.

She grinned back, didn't even mean to. Wiped her runny nose on her arm.

No worries, he said. So, you reckon you can climb?

Sure. The van's just one step up, this'll be easier than the crutches.

Could you climb a fence?

What?

Nah, I'm just gammin with you. I can get us through the gates, I'm working on that.

She stared at him. Someone banged on the door and Rich opened it and stuck his head out. You're gunna have to wait. I might have an adverse reaction here. He shut the door, turned back.

Li said, I better go.

I'm getting out of here, he said. You should come.

She was tired and she didn't know why he was doing this, didn't have an answer for him. Why do you want to get out?

Why? You serious? I mean, I know they call it Transit but have you noticed no one fucking goes anywhere?

Yeah, I noticed. You won't get out.

I got out of worse places than this.

Go on, then. I'm not interested.

Listen to yourself, he said. You don't belong in here.

Who did he think she was? Li shrugged. No one belongs anywhere.

Speak for your own self, woman.

She started moving to the door but Rich got in her way. What is it about this place you like so much? Apart from the free lead poisoning.

I like working. I like not thinking.

You're a patcher, he said. You fixing anything in here?

I don't need to fix anything. I just need to fill the time.

Until what? He grabbed her arm with his gloved hand. Li, listen to me. You lost your kid but you're still alive.

That's right, she said. I lost my kid but I'm still alive.

He let go. She swayed and steadied herself, suddenly nauseous. Her nose wouldn't stop running and her arm hurt like hell from the shot. The need for sleep was a thumping weight.

He said, You know for sure she's dead?

You think a bunch of kids could've survived these last months out there?

The Esso bashed on the door again. Fucksake, we're all freezing our tits off.

Li said, I'm just not lying to myself anymore.

Rich stood looking at her. She walked to the door, easily, steadied herself on the frame before she opened it.

See? she said, with her forehead against the cold metal. I do belong in here.

The runny nose turned into a cold, turned into a low-grade fever and a drag in her bones. She couldn't get herself into the van. The driver backed away, a couple of Essos called her out of the line. It was hard to tell who anyone was now, behind the masks, but she could see in their eyes that they didn't think the masks would save them. They kept their distance walking her over to the sickbox. Coughbox, the women called it. Deathbox. Okay, she thought. This.

She could hear it as she got closer. She wasn't coughing yet, but soon she was. Soon every breath turned into a coughing fit. She lay on a cot someone didn't need anymore and worked full-time on breathing. Not with her brain, just her body. Her body didn't want to quit. All around her women were doing the same work, coughing up phlegm, coughing up blood, coughing till they couldn't breathe and still coughing, a wet desperate sound.

Someone was moaning, an *aaah aaah* that came and went around spasms of coughing. Someone was asking for water, she thought it was Camila. Li was burning with cold and everything was heavy, her hand when she tried to lift the bottle, the blanket. Her neck and stomach hurt. Her lungs had fists and they were bashing at her temples trying to get out.

Something wet on her forehead. Blood? But it was cool, there were hands lifting her head, like she was a child.

The truckie said, Hell of a spot for a date. The water was cold and heavy in her mouth and it tasted of nothing. She went away down somewhere.

When she came back up, Essos in coveralls and masks and gloves were carrying more sick women in and dragging dead women out to make room. The air in the container was foul. She felt paper-thin and all her muscles hurt. The water bottle was empty and she was so thirsty.

Her knee crutch was beside her, when someone should have stolen it by now. She got up off the cot shakily and did up the straps and went outside.

There was a different stench out there, something sweet and leathery mixed in with the dump rot. And smoke. It was still morning, the light grey and indeterminate, a strong wind gusting from the west. Li buttoned her jacket and turned the collar up. She saw bodies lined up by the fence and went over there. They lay uncovered on their backs, or curved against each other, the way they'd slept in the cold. Essos came and went, bringing more bodies. No one told her to report for shift. They moved past her like she was dead, too. She came closer and recognised faces. Jun, who cried when they shaved her head. Tammy, who told them to wake her when she snored. A woman she'd worked a double shift with on the smelter, shared a readybar with, never asked her name.

Then an Esso dragged another body over and went away and left it there, and she wanted to say, No, you're wrong about her, but she knew he was right.

When the boat was sinking, Cami called to a man in the water and the man reached his arms up to catch her baby. Emilio was little but he had strong fingers, she unfastened them and held him over the side and he didn't cry. He looked at her and she let him go, and a wave came and when it passed the man was still holding up his empty arms.

Li felt a deep longing to lie down beside her. When the feeling got too strong she looked away from Cami, out through the fence. Saw more bodies in the next compound, and the next. There were fires in the No Go, smoke on the wind that carried a smell like burning hair and a smell like melting copper. She heard a vehicle heading back in towards maingate , heard dogs snarling.

Behind her, Megan said, You were in there for three days. We've been burning bodies every day. I kept expecting to see you.

Li rested her forehead against the wire. She said, Three days?

Management quarantined themselves in the complex. Megan's voice was flat. I saw the convoy heading out there two nights ago. Then she said, Benj is dead.

Li turned around. Megan's eyes were swollen and she wasn't wearing a mask anymore. Li had watched Benj play footy once, had recognised him because he looked like his sister.

They kept saying they were going to upgrade him. If he'd been in security compound with me he might not have got the cough. Megan wiped her eyes and nose on the back of a filthy hand. He told me I wasn't trying hard enough to get him out.

Did you see him?

Khaled dumped his body, I didn't even see his body. She looked away and Li saw a spasm go through her.

She remembered waking Camila from her dream about her son, always the same dream. Holding onto her while Cami said, It gets darker and darker and his mouth is open but he never cries.

Megan said, Medic wanted to see you if you came through it. He said it's important.

She let Li through the first set of link gates. The rest of them were unlocked. In the other compounds she passed through, there were more bodies on the ground, more Essos dragging bodies. No one stopped her or asked where she was going. It was quiet, just the wind blowing rubbish around. The only labour she saw were queueing outside the food shed, but there was no smell of food from inside. There was no queue outside Medical, and no security. She knocked and went in.

Rich lay on a mattress behind the desk, his mask pulled down. He twitched in his sleep. There was an empty cup on the floor beside him and a small yellow bottle half full of meds.

He mumbled something. Said, No, I need it. You can't. And shook his head and swore fluently.

She said his name but he was lost in it. One hand started to shake. She stood, undecided, looked around, rather than watch him. At the IV stand beside the exam table, tube dangling. The hazardous-waste bin overflowing with gloves and masks and soiled cloths. Piles of paper and half-drunk cups of koffee on the desk.

Rich started breathing faster, his hands clenching and unclenching. Get away from. There isn't any. Then he shouted something and the shout brought him upright, fists ready. He looked at her, unfocused and breathing. After a moment he said her name, his voice slurred with sleep. He said, I'm glad.

You look like shit, she told him.

He cleared his throat. Yeah, well you look about a hundred per cent more gorgeous than yesterday.

She remembered the hands lifting her, the cool, the water. You were in the coughbox?

I was for about ten seconds. It was disgusting in there, dunno how you put up with it. He groped for the empty cup, knocked the pills over. Squeezed his eyes shut. When he opened them again, some of his alertness was back. He looked at the door. Anyone waiting?

She shook her head. How many people have you treated for this?

How many people have I treated? He said it back to her slowly and she thought he was going to put his head in his hands, but he pulled off the mask instead. His hand was still shaking. Well, we run out of everything a week ago – antibiotics, antivirals, whatever they were letting us have. He laughed. They give me a good supply of towelling offcuts, though. So I guess since the last time I saw you I been wiping a lot of foreheads with a lot of flannels and doing status updates for dead bodies. Is how many people I've treated for this.

She emptied the koffee dregs from two cups and filled them with water at the sink. Drank down three cups straight and brought one back for him. You told Megan you wanted to see me.

Yeah. He drank, nodded slowly. Yeah, I remembered something after you left the other day. I didn't know if you wanted to hear it and then there wasn't really time. He got up off the mattress and went over to the computer, pushed papers out of the way and leaned over the keyboard, running a search. After a minute he moved aside. You should sit.

She didn't know what she'd been expecting. Not a child. Not a photo of a child with buzzcut hair and brown eyes out of proportion in her too-thin face, thinner than any camp kid Li had seen.

Li looked up at Rich. I don't know who that is, she said.

He nodded. She got brought in to me just after I took over as medic. Woman who brought her in said the kid turned up on her own in Family the week before. They heard one of the drivers found her wandering and snuck her in. She wasn't in the system. They don't tag the under-twelves, so once she was in, there'd be no reason management'd know.

Rich fumbled in a drawer and found two sachets, tore them open and poured hot water from a thermos into their cups. The salty smell hit the back of her nose, made her salivate. How long since she'd eaten?

They reckon it's soup, he told her.

She picked it up in both hands, burned her mouth on the first gulp, settled for sipping and blowing.

Anyway, the parents in Family were keeping an eye on her but everyone had their own kid to look out for. She wasn't getting fed enough. They thought maybe I could file an unacccompanied-minor claim on the quiet.

Li felt something stirring in her chest, something unsafe. She concentrated on the taste of the soup, the grit between the keys on the board, how the 'e' was almost rubbed away. Kept her eyes below screen level.

So, I done a physical, Rich said. She was borderline malnourished, broken arm at some point that hadn't been set, lot of cuts and bruises. Some frostbite damage, too. We were just in time there. He paused. She was really, really quiet. I had a bit of a queue, so I made a follow-up to do the interview for the claim. He put his cup down and leaned over the keyboard, bringing something else up. He said, You don't have to look, Li, but I need you to listen.

She heard him say, Can you tell me your name?

I already *told* you. Heaps of times.

Yeah, but when you get as old as me you forget stuff. Come on, help a fella out, will ya?

The child giggled, sighed. La*vin*ia Rioli.

And you reckon you're six?

Well, I *was* six, but I might be seven now. Because Alex said I looked more like a seven-year-old.

Alex was one of them?

He was a big boy.

In that mob of kids you were with?

I already *told* you.

Li's fists were pushing down on her thighs, hard enough to bruise. A trembling in her body beyond her control, like it came from underground. She lifted her eyes to the screen. The child's face had filled out a bit from the photo and she had a new dark fuzz of hair. She was looking up at Rich offscreen, half annoyed, half smiling.

Rich said, Don't forget to look at the camera. Where the green light is.

Oh yeah. The child looked, down, up. Straight at Li.

Lavinia, this bit's important. Where were you before that?

In the big camp.

And who were you with?

My dad.

Okay. And what's your dad called? What do grown-ups call him?

The child said something very quietly.

Paul? Is that his name?

She nodded. Rich said, You're doing really good, mate. Can you tell me what happened after you and your dad were in the big camp?

Silence. Li looked into her eyes and saw Nerredin after the fire. The same calm. Outside Medical, the wind was picking up again. She tapped the volume as high as it would go.

— where your dad is, Lavinia? Could he be looking for you?

A woman said, offscreen, She doesn't remember. Or she doesn't – I already tried.

Rich said, That's okay, Lavinia. No worries. You all right?

She gave Li the thumbs up.

So, you liked being with the other kids, yeah?

Sort of. Some of them were mean but Alex was nice and another big kid called Nasir gave me crackers and they stuck up for me. Because some of the kids said I was too slow because I was six but Alex said I was more like a seven-year-old.

Were you trying to get somewhere special?

Yeah. But when we got to the big hill, it was really high and it was *cold* and there was nothing to eat and I got tired of walking. And the other kids said I was a crybaby and they weren't going to wait for me.

Rich said, What about Alex and Nasir?

231

Lavinia blinked. Li hadn't noticed her blink before. Nasir wasn't there then, she said. Alex said he'd wait with me and we'd get a lift in a truck. He said it'd be warm and we'd get there first, but we waited for ages and no trucks came and Alex wouldn't let me go to sleep.

But then a truck did come?

But it was going the wrong way. And it stopped and Alex made me get in anyway but he wouldn't get in with me. He said he was going to to catch up with the others.

The woman said, Serkel does freight over the range.

Lavinia, Rich said, can you tell me where you were trying to go? Before you come here?

We were going to the best place. And Alex said the truck would take me there a different way, but this isn't the best place.

No, Li said. That's not —

The best place has horses. You go over the big hill and there are boats that don't sink and that's how you get there.

Li tried to lift her hands to the keyboard but they were shaking too hard. Rich leaned over and hit pause but she kept staring at the kid, stilled on the screen. She couldn't get her breathing under control. Outside, the wind made a high sound and something slapped the side of the container and bounced off again.

Rich said, behind her, That means something? The best place?

She couldn't get enough air in, no matter how fast she breathed. Felt a terrifying lightness. If she took her eyes off the child she would spiral up out of this chair and through the metal ceiling, up into the wind.

Li?

I want to talk to her.

232

She's dead. Two days ago. Three days ago. There's not a lot of people left in Family. I. He breathed out through his nose. I couldn't update her status cos she didn't exist.

Li had the strongest desire to touch the screen. Those left-behind eyes.

I dunno about your kid, he said. But Lavinia was in a makecamp first. And there was a mob of kids from there still alive about a month ago, trying to get across the range.

Li closed her eyes.

I gave up on someone, too, Rich said. Lost cause, right? But what if it's not? Not for you. His voice was steady in the dark. I saw you run at that fire. You know how hard you fought me when I dragged you away? You need to be out there looking for her, Li. True thing.

The link gates between Medical and Charlie were still unlocked. No one in sight now. Li bent forward into the wind but the wind kept changing, she kept having to stop and hang onto the fence. The ground was strewn with rubbish. It started raining hard, drenching her in seconds. She barely noticed. Something inside her was breaking, burning. It hurt so much that she had to move. All this time, lying to herself, lying down, she had to make it up now. Even if it was too late.

Rich had said he needed to get something, he was going to meet her at maingate, or the first locked gate before maingate. There was an Esso he'd been working on, who might take a pay-off if he could find him. All she knew was that they had to try now while Management was awol and everyone else was burning bodies. She was looking for Megan. Megan had the codes.

Two Essos went past her, hunched over against the wind. One of them yelled something at her but the wind was bashing her around the ears and they didn't stop. A sideways gust knocked her into the fence. The air was full of plastic and cans and she realised it must be blowing from the dump. She felt a glancing blow on the back of the head. An old running shoe. It hit the ground and was plucked up again.

She got all the way to Charlie and then Megan came out of a sleepbox, head down, on her way out. Li yelled her name as she went past and she looked up, struggling to keep her balance.

What are you doing? she shouted over the wind. Get inside!

Li said, I need to get out. I need the codes.

Megan shook her head, staring at her. You should've stayed in Medical.

Just let me out. Please.

What the fuck's wrong with you?

The link gate slammed shut and Megan turned away to wrestle it open again. Li grabbed her shoulder and Megan turned back fast, catching Li's arm and twisting it, forcing her down.

Megan stood over her. Can't you see what's happening?

Li realised that the rain had stopped and the wind had dropped away. There was a kind of waiting hush.

Please, she said. I have a reason.

Megan said, I don't have the maingate code. I never had it. Then she looked past Li and something loosened in her face. She turned to the open gate and ran.

Li looked up. The sky was yellow. A smell like a fresh-lit match. Her body went slack. Brain screaming at her to turn and look, so she would know which way to run. A thin savage howl. The air was full of tussock and sand, and a grey wave was swarming in from the west, unspooling across the sky until it was the only thing.

She hauled herself up and stumbled for the sleepbox. Slammed the door behind her. It was bolted to the concrete pad, it wouldn't give straight away. The howling intensified outside and beneath it a roar like engines. There was crashing, clanging, metal ripping. Things started to slam into the walls. The whole container was shuddering. She needed to get under a cot, cover herself. Oh God, had Matti lived long enough to die like this?

Something moved in the corner. It was Trish, on her knees, trying to stay upright. Her mouth was moving but the words were lost.

Li stumbled towards her. Get down, she yelled.

Trish shouted, We're in God's hands now.

Li felt rage fork through her. At this woman who believed all this, any of it, was the work of something with love in its heart.

There was a sudden pressure in her head. Her ears popped. The sleepbox groaned and the howler was right on them, in her brain and her teeth and her bones. Trish's mouth opened wide and she reached out for Li, but Li turned away and lost herself in the roar.

A wrenching scream of metal. The container flipped.

Can you hear my pencil?

They were lying down together in the tent, under the sleeping bags. Afternoon. Rain falling on the plastic, makecamp gone to mud outside. Li's eyes were closed, her head resting on her jacket.

Can you? Mum? Hear it?

Yeah. I can hear it.

Can you hear my letters?

No. Well, hang on. Li listened, tried to. Did you just make a round one?

An 'O'! You *could* hear it!

They were quiet for a little while, pleased. Matti's pencil scratched. A relief dump had cleared customs and the Kids' Tent had been handing out exercise books and pens but the pens had run out.

What are you writing?

I'm writing my happy memories, Matti said. I've already written two. Do you want me to read you one?

Yeah, go on.

Matti turned back a page. I was six when I started playing schools. Hello class! She glanced up. That bit's a picture. My name was Ms Twinkle. Great work, Amalia K! That's a picture too.

Huh, Li said, I remember Amalia K.

She was one of my cardboard kids.

Remember when you folded all the kids up and packed them away?

Matti nodded. I was getting a bit too old.

What's the other one?

Oh, that's when we went camping with Robbie, and you and Dad made us a flying fox.

You were really little then.

Yeah, I was only about five.

Are you going to write any that aren't so long ago?

Matti closed the book and wriggled closer to Li, rolled onto her back. I think when I'm nine I'll do one about me and Shayla and Sulaman getting these books.

You could write that one now though.

Nah. It has to be a *memory*. Not something that just happened. Matti reached up and tugged at Li's hair, thinking. Five or six is good.

Rich was calling her name in the dark, through the crush, through the other voices calling names. She struggled out from between two mattresses, working to extract her bent leg in the crutch. The back of her head hurt but she could stand. How long had she been unconscious?

She called back to Rich and heard his answering shout. A little light came in through the vents and by that light she felt her way to the door, wading through bedding and dismembered cot frames. Among them, lying face up, Trish.

Li got down and cleared the wreckage from her. A metal shaft wouldn't come free and it was only when Trish's body started to lift with it that she realised it had broken off inside her. She let go and felt for a pulse she knew couldn't be there. There was a hard pain in her own chest. *They shall come to no harm but shall be lifted.* She held Trish's wrecked face and wondered if she was the last person who would remember her.

Rich was banging on the wall, yelling her name. She didn't know what to tell her, only that she wasn't waiting anymore.

I have a daughter, she said.

The door was jammed, the frame bent out of shape. She called back to Rich and they worked on getting it open together.

When she came out into the freezing air, he hugged her. Said, I knew this place couldn't kill you.

There was a gash on the side of his face but he said it wasn't serious. She looked over his shoulder at the still, broken aftermath. Where there had been a network of fenced compounds, now there was a plain of torn-up metal and wire and canvas. The sleepbox had landed on a link fence. Other fences had been flattened or ripped up whole and thrown down somewhere else. Fence poles stuck up out of the ground like spears. Rubbish bloomed everywhere. People moved through the wreckage, but not many of them.

Up ahead, the complex was its own disaster zone – the buildings collapsed in on themselves or fanned out across the plain in pieces. She saw the shell of a helicopter, nose crushed in, blades drooping down like they'd melted.

Li was still staring at all that when Rich took her by the shoulders and turned her around. Look, he said.

The dump was gone, its mountains levelled and scattered. They were standing in a broad channel between two waves. To the south-west, Sumud's XB reared up unbroken in a great curving greyness. To the east, and further away, was the wall around New Flinders, but something was wrong with it. In places, the top of the wave dipped and jagged.

Rich said, Can you walk a bit?

She nodded, without taking her eyes off that distant breach.

I reckon I've got us a ride.

She turned back to face him, saw that he had a backpack on, and something rolled up in canvas. He said, Let's go before some other bastard nicks it.

It was another four-wheel drive, lying on its side about two hundred metres from where the outer fence had been. The keys were still in the ignition, engine off.

Rich crawled in through the boot to pull up the handbrake and put it in gear. He crouched over the driver briefly and then called out that his neck was broken. Li checked for fuel leaks and then cleared and levelled the ground alongside as best she could. They worked easily together, not talking much, keeping a lookout for dogs. Rich found a bent Serkel sign and dug a small hole under the side of the roof and two bigger ones under the wheels nearest to the ground. Then they levered the vehicle up with a fence post on a slab of concrete until it started to tip away from them. It bounced, landing on all four wheels, but it stayed in one piece.

He chocked the wheels and then went into his pack for first-aid supplies and cleaned and covered the cut on his face that was bleeding freely now. Li let the engine settle while she checked the radiator, mounts, fan belt, steer pumps, alternator, everything she could think of that might have sustained damage. The batteries were sealed – no sign of rupture. No leaks or kinks in the fuel tank or fuel lines. The glow plugs on the driver's side had a bit of oil on them but there was still plenty in the pan. As far as she could tell, the engine was sound. She felt a little bit of hope starting but she didn't get carried away. It had hit the ground pretty hard.

There was a tarp caught under a fence not far away. Rich dragged it clear and brought it back while she took the plugs out and wiped them down on her clothes. Then they covered the engine and Rich got out of the way before she cranked it to blow any residue out of the cylinders. Put the plugs back in. Checked the tyres and the suspension. There wasn't much more she could do.

When they pulled the driver out they found a twelve-gauge double-barrelled shotgun wedged against the door. He was wearing a twenty-loop belt loaded with shells and he had a working phone in his jacket.

The engine ran rough and smoky for a few minutes and then smoothed out. Li couldn't believe their luck. She unstrapped her knee crutch and put it on the back seat, climbed in beside Rich. Rich, who'd had no reason to do anything for her. Then she looked up and saw a woman walking towards them. She was swaying on her feet but she moved like she didn't have to worry about dogs or anything else. Rich took the gun and got out and went around to the front of the four-wheel drive. Management, Li realised. She hadn't seen anyone dressed like this woman in a long time – tailored black pants, silk shirt, torn suit jacket. Blood was dripping down one arm.

I'm going to ask you to hand over the vehicle, she said.

Rich was still but his hand on the gun was shaking.

That's Company property. You need to go back to your area. She waved a hand towards the wreck of Transit. Procedures will be put in place.

Li couldn't see his face, only the woman's face as she stepped back, fear moving in even before he raised the shotgun. Roared at her.

Fuck off and die, you murderous bitch.

As they pulled away, Li saw the Company woman staring past them at the wreck of Transit and then back at the wreck of the complex. She turned in a full circle and then sat down slowly.

They drove to the highway and kept driving. *Goodbye, Ange,* Li thought. She felt it come and let it come, a grief and remorse that was like drowning. She wouldn't trade it, would never go back to that dead waiting. Behind her, Transit was finished. It was what it had always been.

The range

Rich drove east and Li didn't ask where they were going. It was enough to be back on the highway, to be moving again. They drove in the howler's wake, through wrecked country where nothing remained in its place but the road. No fence. The tussock and shrubs had been uprooted and thrown down again – sometimes the rubbish and dirt was heaped so thick on the highway that they had to drive around it. Sometimes there were bodies too, people who must have been walking or camped by the highway when the howler came through. Rich said there weren't more bodies because there were no towns around here for people to leave. Everything from here to the range was military.

She watched him, side-on. His shoulders were loose and his eyes on the road were calm, but the shake in his right hand came and went. His anger was an unknown quantity to set against what he had given her back. He hadn't needed to get her out, didn't need her now.

The phone's battery was half charged and there was a signal. No passcode. She laid it on her lap and stared at it like it might disappear if she looked away.

Rich glanced at the grey wall of New Flinders rushing past. We should have reception for a while, he said.

She dialled, entered her status number, language selection, worked her way through the options, pushing hard on the worn-out keypad. For a full minute, she couldn't remember Matti's claim number, thought she'd buried it too deep. She pushed back against the panic, made herself see the three-cornered scrap of card with the number on it that had been taken off her at Transit processing. The shaky eight, the 'W'. There it was, after all, stuck in her brain like a splinter. She punched it in and braced for the queue, trying to keep her breathing steady. There won't be any news, there's never any news. You knew at the start you wouldn't find her like this.

She got through straight away. No ads, no hold music, just a recorded human voice. *We are experiencing unusually high demand for this feature. Due to the number of clients currently in the queue, we do not recommend holding at this time. Did you know you can access all your records —*

When she hung up, her jaw was clamped so tight it hurt.

Rich said, Try again later, yeah?

It started to rain again and kept raining. They didn't pass another vehicle or see any sign of life. No birds, nothing. But from behind New Flinders' wall they heard the faint rise and fall of sirens. Sounds of emergency, as if the howler had wreaked havoc inside as well. It was a deeply strange idea. The wall Li carried in her head could repel anything; the real XB hadn't even withstood its first howler. Nerredin had survived two of them. But then, Frank always said the XB hadn't been built to keep Weather out. It was built to keep unwanted people out of places the builders couldn't even imagine Weather reaching.

New Fingers, she said, remembering.

What's that?

That's what Matti called it. What she thought it was called.

It struck her that right now, while things were chaotic and scrambled, might be the best chance they'd ever have to slip through the gaps. She looked at Rich, his hands easy on the wheel. Are you trying to get inside? Is that where we're going?

Rich looked back at her like he hadn't seen the question coming. What would I wanna be locked up in there for?

She remembered Chris asking her what she thought it was like inside. So where do you want to go?

He rolled his shoulders, cracked his neck. I met this woman in a roadhouse a couple of years back. Two years? She was with a mob that moved around, worked all over. He slowed to navigate a tree that had been ripped up, roots and all, from somewhere south and dumped here on the road. She said they were looking for a medic, so I hung onto her number. I was heading to meet up with them when I got pulled into Transit. Reckon I might see if they're still out there.

Li said, Why didn't you go with them two years ago?

Two years ago I had other stuff to do. How about you? Where are you gunna start?

She looked out through the rain on the windscreen that made the scoured plain around them seem dim and far away. I don't know. If she's alive, she could be anywhere.

That's a lot of places.

Li said, What the girl was talking about on the video, where those kids were trying to get to, the best place? That's what Matti called the Deep Islands. It's where she thought she'd be safe. Where we'd wait for her, if. She waited for the searing in her throat to pass.

You're heading across the range, then?

She nodded, slowly.

He considered it. There's Permacamp on the other side, massive sprawling thing. It's an Agency camp, they keep records. Be the first place I'd look.

She was careful with her thoughts, still, but not the way she had been before. She didn't believe Matti was alive, not really, but she had been alive long enough to drag a bunch of other kids into the Best Place game. Maybe she was still alive when Li went into Transit. She didn't turn away from the pain of that, she'd done enough turning away. The range in the cold season was nature's XB. Heavy rain, flashfloods, slips, probably snow. That's what Matti would have faced if she'd got that far. But trucks still crossed through the cold season and one of them had stopped for Lavinia. The chance was small but it was real.

They followed the curve of the wall until they were travelling due east. She'd never been this close to an XB. It looked like people had said, except for the chunks taken out of the top here and there, like missing teeth. A long way ahead the range was in view, blue-smudged and tipped with white. She'd seen it sketched on the far eastern edge of her map but with no sense of its scale. All the walls did was keep people out. The range split the continent. She looked at it and her whole body trembled. Had

Matti had seen it? Had she walked towards the mountains and imagined the other side?

Looking away, she caught something in the wing mirror. Something bony and hollow, one side blotched darker than the other and pulled tight. It was her face. Stubble on her head, grey-streaked, her eyebrows ragged and half-grown. The eyes were difficult to look at. She felt a stab of grief at what was gone and what was left but she made herself look until she recognised this face.

At first the radio was mostly static but then she found a station that was covering the howler. There were unconfirmed reports of damage inside New Flinders, casualties. She sifted through the frequencies, hungry for these calm voices presenting their arguable facts, after two and a half months without news. The official Source station was reporting that the howler had come up off the Southern Ocean. High category. A state of emergency in South-West. Contact with Valiant had been patchy since it hit. She wondered if Teresa and Navid and Hani were alive.

The coverage switched to a public health official confirming that an influenza outbreak inside Fengdu had been contained, and then an international segment on the situation at the Front. Rich took over the dial and found a country music station.

Her headache was back, tidal. She pressed her palms against her temples to ride it out. Rich hauled his pack over from the back seat. Water, he said. And paracetamol.

The pack was bulging with medical supplies – he must have stripped the shelves before he got out. She found the right pills, swallowed two, calculating the points before she remembered. They passed a water bottle between them and then Li found readies further down and they shared one, just enough to take the edge off. She wasn't sure how long the food would have to last. She hadn't seen an animal, living or dead, since they left Transit.

She fell asleep trying to remember the last time she'd heard music. When she woke it was still raining and Rich was on the phone.

Yeah. Yeah, we'll eke it out, call you if we have to. Yeah, I got a patcher with me. He raised his eyebrows at Li. Dunno. Might be going on east. Well, you can ask. All right, see you there if you don't hear from me first. He disconnected and grinned at her. That was my new mob. They were further north – just caught the tail end of it, so they're wet but they're not dead.

She sat up, looking out at the rain. You're meeting up with them?

They're on their way, yeah. We're aiming for the last road-house before the range, bout a hundred and eighty clicks from here. He looked at the fuel gauge. We're not gunna make it on this tank, though.

He waited for a clear break on the side of the road and pulled over. Li strapped on her crutch and got out. Midafter-noon, they'd been driving for about four hours. The rain had eased but the ground was water-logged and turning to mud – no plants left to hold it together. She turned her face up and caught moisture on her tongue. Had a sudden hunger for privacy. There was no cover, so she walked behind and away from the vehicle and squatted to piss. Twenty metres from her, the body of a woman lay face down, one arm extended as if she was still flying.

When she got back, Rich was putting diesel in the tank. He pointed to where he'd found the jerry can, stowed on brackets between the wheel arch and the tailgate. She shouldn't have missed that. It was held in place with a ratchet strap, and somehow it hadn't leaked or cracked when the vehicle tipped over.

He whistled through his teeth, lightly, easily. I reckon our luck's turning, Li.

She took the phone a few steps away and tried the hotline again. This time she just got an engaged tone that went on and on until underneath it she heard something else, a rumbling. Vehicles coming from the east.

Rich came and stood beside her, holding the can, squinting. She counted four. After a minute he said, Leave this one to me, yeah?

Why's that?

Cos you're not really a sweet-talker, are you?

A spasm of memory. What she'd been willing to do before she gave up.

Anyway, he said, I know how these fellas work. He went back to stow the empty can.

The convoy kept coming until the road was filled with mud-green armoured personnel carriers. The lead vehicle slowed and pulled over and the others followed. Two men in fatigues climbed down, heavily armed. Cautious but not hostile. Rich held his hands clear of his sides and took a step forward. Li did the same. For the first time she noticed the Serkel logo along the side of the four-wheel drive and wondered if that was going to be a good thing or a bad thing.

You all right? one of the men called from the road.

Yeah, we're right, Rich said. Thanks for stopping. He walked forward to meet them. Li leaned on the bonnet and watched how he did it. How at ease he was, accepting a cigarette, rocking back on his heels. They turned together to look west, Rich talking with his hands, the others nodding, serious. Asking questions. Once, they turned towards her and he said something and the soldiers laughed. She looked away down the line. Saw a woman covering her with a pistol through the driver's window of the next vehicle.

When Rich came back he was carrying a stack of army-issue readies and two canteens. Doors slamming behind him, engines starting up again.

What did you tell them? she asked.

Told em the truth. Some of it.

Two short blasts on a horn. He dumped the food on the bonnet and gave a wave that was half a salute. They watched the convoy move off.

I said we worked for Company. Told em what to expect, said there were people alive back there.

What did you tell them about me?

What they wanted to hear. You gunna hold it against me?

It didn't seem like a rhetorical question. She looked for resentment, came up empty. Remembered the shock of her own face in the wing mirror and suddenly the idea of her as anyone's sex object was funny as hell. When she laughed she felt the tug of scar tissue, a stiffness to the mechanics of it. She said, I guess I still look pretty hot from a distance.

He grinned back but it was hard to read. They're disaster relief. Maybe backup if XB Force can't cover the breach. They're not interested in us.

You handled them pretty good, she said with her eyes on the food.

People like me. Told you before.

Yeah. I don't get that reaction much.

I like you, Li.

252

They ate standing, tearing open the readies with their teeth. Meat, pasta, beans in a curried sauce, richer stuff than either of them was used to. Soon Li's shrunken stomach forced her to slow, then stop. She felt dazed, wanted to curl up around the food in her belly and sleep.

Rich started packing up. He said, You know how to drive?

A bit. Mostly tractors.

Four-wheel drive?

Some of them. Fixed more than I've driven.

Have a go. See if you can manage with that. He nodded down at her ankle.

Yeah?

Yeah. He headed round to the passenger side. Just in case.

Straight road, no trucks. Her walking boot felt awkward on the clutch but it didn't hurt. A couple of false starts and Li had the hang of driving. Acceleration and response, straight-line progress. Was this the first time she had felt that her search was on her own terms? Already the flat country on either side was making way for curves, preliminary sketches of the mountains ahead. Travelling this way it was only a matter of measurable time before she caught up. To Matti, living or dead; to the answers she needed.

They got another hundred k east before the engine started smoking. They were out of the howler's shadow, more or less, and there were trees again. The smoke was blue-tinged. Oil in the intake stroke, or the turbocharger. Maybe the piston rings. There were plenty of things she could have missed but it was too dark by now to see if she was right, and they had nothing to fix the problem with anyway. She pulled over, bumpily, turned the engine off and listened to it crackling while Rich called his contact and explained they were stopping for the night. He described roughly how far they'd come, said they'd have a look at the engine at first light and limp on if they could.

They made camp. The rain had passed over but there was still some wind. They had their camp jackets but the temperature was dropping fast and Li knew they'd need each other's body heat to make it through the night, like in the sleepbox. She thought they'd stay in the vehicle, but Rich had a tent and a sleeping bag – what was left of his army kit. While they put the tent up, he told her how he'd slept all over East in it, had them both on him when he was grabbed on the highway west of Transit. They got confiscated with everything else in processing, but then when he got to Delta compound there wasn't enough room in the sleepboxes, so the Essos reissued him his own kit.

Generous bastards, he said, and Li heard herself laughing. Laughing at Transit.

They were clear of the worst devastation here but the wind had still blown through hard enough to tear branches from trees. They built a fire close to the tent and dragged more branches around in a circle to make a windbreak. The routine was familiar but sharing it was new. Rich heated up readies on stones by the fire while she checked on the engine. It was still clicking, but slower now. When she raised the bonnet, smoke and heat gusted up and she stood over it, warming her hands. Rich came over and laid a couple of readies directly on the hot metal. She remembered a Cup Night barbecue in Nerredin. The charred meat smell, kids hyped up and running amok, Frank a bit pissed, getting into an argument about a fifty-metre penalty. Matti saying, My one wish is the Mynas make it to Regionals next year.

Rich flipped the readies to warm the other side. When're the neighbours getting here, love? he said. I'm starving.

They ate by the fire and then Rich heated one of the canteens in the embers and added koffee and sweetener. Two meals on top of each other. Li was full for the first time in months. They passed the canteen between them and she looked away from the fire at the other source of light – a haze bouncing off the clouds to the south. The lights of New Flinders.

She said, What's your plan?

Huh?

If you don't want to get inside. Just drive around with this crew? Go where they tell you?

He said, I want to go to North, Li.

North? Sacrifice-zone North? But she wasn't surprised, even though she couldn't have known this. Said it back to him. Have you got a death wish?

And he laughed and leaned in to tend the fire. D'you know where you were born?

Ah, yep. Place called Granity. Val had told her that. She didn't remember living there but she'd been through it plenty of times on the circuit. Nothing little town, she said. It'd be gone now.

I dunno where I was born, he said. Who my parents were, my kin. I grew up in a place called Tom Creek. Dunno how I got there either, it's just the first place I remember. I used to sleep on the riverbank, down between the tree roots, sleep under houses in winter. There was a lot of stray dogs I used to cuddle up with, kept me warm. And I'd hear the noises through the floor – kids eating dinner, parents yelling at them, yelling at each other, kissing them goodnight.

Li couldn't tell where this was going.

He said, When I was ten or eleven I got caught stealing food, stealing grog. Cop didn't know what to do with me, so he asked this couple if they'd take me in. Lorraine and Vince. Their kids

255

had grown up and gone away. I was with them five years, till I joined up. They were from North, before the sacrifice zone. Got forced out. The way they talked about it up there, I never heard anyone talk about any place like that. It was like it'd been cut out of them but it kept growing back. You know what I mean?

No, said Li.

Yeah you do. Auntie Rainey and Uncle Vince had to talk about North, they had to tell those stories. They were still grieving it. He swigged at the koffee dregs, passed her the canteen. His skin where their hands brushed was hot. I'm gunna walk that country.

It's not there anymore, Li said. North's just poison now.

He said, Don't you reckon though, we've been hearing about the sacrifice zones so long we don't even question them? North's some kind of horror story people tell their kids, like it was never a real place, but that's all happened in our lifetime. People lived there, Li. Maybe they still do. Maybe what we got told isn't the whole thing.

Li was tired. Her stomach was stretched around the food, her head ached and her foot ached and she could feel the cold at her back. She wanted to piss and then crawl into the tent and sleep until she could start moving again. You saw what took out Transit, she said. Think it isn't worse up in North? You go up there you'll just die, like all the other dickheads who tried it.

He sat quiet for a while, poking the fire. Li pulled her crutch towards her and started putting it on. She was angry with him, and sad in a way she couldn't account for. They were always going to split up tomorrow. She heard the rattle of pills. Out of the corner of her eye, she saw Rich swallow something down.

This mob I'm joining, he said, they've been up there. They're still alive.

Something unlikely shifted out from the back of her brain.
Your contact, the woman you met, what was her name?

Eileen. He paused, watching her face. You know her?

No. I just heard a few stories about mozzies on the road.

In the tent, Li lay awake, consumed. Her guts cramped and there
was a pulse behind her eyes. It had to be them. She should warn
Rich, but she wasn't going to. Because if it was them, then she
had a chance of getting her stuff back. But she also had a chance
to make them pay. Make Jasmine pay. For the two and a half
months in Transit, wasted on despair. Months that might have
kept Matti alive. She wanted to beat Jasmine into the ground,
her dreadlocks and sweat and greed, and take everything away
from her.

Rich jerked and shouted. He struggled against the sleeping
bag and released a stream of unwords. They were zipped in
together, animal-close. At the last minute he'd told her he was
going to sleep in the car, said he wasn't much fun to share a bed
with. She remembered him twitching on the floor of Medical but
she told him if they didn't share the sleeping bag, one of them
would freeze to death.

He subsided again into unsettled sleep. She slowed her breathing, tried to stay close to his heat. She felt each place where
their bodies met. There were times when she had a deep hunger
for Frank, for his body, but it always led to the same place, to
the shipping container on the wharf where the clock ticked
and Frank's body came to its conclusion. Rich was all bulk and
muscle but she knew there would be a moment, right before
sleep, soon, when she would let herself imagine he was Frank.
That this was that tent and they had walked all day in the heat

and might still have been hungry for each other if their child hadn't been sleeping between them, but they could let it simmer because there would be other nights. She would let herself, but it wouldn't help.

She'd been following their tracks in the snow for a long time, their bare feet, and then they were there ahead of her but she couldn't call out so she ran along the straggling line, pulling them round to face her, one by one, thin as cardboard. Something roaring and cracking behind her. One face after another, looking at her with round, felt-pen eyes. And then one of the cardboard children blew over, and the others were blowing away and the thing was behind her, she kept running looking heart busting she was almost at the front of the line and then she pulled one around and it was Robbie and he opened his mouth and mud poured out. She was shouting and something had her gripped from behind, hot breath on the back of her neck. She bucked and flailed.

Li. Li! I got you.

She went loose, shuddering, keeping her eyes open in the dark because it was still right there. He had his arms braced around her. His heart thudded against her back.

Easy. Easy, you're okay now.

But the dream was still inside her. Her breath came out raw and she needed him to keep talking. She said, Who was it? Your lost cause.

His grip tightened for a second.

You said you gave up on someone too.

Rachael.

She lay still, waiting.

And then he said, We were in the same intake, both signed up as soon as we could. We did basic and then I got into medic and she trained as a combat engineer. She and her mate pushed in in front of me in the mess-hall queue. I told them to get in line, she looked me all the way down and up, said she was hungry. He laughed like it hurt. She was, ah, she had so much life in her, you know? Gutsy. Loved blowing things up, good with her hands. Bit like you that way. Nah, I'm just trying to make you feel good. She wasn't anything like you, Rach was real sweet. Filthy mouth on her. And funny. She had this laugh like a chook getting strangled, crack you up just listening to it.

Li shifted and he let go of her. She closed her eyes and let his voice flood her system like coolant, the nightmare receding.

I wasn't planning to settle down. But. Auntie Rainey and Uncle Vince were both dead by then. She had this cancer we couldn't afford to treat and he just didn't last without her.

Me and Rach were posted all over, different bases, disaster relief, XB skirmishes. Lot of time apart. Years. But whenever we got back together it just felt like home. She didn't want to get married or nothing like that but it was us two, everyone knew it. Rich and Rach, you know?

He was quiet for a minute but she knew he wasn't done – couldn't stop now. We shipped over together. When it come up, they gave us that time. There was this big joke about our honeymoon cruise.

She said, You were on the Front?

Career army, Li. Part of the deal. And the brass talked about it like it was containable, like they knew what we were getting into.

What was it like. Over there? It wasn't a fair thing to ask but she was afraid he was going to stop talking. And maybe if she could understand where he'd been, the place he was going would make more sense.

He said, It was the worst thing I ever done.

First there was the imperative to redraw borders around new oil and mineral and ore discoveries on other continents: for certain global powers to dissuade other powers from trying to keep existing deposits for themselves. Li remembered that phase from her later childhood – a distant conflict that affected them because of the supply disruptions that government insisted would be temporary, and the waves of refugees flooding into East.

The Front made it their Wars too. Their allies demanded troop support because they couldn't keep producing the hardware, all the technology of targeted strikes. There wasn't enough steel or copper, or silicon, aluminium, terbium, graphite, chromium, iridium, petroleum. There wasn't enough water. All the things they were fighting for were the things they were fighting with. But you could always find metal for bullets, and there were no export restrictions on human bodies, no supply problem. Not once they brought in the ballot.

He was there for four years. A six-month tour of duty that kept rolling over because there were never enough medics.

There was never enough anything, Rich said. I mean, I had kit. You saw what Transit was producing in medical supplies – most of that gets shipped to the Front. But we were always running out of stuff. Back in training I done a whole unit on utilising plants in the field, but on the Front there wasn't anything alive you could use. It was just mud.

He rolled onto his back and her body went with him in the confines of the sleeping bag. The intimacy seemed ordinary and familiar. Sometimes, whatever I reached for, I had it on me. And other times I'd be out there with my shears and some duct tape. And I started getting those times mixed up in my head, you know? Someone's screaming my name and I've frozen up, trying to remember if I've got what it takes.

Soldiers weren't just bleeding out or getting blown up either. They were dying of dysentery and frostbite and blood poisoning. They were dying of flu. Rich said, It was like, the longer I was there the worse I got at keeping people alive.

He and Rachael hadn't been posted near each other but people higher up did what they could for them. They talked most months, got R&R together twice. Her job was more dangerous than his; when they were apart, he worried about her obsessively. But when they were together, they only talked about the past or made plans. One thing they decided, easily, was not to have a kid.

The nightmares started on his second tour. He started self-medicating. Started a list in his head, of names and circumstances, injuries, locations. Men and women he hadn't been able to save. Kids. He came and went. The sound of a soldier snoring beside him in a base camp was also the sound of a fifteen-year-old conscript trying to breathe through blood.

Rachael's tour ended and she got the offer to ship home. Rich tried talking her into it but she wouldn't go without him, signed on again. They were both hospitalised, at different times: shrapnel in his legs, soft-tissue damage to her face and neck from a mine, dysentery.

Four years, he said. Luckiest bastards in the world.

They got sent back on different ships, her first. They had a phone call before she left.

She was talking about getting inside, he said. That was always her plan. Survive the Front, get lucky in the returned service ballot. Why not us?

When he got back, he couldn't find her.

Army couldn't tell me nothing, he said. There were too many MIAs and deserters by then, they couldn't keep up with the filing. I logged an MP claim, nothing. They wouldn't give me a discharge so I just pulled the pin, took off.

He searched for two years. All over East, every town, every camp. The whole time he was thinking how she'd survived four years' active duty in the worst hell you could dream up – what was there back here that could even touch her?

And then down in Port Howell, after you took off, I ran into some ex-army fellas. One of them knew someone who shipped back with her. That ship never made it. She'd been dead the whole time I'd been looking for her.

It had started to rain lightly, drops smacking the tent. Smell of wet dust and each other. His grief its own sharper smell.

She's still in my head, he said. I can't get her out of me, can't get past her. I go to sleep or I lose track for a minute and she's going down in the dark, screaming. Not just her – there's a whole lot of people screaming my name. It didn't help them.

You saved my life.

No. Nuh. I done the same for you I done for hundreds of other people in Transit and most of them are dead.

She said nothing. Nothing would help.

I got so much pressure in here. He felt for her hand, pressed it against his chest. Feels like it's boiling up and there's nowhere for it to go that's good. Only good thing I got is those stories, those North stories. There's rivers up there I never seen but I can

262

feel them. I need to go there. Need to be somewhere I haven't looked for her – somewhere that's not about that.

Would she have gone up there?

He barked out a laugh. I never tried that hard to talk her into it. Didn't seem as important then. The way I saw it, being stuck inside with her would've been worth it.

Li understood that. And how North would be a release from a promise. But he hadn't given up on Rachael until he knew she was gone. She said, I told my daughter once that you could do bad things and still be a good person. She wanted to know how many things.

What'd you tell her?

What had she told her? Something she didn't believe, just borrowing Frank's generosity, his faith in endless second chances.

Rich rolled away, fumbling for something in the dark. Pushed the phone into her hand. Try again, he said.

She held on in the queue for forty minutes. Beside her, Rich slept uneasily. She had turned away from Angie's grief. The couple with the baby had helped her but she hadn't left them the gun. She'd had a child in full knowledge that the ballot would not end, that Wars would not end, that Weather would only get worse. She'd given up and poisoned her body. She'd hated Trish for trying to have faith. She hadn't warned Rich about the mosquitoes who had maimed her and robbed her and left her to die. She'd lied to Frank about Chris when asking for his help might have saved them all. She left Matti alone in the camp. She left her.

The advertising cut off into four long beeps. *There is one. New. Update. On this claim.*

The battery icon was blinking as she rang Chris's number. Let him pick up, pick up. Goddamn you, pick up.

Another recorded voice. She talked fast into the answering machine, falling over her words. There's an update on Matti, something new on the claim, but I can't get through to anyone and my battery's about to die. I need you to call them or log onto my claim and call me back. She reeled off her status number, password, the claim number. Did you get that? I'll get this phone charged. Chris, please, call me back and tell me what they know. Keep trying me. I'll give you the numbers again.

She was halfway through repeating them when the phone died.

Rich was awake, listening. He said, It's good, Li. It's news.

It means she's been processed or they've ID'd her body, she said.

The answer was on her missing-minor claim, or on Matti's record or both, but it would sit there longer than she could sit in a queue; sit there until someone with the right status started asking. The nearest working Source connection she knew was about fifteen hundred k in the wrong direction, back in Kutha. Or she could go east, where Matti had been trying to go. Where Permacamp was. I have to get across the range, she said.

Get some sleep. This mob we're meeting'll have a charger. You can call that fella back or he'll call you. Then make a plan. Just sleep first, all right?

But she felt fevered. Eight words had upended everything. She strapped her crutch on and crawled out of the tent. It was the coldest time, the clouds had cleared and the dark was thinning, the stars losing their force. Somewhere on the continent, someone had seen Matti. Be alive. Be safe somewhere. Be fed, be sheltered. She was walking, shivering, east of their camp, like she could do it on foot again. Turned herself around and went back to the tent. It would be light in a few hours and she would try to get the four-wheel drive running.

A heavy sound woke her, thumping through the ground into her body. Her brain was thick with sleep. Rich had lunged for the shotgun before she even registered the engine running under the full-volume drum and bass. Then she heard the vehicle brake at close range.

Adrenaline kicked in. She tightened her boot and fumbled for her crutch – they couldn't lose the vehicle, not now. The music cut off, car doors slammed. Frenzied barking. Rich was already out of the tent. She crouched, yanking at the straps, waiting for his shout of alarm or anger, for shots.

Did youse get sick of waiting for us? he said.

The tent faced away from the road. When she crawled out, there was time for her to look around it and see them first, for the fist of rage that almost choked her. *We do this all the time.* Eileen out front. Rich hugging her, the shotgun discarded in front of the windbreak. Stokes and Dev behind them, Mira climbing down from the back in Li's blue thermal top, releasing the dog to run at Rich and then divert in crazy circles. Lucas was still in the tray, with a younger man she didn't recognise, sawn-off propped up between them. Shaun was behind the wheel, the passenger seat empty. She couldn't see Jasmine.

She came forward fast, grabbed up the gun from the ground and knocked the safety off, seeing their shock with vicious satisfaction. Eileen stepped back and Rich spun around. Lucas swung up the sawn-off but she leaned in and fired over his head. The kickback felt like it had split her shoulder.

Where is she?

Stokes said, Jesus. We thought you were dead.

Li? What the fuck? You said you didn't know them.

She moved past Rich without looking at him. Where is she? Where's Jasmine?

Eileen said, She's not with our mob anymore.

Li looked from her to Stokes. He nodded. We didn't think she was reliable.

Rich said, Put it down, Li. Come on, don't fuck this up.

She heard the urgency in his voice, saw that Lucas had got the sawn-off to his shoulder, but Stokes acted like the guns weren't even there.

What happened? he said. We heard the chopper when we were driving away, heard shooting.

She said, Those people are dead.

So, how did you get away?

You know I didn't get away. She was shaking, trying to keep the gun steady. Your operator broke my ankle. I got picked up and I spent the last two and half months in Transit, while my daughter —

Rich came up beside her. The steel-cap was their operator?

She saw Stokes put it together.

Shit, he said quietly. His eyes moved down to her leg. Jas told us you panicked and did a runner. It sounded wrong but we didn't have time to hang around. Then later Mira saw she had your tools. He shrugged. By then we didn't trust her anyway.

Something wrong with that girl, Eileen said. Right from the start.

Li looked at her and back and Stokes. The shotgun felt pointless suddenly. She put the safety back on and lowered it. Didn't even look at Lucas but she felt the tension go out of Rich and figured she wasn't going to get them shot.

Do you have my tools?

Nah, she took them. Took a bunch of stuff that didn't belong to her.

So they hadn't sent Jasmine away – she'd run out on them. Maybe saw what was coming. It didn't matter. She'd wasted enough time on Jasmine. She looked at Rich but he didn't look at her.

We've got most of your other stuff, Mira said. We can put it back together for you.

The gear would help her get across the range. In Transit, she'd heard about people crossing the lower slopes in four or five days but that was in the hot season. If she could get the four-wheel drive going, Rich would take her as far as he could before he turned north. He was angry with her but he'd do it. Otherwise, they could strip it for parts and she would make them give her a lift to the foothills. They owed her that. But first she needed to see if the engine was fixable. Maybe Shaun would let her use their tools.

She was already walking back to it when Eileen said, Why don't you come along with us too?

Li stopped.

Stokes said, We don't have an operator or a patcher now. Mira's training up pretty good but she'd do better with help.

She turned to face them. No. I'm going east.

Across the range? On foot?

Rich said, She's taking our ride.

There was some argument. The mosquitoes liked the idea of a second vehicle.

You're getting a medic, Rich said. She gets the transport.

Why hadn't she known he would do this? They'd never discussed it but she'd thought of the phone as hers, unquestionably. The vehicle was his. His independent means to get to North if things didn't work out with this crew. He was giving that up for her. Even though she'd used him and he was talking about her like she wasn't there. He kept helping her and helping her, like the act of helping meant something and she didn't know how to thank him, didn't even know what she was to him. Was she some form of Rachael that could still be saved? Or one of the others on his list? Or was she him, before he gave Rachael up?

Things were rearranging in her brain: speed, distance, time. *One new update.* She would drive across the range and into time again, through time. To Matti.

Shaun had everything. Working together, they cleaned the plugs thoroughly, wiped out the tubes and the air intake, changed the oil and the coolant, checked the fuses, the battery. Shaun replaced a couple of worn piston rings in the cylinder block. He conferred with Stokes and then half-filled the tank with diesel.

I don't know if that's gunna get you over, he said, but it's all we can spare.

They worked all through the clear cold of morning while the others got the fire going again, brewed tea and made damper. She looked up now and then at the range in the distance, flickering bluely in the air above the fire. Stokes and Eileen sat talking to Rich while he dressed an ulcerated sore on Eileen's arm. He'd taken the tent down, packed up his gear. Lucas was cleaning and oiling the shotgun. Mira threw sticks for the dog while she powered up the phones with a hand-cranked charger, and then the dog left the game and went to Rich and lay looking up at him. Dev was repairing a torn pack. The new guy crouched a little way from the fire, cleaning and polishing everyone's boots. Now and then he looked across at Mira and Li saw he was even younger than she'd thought.

Shaun said, We've got him on the shit jobs till we see what he's good at.

When they were done, the engine started first try. Mira brought Li's phone over, fully charged.

Shaun wiped his hands on a rag. There'll be ice on the road further up. Don't rush it – you're sitting high, easy to flip and roll.

There was no message from Chris and when she called she got his answering machine again. I told you before, she said. They'll just put me in a queue till my credit runs out. So I need you to do this and I'm going to wait for you to call me back.

It was early in the afternoon now, a thin grey wind coming up, and she had a great need to start driving. But Stokes asked her to eat with them first, and when she looked over, Rich was looking back at her, so she went and sat across from him at the fire, between Stokes and Shaun, and listened to them talk about the howler, about supplies, and the route they were taking to North this time. Rich was sketching or writing something on a piece of paper between mouthfuls. Mira came and sat beside the new guy and then Dev squeezed in between them with his plate. Eileen started laughing and Mira said, Dad! Seriously? And Stokes said, Dev, Dev, give it up, bro. You can't fight love.

The dog lay quiet on the edge of the circle, watching them eat. Li saw how they had knitted together without Jasmine, how easily Rich would fit. She got up and cleaned her plate and went back to the vehicle.

Stokes brought her gear over. She put her hand on the pack and was walking again, in pain and dust, dry-throated, sick with fear. Jerked clear of the memory.

He said, I heard your kid might be alive.

I'm going to find out.

Good. That's real good. He hesitated, as close to awkward as she'd seen him. I looked for my folks for a long time, he said. Kids don't give up easy.

She nodded, hoisted her gear into the back.

Your waterbag's full but we couldn't find any fish. And, ah, we've all been wearing your clothes. Sorry bout that.

She remembered the way she'd thought about him, about all of them, in Transit. They would've taken them off me anyway, she said.

There's a couple of phone numbers in the top pocket, he told her. We could use you. Any time. We're a family-friendly operation.

The last thing Rich gave her was the tent. He came up and threw it in the back with the rest of her gear. She looked at him, making sure.

I want it back, he said. And he put a folded piece of paper in her pocket.

The trees around them were noisy with wind.

Rich said, Why didn't you tell me what happened with this mob?

I thought you wouldn't bring me with you in case I fucked it up for you.

Li. He shook his head but he wasn't angry anymore. You gotta have a bit of faith.

How long since they'd met? A hundred days, not even, back in that factory in Port Howell. He had restarted time for her in Transit and there were things she should say to him that she hadn't worked out, but now she could feel the range like a magnet and everything else was background.

He took her hands, grubby with oil, turned them over and touched the shiny new skin. They healed up good, he said.

She shivered, though it was hardly even sensitive anymore. I should have thanked you for that.

You should have thanked me for a lot of stuff. You're shit at it.

She shrugged. Sweet-talk. But her gratitude to him was an anchor.

If you find her. Or if you find out. Would you think about coming up to North?

She took her hands back. I don't know.

All right. He nodded. Stokes gave you the numbers, so just let me know. About Matti at least.

When he turned away, she remembered that she did have something for him.

Hold on. She opened the driver's door, reached across the front seat for the Saint Anthony medallion. Held it out carefully.

Rich picked it up, looked at it with recognition and then pleasure. Lost things, right?

Maybe I'm wrong. Maybe there is something up there.

He gave it back. I don't know if I can take that. Don't you need it?

She hoped he lived. Put it in his hand and closed his fingers over it. You already found her for me.

The map she'd carried from the lake and lost at the roadhouse lay open on the passenger seat, as she drove, the range its easternmost limit. Beside it was Rich's hand-drawn map of the southern pass over the range, the lowest, least Weather-bound route, sketched from memory.

There was no sign of the howler's passage this far east. Beyond the roadhouse where Rich had planned to meet the mosquitoes, she drove up an old river valley. Fire had gone through this country, but there was new growth among the blackened trees. Big rock formations and new colours, too, less red and scrub, more shades of blue and brown.

Rich had told her not to stop along this stretch between the roadhouse and the range. She passed warning signs about training exercises and unexploded ordnance. Now and then she saw an army vehicle in the distance, but the base wasn't visible from the road. Sometimes a truck or a convoy of trucks, army or Company, passed from the other direction. Once a ute overtook her, the tray crowded with people and dogs staring back at her.

Chris didn't call and whenever she tried him it went straight to answering machine.

It rained heavily, cleared and rained again. The range was always there, but its snow-coated peaks came into view without warning. Li felt a high straining in her stomach. She didn't know how to prepare for whatever was waiting for her. *One new update on this claim.* She watched the speedometer and saw distance and time folding together, clicking over.

Late afternoon, the mountains closed in around her and she started to climb. Up and up, one tight curve after another with no reprieve. She was struggling with her walking boot now, wanted to take it off, but there was no safe place to stop. The road didn't seem wide enough for anyone to pass her. She slowed to a crawl, keeping an eye on the fuel gauge and seeing it wasn't going to get her over the pass. An orange light was layered across the valleys deepening into shadow below her. She felt the temperature dropping inside the vehicle.

Two hours later a truck came at her around a bend in the dark, across the centre line, lights on high beam. Blinded, she swerved left and braked hard and skidded out against the barrier. Sat, panting, at the side of the road until the tail-lights disappeared. Then she drove on slowly until she found a rest stop, backed onto a wall of earth and rock that gave some shelter from the wind. She was asleep almost before she turned off the ignition.

Cold woke her. She was stiff and groggy, and she needed to piss. She lurched out of the car and slammed the door behind her to trap whatever warmth was in there. The sudden drop in temperature was brutal. She was outside for less than a minute but by the time she got back in she was shivering uncontrollably and there were pins and needles in her fingers and toes. Stupid, stupid, not to have put more layers on. She started the engine again and blasted the heater, then fumbled urgently in her pack for her thermal gear – the top smelling of sweat and woodsmoke as she pulled it over her head. Gloves, balaclava, hunting cap. It was so important that she lived. She couldn't work her fingers on the straps and buckles of her knee crutch, and she started crying out of rage but she got the thing off and got into her sleeping bag.

In a little while her body started to regulate. The shaking eased until she was able to get out of her boots and pants and pull on the thick socks and leggings. The smell of other bodies was warm and human. She unrolled her groundmat and got it under her. The rain came sleeting on the glass, filling the car with noise. She ate a packet of curried instant noodles, swallowed a mouthful of water. Killed the engine.

Later, she woke again in absolute certainty that Frank was there, just outside. Had she been dreaming about him? Her head was clear. The rain had stopped and it was quiet, the car windows iced over. She was very cold but not dangerously cold. She sat up and listened. Heard breathing distinct from her own.

Li cleared a patch on the window, flinching from the burn of the glass. In the moonlight she saw a dingo sitting still at the side of the car. White. Black-lipped. It sat upright with its front paws together, calm and enormously alert, brow furrowed in a long angular face. Clouds moved across the moon but when they cleared again, the dingo was still there. Under the shaggy coat it was almost skeletal. It must be able to smell her but it couldn't get in unless she let it in. She touched her waist, where she'd kept the knife. Closed her eyes. She felt so close to Frank now. Not the stab wounds of memory, or the surrender of Transit, but something illuminating. She could almost reach him, almost make him understand. I didn't know what else to do. There was no safe place. I made a choice and I lost her.

The dingo was still. She couldn't believe how still. Only the tiniest movement of one ear, the ferocity of its attention. Every time I remember it I try and turn around, make myself turn, see what she wanted to show me. I can't change anything.

In the dark behind the still, silent dingo there was howling. It rose and fell and rose again in waves of longing or warning. The dingo got up unhurriedly and padded away. Li pressed her ear against the frozen glass. Why would I get another chance? she asked Frank. I wouldn't know how to do it any different.

The next time she woke it was early morning and raining again. The engine was slow to warm up and she got out to scrape ice off the windshield, bone-cold and stiff. Thought about the dry firewood in the boot, how she would build a fire tonight if the rain held off long enough. There was muesli in one of the army readies, she ate that and drank a little water. Took off her walking boot and put it on the floor on the passenger side. Before she pulled out she turned on the phone but there was no signal.

For the first hour the road climbed and twisted relentlessly. It was easier managing the clutch with the boot off, although it felt strange, after so long, to apply pressure directly with her left foot. She craved paracetemol but she couldn't risk taking her hands off the wheel, her eyes off the road. Anyway, the pills wouldn't last. The headaches were just one more thing she'd done to herself that she had to live with. Except Rich didn't think she'd been exposed long enough to do permanent damage.

So I won't always be like this? she'd asked.

And he'd grinned that complicated grin. I wouldn't've thought.

There was black ice and she had to slow, nervous about locking the wheels again. She was tensed all the time for the sound of trucks. Three of them passed her, two westbound and one roaring up behind her. She pulled over as far as she could and they bore down without making any concessions. It was a physical relief to come out onto an open stretch of highway, ribboning ahead through tussock and outcrops of rock, with an occasional tree or patch of trees. There was still a quarter of a tank. She'd seen no one on foot since she left Rich, but she felt confident that when she had to walk she would be able to.

A bird of prey spooled up up up on a current and then coasted, splitting the sky between the white of its belly and the grey above it. *One new update.* Matti should be dead, but Li could feel her again, thought she could, on the other side of all this rock and dirt.

The road climbed above the tree line. She'd never been this close to snow. Pulled her visor down against the glare and turned the heater on in short blasts to keep the temperature manageable and the windows from fogging up.

The highway hugged the cut face of the mountain now. When snowflurries blew across the pass she slowed to a crawl, barely able to see a metre ahead even with the wipers on. To her left was the gravel siding and then a metal and concrete barrier. Sections of the metal had been salvaged, exposing a broken fenceline behind it and then a high emptiness, a suspension, before white folds radiated up to the next peak. Li only saw this in grabs – mostly her eyes stayed on the next bend.

She heard the road train before it lumbered into view, taking up more than its share of road. She slowed, veered a little more to the left and then held her course, buffeted in the wake. The driver blasted the horn as they passed each other and she sensed him gesturing through the open window of the cab but she kept her eyes on the empty patch of road behind the last trailer. It wasn't until she was safely past that she registered the Serkel logos along the side and remembered the matching logo on her driver's door. It didn't matter. He might radio back to his depot but he wouldn't be turning around on this road.

Early afternoon, the gauge was very low now. She didn't know how far it would run on empty but if she made it over the top, maybe she could coast part of the way down. She came out of the sunlight into the mountain's shadow again. The wheel was wrenched out of her hands. She felt the back slew out, braked too hard and the tyres locked. Her face was hot and everything was slow. She pumped the brake, a useless instinct. The metal box began to spin and kept on spinning, building momentum. Mud sprayed up behind her. Li caught the wheel and held on. There was the far mountain and the near fence, snow, bank, road, a river of places. She leaned over the wheel, leaned into the current and swam for the bank.

There was blood running to her head. Cold air, the upward pressure of the seat belt, the work of breathing, smells of earth and diesel, a clock ticking too fast.

She opened her eyes. The windscreen frame in front of her was full of road but it was wrong, too close, and when she looked up she saw the bonnet. Upside down. No, she was upside down and the engine was still running. She breathed in the spilled fuel again and her focus contracted. Reaching out and up, she located the steering wheel and then the key ring with its Serkel logo. Turned off the ignition. Breathed for a moment, checking her pulse, waiting for the pain to surface. Something was trickling from her cheek to her forehead and when she ran her hand through her stubble it came away red.

She reached down to brace herself on the ceiling before she tackled the seatbelt. The buckle strained against her weight and then gave, and she slumped onto the roof. Dragged herself out through the empty frame of the windscreen, and the gap between the bonnet and the road, into the open. She stood looking at the crumpled vehicle with the slip banked up half-way over it, glass and metal spewed across the road, right to the barrier. She saw how the barrier had caved at the point of impact, the drag marks, but she resisted the urge to go and look down, as if she might see a tiny vehicle crushed and burning on the valley floor.

She was intensely conscious that she was still alive. There were shards of mirror around her feet, she picked one up and held it in front of her face. Her pupils were dilated and blood was smeared in tracks down her cheeks and up into the fuzz on her head. There was a gash under her collarbone that accounted for most of the blood. It wasn't deep but she was going to need to clean it up and bandage it or it wasn't going to stop. That chain of events didn't seem to affect her personally, though, in the same way that she had started to shiver but didn't feel cold. Li tried to order things in her head. The first thing was to not keep standing in the middle of the highway. But she needed her stuff.

Her walking boot was upright metres from the wreck, as if someone had just stepped out of it. She limped over and put it on and then went back to the vehicle and managed to wrench the back passenger door open. Retrieved her knee crutch, then the rest of the gear, bit by bit, and carried it across the road to the siding. She pulled her balaclava down over her forehead and then dug out the first aid kit, cleaned her hands with snow and then with saline, cleaned the wound and covered it with gauze and adhesive.

The phone was the last thing she found. The screen was cracked and it wouldn't turn on. She fumbled taking the back off, and saw that the battery had jolted loose from the terminal. She started laughing at how easy everything was getting. She had survived the crash and now, when she needed to walk, it had stopped snowing, and those things seemed like some kind of sign.

If there was a message from Chris it would be proof, but when she turned the phone on there was still no reception. The diesel fumes were making her dizzy and laughing hurt her head. She was standing there, holding her knee crutch and trying not to laugh, when a truck came round the bend towards her.

It was an aid truck, westbound, marked with the cross that meant an NGO of any precinct. As soon as it was clear of the bend it pulled over. The driver put the hazards on and got down. She wore a baseball cap with *Wet Creek Hotel* printed across the front.

You okay? she yelled over the engine.

Li nodded, still fighting the urge to laugh.

The woman came closer. You're bleeding.

It's not serious.

The driver looked over at what was left of the four-wheel drive, the wreckage on the road. I guess I'd be happy too.

She led Li back to the truck. Li let herself be led, climbed up into the humming warmth of the cab, accepted the emergency blanket the driver wrapped around her. She didn't know why she was being helped, none of this lined up, none of it felt earned but she didn't want to question it.

The co-driver's seat was occupied by a yellow mastiff. It assessed her steadily and then looked at the woman.

All right Nellie, she said, shift over. Then to Li, You sit here for a bit. You hear anything coming, honk the horn, okay?

Li nodded again. The driver poured koffee from a thermos and put the cup in Li's hands. Then she took a pair of heavy-duty work gloves out of a compartment between the seats and went to clear the road.

There was music on the radio, a deep bell tone, then a flurry of high strings descending and then the bells again. Li felt her body thawing and warming, the sweet scald of the koffee going down, something more painful than bewilderment. The dog whined. She offered the back of her hand and it sniffed, licked and turned back to watch the driver hauling the windscreen to the side of the highway. Apart from the dog, the only visible concession to the dangers of a solo run was the tyre iron stowed down beside the driver's door. Li touched the silk at the base of the dog's ear, kneaded it gently.

The woman came back and climbed into her seat, shunting the dog back over towards Li. I can't stay stopped here, she said. Someone'll come round the corner in a minute jacked up on wakey and plough into the back of us.

Li looked full at her. She said, Thank you.

You're all right, there's no need.

Her name was Emily. She told Li she was running relief to a new camp on the fringe of the howler's radius, but her brief included any survivors she met on the way.

You're welcome to come for the ride, she said. We like company, don't we Nellie? She planned to make the return crossing in a week, all going well, and she could drop Li at Permacamp then.

Li shook her head. I don't have time.

Okay, the driver said, like she'd expected that. Got some relief packs in the back.

She went through one with Li, sorting out what she could use: high-efficiency biofuel pellets, protein bars, a pair of lightweight gaiters, fifty dollars' worth of phone credit. And a square block of chocolate, silver-wrapped. Li remembered the melon. She put the chocolate carefully away inside her jacket.

Emily thought Li could make the top before dark and she'd get a glimpse of Permacamp from there, but it would take a few days to walk down the other side. You won't get a lift from Company, she said. But if it's army or aid, try to flag it down.

She left her on the side of the highway, facing east. Li walked away from the four-wheel drive without looking back. The incline wasn't too steep and the gravel siding was a good surface for the base of her crutch, where the rubberised tip was wearing through. The sun came out as she walked and soon she was warm enough to fold the emergency blanket away.

She was thinking about Emily, and about the other driver who'd stopped for her, whose name she didn't remember now. About Megan with her gift of talk and cigarettes. Sanaa and Amin and Abraham bringing water for Matti in makecamp when she was sick. About Yara riding around the industrial zone with her list and her pencils. Angie and Carl, who had never made her feel that they were Frank's friends. She felt a sharp pain thinking of Trish, who shared her gum and tried to keep them from despair, and Miriam who had talked about how things might be when she knew as well as any of them how things were. She remembered the couple with the baby called Billy, the uncle with the dustmask. The mosquitoes. Rich.

She stopped thinking and saw that this place she was walking through was beautiful. It had snuck up on her. The complex folds of the range made simple by snow, the fine-grained light, an immense purity and space that reminded her of the lake. There were occasional animal tracks on the slopes and twice a truck passed without slowing. Otherwise she was alone. The light was lucid on the snow. She looked until her eyes burned and when she closed them, the dazzle was still there. She crouched down and touched it, scooped up a handful. It was soft and then hard and when she licked it she caught the tang of diesel.

*

There was about an hour of light left when she found the children. They hadn't made it to the top. They were in a rest stop, curled up together under an overhang of rock. It was set back behind the rubbish bin and the picnic table but she saw them from the road. Anyone could have seen them.

The boy was smaller, maybe six or seven; it was hard to know, they were so thin. He wasn't wearing his shoes. His socks were blackened and worn away at the soles but Li could still see hotdogs running after each other on stumpy yellow legs. The girl had a red elastic band in her hair and she'd lost two top teeth, like Matti the last time she saw her. They'd taken off most of their clothes and they were holding hands.

Li knelt in front of them for a long time, crying. She wrapped them in the blanket. They'd tried to make a fire with rubbish from the bin – the packaging had charred but it hadn't caught. Matti and Robbie were always lighting fires. It would be dark soon and they would be alone. Li set up her tent under the overhang and built a fire with the pellets. She wanted to carry them inside where it would be warmer but some protective part of her understood if she did that she wouldn't ever be able to put them outside again.

As the heat blazed up she sat close to the children and thought about where they needed to be now. She thought about Rich's North stories, how a story could be a map, and she tried tell them about the best place the way Matti used to tell it. She told them they'd have to cross the deep sea but there were boats that didn't sink. And about all the colours and how the animals all had families. That there was water that came from inside the rocks, and kids rode horses to school and on the way home there was a shop that sold lollies for zero money. And you never got old enough to go to Wars and no one in your family died.

But if someone had already died, or you'd lost them, the best place was where they'd wait for you and when you got there your room would be ready.

It was no good. She couldn't hear Matti's voice anymore. She only had her own words, her own understanding.

It was dark when she stopped telling the best place. She didn't want to eat but she ate something. It was okay to take the blanket back, they didn't need it and she still had to live, but she piled their clothes over them and left the fire burning. And when she was in the tent, in her thermals and balaclava, with the blanket wrapped around her inside the sleeping bag, she sang the song that came from her mother, just the little bit she remembered.

Guardian angels
watch beside us
all through the night

The last time she talked to them was a Sunday and she was nine. Almost nine. At the beginning they called every Sunday, then later it was once a month, and by that last time they hadn't called for three months. She used the calendar Val got from the free hospital to keep track of his medication. She checked every Saturday that his phone was charged and he had credit and they would be somewhere with reception. When she asked him why she couldn't call them instead, he said they didn't have a phone yet, that it took time to get set up inside but he knew they'd call as soon as they could.

She and Val were inland on a sheep station called Yanderup, about halfway round the circuit. They got a lift into town with the boss and Val bought tinned food and flour and powdered milk and tobacco and cigarette papers, and an orange for Li because he worried about vitamins. When it was nearly time he bought a newspaper and sat at a picnic table by the playground pretending to read, and she pretended to play, and when the phone rang he grabbed it off the table and said, Howaya? and then, All right, so. She's here now, I'll pass you over.

She talked to Chris first. He was three years younger and not good at phone calls – he would nod instead of saying yes, or forget to talk, or try to show her things. She asked about his birthday the month before and he said he had to choose between a footy or a cake so he chose a cake. They were living in a different place again. She asked if he had any friends at the new school yet and he told her about a kid who'd fallen off the big climbing frame and broken his arm. He asked about Tolly and some of the other kids whose families were on the circuit. She said she was helping Val with patching jobs now, that they might get a job on a kelp farm next season.

Then she said, Is Mum there?

Yeah.

Can it be her turn next?

She's gone in the other room.

Then her dad came on the phone and asked if she was being good and listening to Val. He wanted to know where they were now. He asked how often she was getting to school and if she liked the postcard they'd sent with the last letter to Val. There was a strangeness in his voice, he was talking a lot and not leaving space.

She said quickly, Did you get a phone yet?

A hesitation. No, no not yet. Me and your mum are still looking for work, it's all taking a bit more time than we thought.

And she didn't ask for her, she didn't ask, but he told her anyway. Mum can't talk this time, love.

286

Did she lose her voice again?

She's been a bit sick, yeah. She sends her love, though, she's blowing kisses down the phone. There was a kissy noise and then her dad's voice straight after saying, Did you catch them? Put them in your pocket, quick. Like she was a little kid. But Li couldn't answer because something was pushing up into her throat. She pressed her ear against the phone in case she could hear her mum in the other room, in case she was trying to say something, but after a minute her dad said, All right, love, I need to have a chat to Val now, okay? We'll talk next month. Okay? Everybody loves you.

She played The Floor is Lava with a kid she didn't know while Val talked to her dad. After a while she looked over and he wasn't on the phone anymore, he was just sitting on the bench, so she went over and he looked up at her with a look she didn't understand and then he said, How about an icy pole? And pinball.

She said, Can we afford it?

We can this month, yeah.

When the month came up on her calendar again, they were further north, further inland, at a camp in the bush. She kept reminding Val and he kept saying it'd be fine but on the Sunday they were out of range. That was the only time she got angry with him. When she screamed at him that he was trying to steal her from her parents, he just sat and listened with his head down and told her he was sorry, he'd fix it next month, next month wasn't far away.

For a long time she thought, They'll come back for me. Later she thought, They'll call. She didn't remember when she stopped thinking that, when she put it away. She stopped asking Val if he had credit, and then she didn't mark off the days anymore, and then she never spoke about them again. She turned to Val completely, tried to keep him in her sight at all times. And she felt so sorry for abandoning them, for not being there when they tried to call.

In the morning the rest stop was heavy with snow and snow was piled up at the edge of the overhang, and still falling. Without Emily's blanket, Li didn't think she would have made it through the night.

No headache but her hands and feet were numb and un-cooperative. She put on all her clothes and packed up and then stood under the overhang, looking at the children beside the dead fire. They had come through the night unchanged. She couldn't bury them, except under snow. It was too high and too cold for dingoes now, at least she hoped it was. Better to leave them together like this, visible to any driver who cared enough to lift them and take them on the rest of the journey. She looked through their clothes for status cards or anything that might identify them, so that someone could know for sure, but there was nothing, so she pulled a few hairs from each of their heads as gently as she could, gold and brown, and wrapped them in a corner of the pellet packaging, and put them in the buttoned pocket where she'd carried the horse.

She walked out into steady falling silence. There had been enough traffic in the night that the road was fairly clear so she walked on the road, listening for trucks. Each time she heard one going the right way she turned to face it and stuck her arm out, but they passed her like she wasn't there. She wore the blanket and draped a plastic sheet over everything. As long as she kept moving, as long as it was light, it would be okay. When she was thirsty she wet her mouth with snow.

Li arrived at the top almost without noticing. There was a lookout but whatever there was to see was hidden behind low cloud and drifting snow. She felt no closer to Permacamp, or anything that was here in front of her. Now that she had let herself remember, she couldn't stop. If she listened hard enough, was there still time to hear her mother in the other room? Was she crying? Had they always meant to come back and get her, like they said they would, and take her inside? Had they meant it at the start, at least, until things got too hard? Or had they always known it wouldn't be possible? They got in on a one-child visa, she knew that much. Fengdu brought in One Child years before everyone else. That was the condition, and they took Chris. She assumed they'd left her because she was older, more capable. Or maybe Fengdu wasn't looking for girls then. Val was their closest friend on the circuit, the one they trusted most, and he'd been dry for years. She knew they'd sent him money for a while. Had it been a slow, deferred decision, creeping up with an inevitability that surprised them, even while they resisted it? Had her mother always lost her voice on Sundays because the alternative was unbearable?

She didn't know, she never would. There was no sound from the other room. She could push past the fear, the refusal, in Chris's voice and ask what he thought, if they ever spoke about it later, about her. But what would be the point, now? And it wouldn't be fair. It wasn't his fault that he was chosen.

After she'd been walking downhill for a long time, she heard another truck coming up behind her and stuck out her arm without turning. It went past, but slowly, and she heard the gears changing down. She watched it round the bend and then heard the whump and squeal of hydraulic brakes. Tried to run but only managed a stumble. The truck was waiting, pulled over on the siding. She saw the Homegrown logo on its side and thought somehow it would be him again, the driver with the melon. You couldn't stop for everyone, he'd said, but he'd stopped for her.

The cab window slid down and she looked up at a face she didn't know.

Jus you, is it?

She nodded but he looked back past her anyway.

How'd you get this far?

I had a vehicle. Wrote it off yesterday.

Black ice, hey? He nodded unhurriedly, sucked his teeth. Lucky you weren't a gonner.

His face was ruddy with the heat from the cab, freckled forearms bare. I'm not sposed to take passengers.

I know, she said, and she was ready. She lifted her heavy arms clear of her sides, letting him see.

He nodded again and kept nodding, thinking it over. Nothin in the pack?

You going camping?

I'm not going camping.

Then there's nothing in the pack.

If he drove on now, took his cubicle of heat and left her in the snow, she didn't know what she would do. All she could do was stand there and let him look.

Fair enough then, I spose. Can't have you freezing to death.

He kept the engine running. Her fingers wouldn't work so he got down and helped her with the buckles of her knee crutch. She was greedy for the heat but she almost couldn't feel it when he pushed her up and through to the bed in the back of the cab, helped her get the plastic off and the pack, the blanket, the coat.

Jesus, he said, good thing I didn't ask for a striptease. He unbuttoned her pants. Threw his hands up when he saw the leggings and left her to fumble them down while he hunted for a condom in the glovebox. Made her turn around. No offence. I can tell you were a good-looking woman.

She heard him spit on his hand and then he pushed her legs apart and shoved himself in.

You like that? he said. Do you? Hey?

His spit barely lubricated her, she rubbed raw. His breathing was loud in the cab, opening tiny splits inside. The shelter house, crawling away from the shelter house with him in the dark behind her. She gripped the back of the seat with her numb hands and looked out through the fog on the windscreen at the road and the mountains descending east, she thought it was still east, this is nothing. He had her by the hips, grabbed at her hair but there wasn't enough of it so he ran his hand down her face, forcing her mouth open, down to her throat. She yanked his arm away with both of hers, falling forward and hitting her cheekbone on the headrest. He came out of her, swore and pushed her head against the seat. Held her down that way, breathing over her, the stink and slap of flesh as he worked in and out.

When he was done, he offered to help get her clothes on but the feeling was coming back into her fingers in stabs by then, and she wouldn't let him touch her again. He fiddled with the radio and she knew that if he told her to get out now she would have no choice. But he put the truck in gear and pulled back onto the highway.

He asked her if she liked classic rock and when there was a newsbreak he asked if she'd been anywhere near the howler, if she'd heard about the flu outbreak in Fengdu. Then he just drove and she leaned against the window and counted each turn that brought them down the pass.

Hey, wakey wakey. The driver was nudging her shoulder. She sat up fast, shrugging him off. Don't be like that, he said.

The snow was gone and the sky was brilliant. Her eyes followed a hawk labouring up and up and then diving in a steep V. The mountains were hills now, green with bush. A fast-flowing creek running alongside the road.

This is the last bit, he said. Thought you'd want to see. He palmed the wheel into a slow turn, humming to the radio. Around the bend, the view opened onto a wide valley, and there was the XB again, running through it under the sun, as if the range had just been a minor interruption. But this was a different XB, this was the first one. Fengdu. Its wall ran north and south, beyond her sight, but she could only see one gate, fortified with barbed wire and guard towers. The road cutting through the No Go to the gate was fenced in and lined with concertina wire. A queue of vehicles and a queue of bodies. That human queue was built on hope, on the hidden promise of something better, but Li was still high up enough to see over the wall. She had a brief impression of a long metal cage running between the wall and a second barrier. On the far side of that, smoke rose from a vast industrial zone. A flash of greenhouses further north and the start of a metropolis that made Valiant look like a suburb. But Li tracked back over the wall to what was outside it.

The driver said, That's where you're headed, right?

Permacamp sprawled north and south along the No Go's perimeter fenceline, like makecamp, but it carved into the No Go as well, and it was gated and fenced like Transit. It wasn't like either of those, though, not really. There were checkpoints and guard stations, roads branching out through defined settlements. Precise, endless rows of army tents interspersed with toilet blocks and washing lines and solar panels, and small container settlements and fenced-off administration areas with real buildings, and patches of cultivated land. It looked like Agency. She imagined the numbers of unsheltered living in this camp, moving through its ordered world, where everything was recorded and accounted for.

She tried to imagine Matti in there but she came up empty. So she looked east instead, across Fengdu, squinting against the distance, and imagined she saw the grey shine of ocean. Boats that didn't sink.

I can drop you on the outskirts, the driver said. I can't risk getting spotted setting you down before I clear customs. There's taxis running to the camp all the time down there.

She saw where the highway came out on the valley floor, how much traffic there was on it, the trucks queuing up outside the gates of Fengdu. The fringes of the camp started at the side of the road and there it looked scrappier, dustier, less regulated, like you could jump a truck, or maybe just walk a while before anyone stopped you.

A beeping started up inside the cab. The driver glanced at the CB and then at his phone in its dock, frowning, but Li already had the phone out of her pocket. Two messages.

You didn't say you had a phone.

Two messages. She couldn't listen with him there, the smell of him, his body filling up all the space. Can you pull over? Let me off here?

I would've traded for the phone.

Li looked at him and what she felt must have been in her eyes because he shut his mouth, turned back to the road. A few minutes later there was a passing lane and he pulled over. She threw her pack down and got out without speaking or looking at him again.

The first message was from Rich. I wanted to call you before we get out of range, see if you heard anything yet. Might be a while before I can call again. I hope you made it across, Li. And I hope you find her. I'm not worried about you cos. He laughed, scrambling the reception into static. Haven't seen anything yet that could kill you. But just take care of yourself. And wish me luck, yeah? A pause, she thought he'd gone. There's so many birds up here, Li, never saw this many birds, true to God. Following the river now. I got your saint looking out for me, so we'll see what we find.

She saved the message, the glint of him following those northern rivers back to the source. Went with him for a moment because, after everything, she wasn't ready. *To listen to the next message, press one.*

She had stopped walking, was standing where the gravel met the open side of the hill, facing east. Torn-off pieces of cloud and

below was the valley and the wall and the camp outside the wall.
To listen to the next message.

She pressed one.

Li. She's alive. Call me.

Li sat down on her pack to make the call. She dropped the phone on the gravel, scrabbled to pick it up with hands that didn't belong to her. She felt boneless, unable to take the next step. A living child. Not a body. Not a witnessed statement of time and cause of death. She was the living mother of a living child.

She looked at the hand that wasn't holding the phone and then slapped her face with it, hard. Then she called Chris back.

He answered like he'd been waiting. She's in Permacamp with the unaccompanied minors. They processed her more than a month ago.

A month ago. When Matti was crossing the range Li had already buried her. Couldn't let herself believe in her again yet. Not till she was sure.

How do they know it's her?

DNA match. And she verified everything on her record: status number, parents' name, date and place of birth. It's her, Li.

Then what was wrong with his voice? Why was he talking so slowly, what hadn't he told her yet? She said, How did she get there? How did she get across the range?

She came in with a few other kids in a truck. Apparently they got picked up early on, that's why they made it. She said there were a lot more kids. Some of them died, some of them got into other trucks. A lot of them are still unaccounted for. She was lucky.

Lucky. That slowness in his voice again, like he was medicated. You've talked to her?

No, I read her file. You gave me access, remember?

What else did she say?

She confirmed her father's place and cause of death.

What about me?

He didn't answer and it made her afraid. Does she think I'm dead too?

No, he said reluctantly. She doesn't believe you were in the camp when the fire started.

And what, Chris? What else?

She says you were claiming for the Deep Islands. She thinks she's going to meet up with you there. Apparently she's tried to get out of Permacamp a couple of times.

Everything that had been too big, too borderless to wrap feeling around, came down on Li now. She couldn't breathe. This this this.

Li. Li? She's all right, are you listening to me? She's alive.

Then what's wrong? There's something wrong. What's wrong with her?

He sighed, a terrifying sound. She waited for him to find the words he needed and lift them, one at a time. It's not her. It's Aaron. We lost Aaron.

You lost?

He died. Three weeks ago. Flu.

Lucky, she thought. She was lucky, said Chris.

He said, We thought. Never thought we could have a kid. Suyin tried before. But then we had him. But we were right.

She felt the distance from their childhood to now, with this waiting for them all the time. I'm sorry, she said. I'm sorry for you. Both of you.

He was silent. She wondered if Suyin was there, listening.

Chris?

I'm still here.

Thank you. For what you've done. I won't ask you for anything else. I'm going to go to the camp now.

Wait, he said, but she had to hang up the phone, the weight of it. When she placed it carefully at her feet, she felt the gravel against her knuckles, skin on stone, barely tethering her to the hill. Her child was alive. Her brother's child was dead. Get up, she told herself. Go and get her.

But was this how it worked? All the weight that had lifted off her had to fall somewhere else? Robbie had to drown so Matti could run towards her through the miracle rain? And Carl and Angie had to carry it. Chris had to. He was her little brother but when they played families he was always the dad.

She was suddenly terrified of Matti. Of what had happened to her and what she was now. What she had cost. Of standing in front of her and looking into her eyes.

Mum! Look! She tried to. And in and out of focus she started to see her again. Her road-to-Valiant freckles and the gaps between her teeth, the nut-coloured crop of her hair three weeks after lice. All lost to the months of searching. But there would be new teeth, new gaps. The top of her head had come up to Li's bottom rib but she would be taller now. Li was starving to see what she had become. It opened her up and shook the air around her, the idea of Matti down there in the camp, holding onto the idea of Li.

Get up, she's waiting for you.

She could make it there in daylight. And if she couldn't, and if they wouldn't let her in after dark, she would sleep outside the gates.

She put a hand on the pack underneath her, saw that the phone was ringing. Grabbed at it with both hands. Matti.

Li, Chris said and his voice was different. Don't hang up. Listen. We can claim her.

What?

That's what I wanted to tell you. Suyin and I can claim her now, under One Child. If that's what you want.

She didn't understand. If that was what she wanted?

When was the last time you logged on at a Source Centre? He said. Not on the phone.

His words had speeded up but Li felt stupid, slow. Three months ago, she said, maybe longer? Town called Kutha.

Where is that? Listen, Li, would that be in the howler zone now?

Maybe. What do you mean, claim her?

He said, I can convince the Agency you're dead. I can match DNA and claim Matti. We can sponsor her, bring her in.

Li heard her voice come out but she didn't recognise it. Matti doesn't know about you.

Oh. Yeah, I figured. We didn't tell. Aaron didn't know about you either. I was going to tell him when he was older, when he could understand.

She could hardly hear him over the blood rushing in her ears.

He said, It would only work if you stayed dead, Li. They're saying they'll never be able to ID all the unsheltered who died in that howler, but you'd have to disappear, go somewhere there's no Source, no Agency, no reason for anyone to run your status.

She understood now. He meant no goodbye. He meant all she had to do was stay lost. Turn around, was what he meant.

Chris said, I was wrong, Li. I do owe you. I got this life and you got that one. I can change that for her, if you want.

She made herself speak. Is that what she wants too? Suyin?

Suyin wants Aaron back, he said simply. She'll come round, she'll see this is right. Matti can have a life here. She can have Aaron's life. He stopped for a minute. Inside, it's not what you think it is but it's better than out there. She'll get more time. And maybe, who knows, maybe we'll get to the Deep Islands.

There was a flower growing up through the gravel, a weed. Sour yellow stem and frail cup, white with blue veins. The cold season was almost done. She said, I need to call you back.

Okay, I know. Do you have credit?

Yeah.

Okay. I'll wait for you to call.

Chris.

Yeah?

Was there a photo? Did she look. How did she look?

She waited, hardly breathing.

Li-Li. She looks like you.

She sat still at the side of the road, holding everything in, and she'd never hated Chris for being chosen but she hated him for giving her this choice. Because he was right. She got the other life. Her deep desire was to go down now and walk until she found Matti and touch her to know she was real and say, I'm here, I won't leave you again. You are my best place. But it wasn't enough. What could she offer her? A lifetime queueing for islands not even sheltered people could get to? A long drive north into the heart of Weather? She touched the shape of the chocolate in her pocket and it felt pathetic, someone else's gift, not even hers. Chris had been loved, raised, sheltered – didn't Matti deserve that same chance?

A truck went past, spitting gravel. She tried to lose her thoughts in the roar but they found her on the other side. How did her own mother make the choice? Knowing so little, having so little power. Did she just do the best she could? Save one child and trust someone else to save the other one? What did it mean to her at the moment she decided and for the rest of her life? What would she tell Li now if they were face to face and her voice didn't fail her? She listened for a sound from the other room but she was alone with this decision, just like her parents had been alone. If she went to Matti now and put her arms around her and told her she was loved and safe, half of that would be a lie. Matti wasn't safe with her, not out here. All Li knew how to do was walk, seek shelter, find the next place, make the same mistakes. And she would leave her again. Matti wasn't safe in there either but she would be safer, for longer. And Chris would love her. She had heard the slow wonder in his voice remembering Matti's photo, when he saw his eight-year-old sister in her face.

Was this what she had needed to see? You're not the one who can save me. You're not the one.

Somewhere down there in the managed sprawl of the camp, was Matti. Matti was alive. There was all this joy inside Li, this blazing joy, but it was held in check, waiting for her to choose. Could she turn around now and walk back into the cold, and love Matti without wanting her? Hadn't a part of her been doing that from the beginning? She closed her eyes and was in Nerredin again. Dark, early, the cold pressing in around the bed. She felt the sunken space that Frank had left, smelled woodsmoke from the kitchen stove, koffee, heard the radio on low.

Matti's arm was flung back across her throat, resting there. A school morning. She felt through the arm that her child was awake and not ready to be awake. She kept her voice low. Do you want a piggy back, a carry, or do you want to walk?

Matti laughed quietly. All small kid things.

Even walking?

Except walking.

So, do you wanna walk?

I'll walk.

*

Li came back to the hill and the road and the sun, the end of the cold season. When it came she let it come in a great hot rush that brought her to her feet. She lifted her pack and faced the camp and started walking.

Acknowledgements

This story takes place on a continent that floats somewhere above the one I grew up on. I want to acknowledge the Traditional Owners and custodians of Country all throughout Australia, and their Elders past and present. I pay respect, especially, to the Whadjuk Noongar people, whose plains I was raised on, and the Arabana people, whose extraordinary country fuelled a central part of my imaginary one. 'Kutha' is the Arabana word for water. I'm grateful to the Arabana Aboriginal Corporation for letting me give that name to the last town before the lake.

Thank you Leon Davidson for years and years of belief, encouragement and collaboration. And for always being right about what was wrong, even when I didn't appreciate it.

To Franka Christine, the number one storyteller in the family, for all the great ideas and all the great titles, for offering to be my publisher, for making sure I never give up.

Thank you to my father, Vincent Bartolo Moleta, for your steadfast example of the life of the mind, and your translation of Montale's 'A Liuba che parte', way back at the start. And to

Sophie, Gabrielle and Benedict Moleta, with my admiration and aroha.

To my supervisor and workshop convenor Emily Perkins for every single thing you said. I reckon you knew Li before I did and I was so lucky to have you on the road with me.

To my workshop whānau: Anthony Lapwood, Antonia Bale, Frank Sinclair, Kirsten Griffiths, Lynne Robertson, Maria Samuela, Mia Gaudin, Nicole Colmar and Sharon Lam, for your company and your many contributions to this pukapuka, and for the way you always get to the heart of things.

I'm grateful for the support of everyone at Te Pūtahi Tuhi Auaha o Te Ao | the IIML, and the writing community that thrives around it. Thank you most of all to Katie Hardwick-Smith for your friendship and for making 2017 possible.

My thanks to Alyson Barr and Chris and Margaret Cochran for New York Street, where I got to the end. And to Anna Smaill and Yadana Saw for good advice, early and late.

I owe a lot to my perceptive and generous early readers: Elizabeth Knox, Fergus Barrowman, Rajorshi Chakraborti and William Brandt. Particular thanks to Alison Arnold, for a structural edit that made all the difference.

Thank you to the magnificent Jenny Darling for that first phone call and every one since. I can't wait to meet you kanohi ki te kanohi.

To Ben Ball, ngā mihi nūnui ki a koe for your faith in this story and its unknown author from across the ditch and outside the bubble. And to you and Meredith Rose for your care and attention in editing: especially all the pātai, big and small, that made things clearer.

I'm grateful to Ebony Lamb, Kate Breakey, Lisa Bailey, Sandy Cull and Stan Alley for their invaluable artistic contributions, and equally to Anna O'Grady, Anthea Bariamis, Elena Gomez, Michelle Swainson, Sandra Noakes and all at Simon & Schuster for their time, skill and manaakitanga. And a big thank you to Emily Maguire.

The fragment of lullaby Li sings to Matti and to the children on the Range is my memory of an old Welsh song 'Ar hyd y nos' | 'All through the night'. The real lyrics turned out to be different from how I remember them, which is maybe also true of childhood.

Aroha mai to the many other people who have shared kupu āwhina, pūkengatanga and whanaungatanga over the last few years. He mihi tino nui ki a koutou kātoa, mo tō koutou tautoko. I hope I can thank you in person.

Clare Moleta was raised on Whadjuk Noongar Country in Western Australia. She now lives in Pōneke | Wellington, Aotearoa, where she was born. *Unsheltered* is her first novel.